Kiss Cam

Anie Michaels

To all my friends in Anie's Awesome Teamsters who loved Camden and Riley so much they demanded more.

Kiss Cam
© Copyright Anie Michaels 2017

Edited by Hot Tree Editing.
Cover design © Pink Ink Designs

Chapter One

Riley

OMG, you have to hurry back. I think the guy sitting next to me is getting dumped by his girlfriend. AWKWARD!

I hit Send on my text message and then subtly looked to my right to make sure the man sitting next to me wasn't reading my screen over my shoulder. Luckily—for me, not for him—he was too busy being dumped to notice I was texting about him.

"I'm just sick and tired of always coming in third on your list of priorities." His girlfriend was obviously so over their relationship and honestly, just by looking at them, I couldn't really see why they were together at all. They couldn't have been more opposite if they'd tried.

He looked like he belonged in Portland—slight scruff of a beard, as if he'd skipped shaving a few days, longish brown hair, baseball-style shirt with sleeves pushed up to his elbows, jeans that looked just tight enough to hug his thighs (which, by the way, were like eye magnets since I hadn't stopped staring at them since he sat down next to me), and shoes that looked like they'd been worn in the rain. He was attractive, but he wasn't start-a-fight-in-the-middle-of-a-Renegades-basketball-game attractive.

I came to watch the game. To see the players. To drink the beer. And these people were slowly but surely ruining my night. Well, her more than him.

She was high maintenance. No doubt about it. Her hair was styled. Not just fixed or done, but styled. She'd paid someone to do her hair for the game. Her nails were fake, so were her lashes, and I was sure not all that hair was hers either. Her shoes were completely unrealistic for the stadium, with heels taller than my beer glass. Her halter top was sequined, her pants too tight.

I tried not to appear like I was eavesdropping on their breakup, but I totally was. The Renegades were kicking ass and up by fifteen points, so I could spare a little attention to the drama in the seat next to me.

"We've been dating for, like, two weeks. How fast were you expecting to climb ranks, Sophia? I'm not ditching my grandma's hundredth birthday party to go to your cousin's husband's nephew's bar mitzvah."

Seriously, you have to hurry! I think she's going to throw her drink in his face!

"Is this how it's always going to be? If we get married, is your family always going to come before me?"

"Married? Sophia, this is our *third* date. We're not getting married."

My eyebrows spiked toward the ceiling and I couldn't help but turn to watch her head explode.

"If you don't see us getting married, then why are we even doing this?"

His head dropped into his hands, elbows resting on his knees. "I have no idea."

I felt bad for the guy. I almost wanted to pat him on the back and give him some encouraging words. *We're not all batshit crazy, guy with amazing hair and freakishly sexy thighs. Trust me, there're normal girls out there.*

"I can't be with someone who doesn't put me first, Camden."

I heard him take in a deep breath, and then watched out of the corner of my eye as he lifted his head and turned to her. "You're right, Sophia. You deserve so much better than I can offer. I think it's best if you leave me behind and move on, try to find someone worthy of all your beauty and grace."

Sophia was silent for a moment and I desperately wanted to fully turn my head and eat my cotton candy like I was in a movie theater.

"You're going to regret pushing me away. I'm the best woman you'll ever manage to get, and you're just going to let me walk away." Her head was so high, she was literally looking down her surgically altered, slim little nose at him. She seriously sounded like she was about to splash her Diet Coke all over him. If she ruined my pleather jacket, I was going to freak. "Have fun watching your boring little baseball game."

Luckily, she decided to take her beverage with her, toddled down the aisle in her five-inch stilettos, and slowly climbed the stairs to the exit. Her boyfriend, er, ex-boyfriend, watched her go for a few seconds, but then let out a huge sigh and then turned back to face the court. He must have noticed my curious stare because he caught my eye. All I could offer was a sheepish smile. The very corner of his mouth turned up in a lopsided smile, but then he looked toward the court once more.

"Dodged a bullet with that one," I said quietly, mostly to myself, but his head turned to face me again.

"You think so?" His smile was a little fuller, but his question was sarcastic. "She was a setup. Someone my dad

3

wanted me to date. Thought it would be good for my image."

"You have an image?" My eyes roamed over him; he was still good-looking, but not someone I would peg as worried about his outward appearance. Then he thrust his hand out toward me.

"Camden Rogers. Son of Andrew Rogers."

My eyes couldn't have grown any wider. "You're the mayor's son?"

"Didn't anyone ever teach you it's impolite to refuse to shake someone's hand?" His eyes darted down to his hand which was, in fact, still held out toward me and still very empty. I placed my hand in his, still a little shocked to be sitting next to a celebrity. Well, not really a celebrity. A political celebrity. The Prince William of Portland royalty. He called me on my gaping mouth, which was still silent. "And your name is?"

"I'm Riley. And you're the mayor's son."

He laughed as he released my hand. "He's my stepdad, but yeah."

"Well, your girlfriend is a lot dumber than I was giving her credit for." I hitched my thumb over my shoulder.

"Ex-girlfriend," he corrected.

"Yeah, good for you." I pumped a fist in the air for good measure. "She doesn't even know the difference between baseball and basketball." That alone seemed blasphemous at a Renegades Basketball game.

He gave me another smile, but then Hadley dropped in the seat next to me, handing me the beer she'd gotten for me when halftime started.

"Did I miss the drink tossing?" Hadley whispered this to me, but not quietly enough that he didn't hear her.

"I was sure she was gonna toss her drink. But she went instead, for the 'You'll never find a girl like me' speech." I fluttered my eyelashes and pressed a dramatic hand to my chest.

"How'd she know about the breakup?" He leaned forward, his gaze darting between Hadley and me.

"Camden, this is my best friend, Hadley. I was live texting her your breakup."

"Nice to meet you," Hadley said, shaking his hand. "I'm sorry for your loss."

I couldn't hold in my laughter. "It was her loss." I turned to look at him, trying to include him in my joke, but his eyes were on me, and now he was really smiling, all the way up to his eyes. My laughter died, but his eyes didn't leave mine, neither did the gorgeous smile.

"So, do you come to these games often?" Hadley's question broke us out of our gaze-lock.

"Uh, yeah," he answered, running a hand over his chin. "I've got season tickets."

"Big Renegades fan?" Hadley asked, her voice polite and curious.

"Yeah, I've grown up here so it's hard not to be. Plus, these last couple years they've been doing incredible.

Do you guys come to a lot of games?" He asked us both, but the question was directed at me.

"I usually watch the game at a bar down the street from my apartment, but I got a promotion last week, and this was kind of a splurge."

"Ah, congrats. What do you do?"

"I'm an event planner."

"Don't let her fool you, she plans parties for a living. And she's fantastic at it," Hadley threw in for good measure.

"You know, I met you five minutes ago and I can already tell you give good party." His smile was still sparkling and I could feel myself blush at his goofy compliment.

"What do you do?" I asked.

"Ah, it's pretty boring. I'm a lawyer." He could have told me he was a wizard and I wouldn't have been more surprised than I was to learn he was a lawyer. And I was not an actor, so my shock was evident all over my face. He laughed and continued. "It was sort of a familial expectation for me to go into law. But I'm not, like, a stuffy lawyer. I'm in entertainment law, actually."

"I don't care how you dress up a pony, it's still a pony, and you don't look like you give good lawyer. No offense."

"None taken," he said, still laughing. "The day someone tells me I look like a lawyer is the day I have my first life crisis."

My eyes fell to the court where a man who didn't look at all familiar with a basketball was trying to make a

6

half-court shot to win five thousand dollars. Halftime wasn't my favorite, but only because I liked to watch the game. At least if I was watching the game on TV I could listen to commentary and stats. But in person halftime was filled with lame competitions and the RenegadesDancers shaking their asses. I'd have gladly gone to get our beers, but Hadley insisted since, technically, this was my celebration.

"Riley loves basketball, but hasn't been able to find a guy who likes it as much as she does, thus creating a divide between her and all her ex-boyfriends."

I turned to look at her with wide what-the-hell-are-you-doing eyes. She just smiled at me.

"Their loss," he said, smiling brilliantly.

I just lifted my cold beer to my lips. That was my only requirement for watching basketball games. Widmer Hefeweizen had to be on tap—my favorite beer. However, being there in person and getting to watch Damian Lillard and CJ McCollum in action was a perk too. I cheers'd myself for getting my promotion and took another drink.

"Ugh," I groaned. My least-favorite halftime event was starting: the Kiss Cam. Sporting events and kissing didn't go together *at all* in my opinion, so I never understood why the Kiss Cam had become popular. Watching people kiss was uncomfortable for everyone. A lot of the time it was an awkward kiss, or a gross kiss, or a kiss that was more suited for a soft-core porn flick.

"Riley's favorite," Hadley chimed in.

"Not a fan of kissing?" Camden asked, his voice a little heavier and thicker than my pulse would have preferred. His words were punctuated by the image of a fiftysomething couple giving each other a polite peck on the

7

lips as the lights around the Jumbotron flashed in time with the music playing.

"I don't mind kissing in general, I just don't understand how it correlates with basketball." I turned to him, trying to make my point.

"Really? You don't see the correlation?"

I gave him a skeptical look. "There is no correlation."

"Basketball is just like sex," he said, matter-of-factly. I heard Hadley choke on her beer next to me, but couldn't pull away from Camden's eyes to check on her. He leaned closer to me, our faces just inches apart. "Dribbling the ball, passing it back and forth between players, it's exactly like sex. You get all excited, just teasing the basket, then finally, when the ball finally goes in, it's the climax."

I swallowed and never had my throat been so dry, even though I'd been drinking my beer. "And where does the kissing fit into all that?" My voice was just an echo of its former self; I was all raspy whispers.

"It's foreplay, Riley."

"Oh, shit," Hadley said from next to me, and I heard a buzz begin in the crowd around us. "Um, guys, you're on the Kiss Cam."

"What?" I looked toward the giant television screen floating above the basketball court and, sure enough, Camden and I were two giant heads with hearts floating around our faces.

"Looks like they want you to lay one on me," he said, not sounding disturbed at all by what was happening. I whipped my head back to face him, panic coursing through me.

"We can't kiss. I don't even know you," I exclaimed, the panic now tingling in my fingers.

"Kiss her!" someone yelled from a few rows behind us.

"Get it, girl!" another enthusiastic person screamed from the seats surrounding us.

Camden wasn't bothered by any of it at all. He just sat there, smiling at me, as if he were waiting for me to just *agree* to being kissed by a complete stranger.

"Riley, just kiss him and get it over with," Hadley said with a sigh. We would have to discuss her lack of sisterly solidarity later.

"Kiss her. Kiss her. Kiss her. Kiss her." The chant started slowly with the people in our section, but in just a few seconds, the entire arena was demanding we kiss. I was blushing so hard I was sure my face would melt off at any moment. I was looking around at all the traitorous spectators surrounding me, silently willing them to shut the fuck up, when I felt a warm hand on the side of my neck.

"Riley," he said gently, making it impossible to not look back at him. "They're not going to stop until we give them what they want. I'm going to kiss you, okay?" His hand was slowly moving up my neck to cup my face, but his eyes were searching mine, looking for an answer to his question.

I nodded slightly, then watched as he closed the distance between us. My eyes closed out of habit, but also because I didn't want to watch the train wreck that would be our kiss on the Jumbotron.

I'm not sure what I expected, but I'd never, *ever*, been kissed like that before.

His lips pressed softly against mine, but captured my bottom one. He held my lip ransom between his own for a moment, and I thought he'd pull away, that the kiss would be over, but he didn't. It wasn't. Instead, he pulled back just a fraction, only to dive back in again, this time with more enthusiasm than I was prepared for. And for the record, he wasn't just kissing me with his lips; his hand was cupping my face, his other arm slipping around my back, and dammit if his head wasn't tilting at just the right angle to kiss the hell out of me.

When I felt the wetness of his tongue teasing, I had two options—pull away and end the kiss, or get lost in it, in him. I opened for him, whimpering as I did, and I immediately wondered how they were going to scrape me off the floor of that arena because it. Was. Over.

His tongue swept in, tangled with mine, and then he went back to paying special attention to my bottom lip, and then continued on and on in an endless cycle of the sexiest kiss I'd ever had.

The entire arena was hollering at us, whistling loudly, yelling obscene things in our direction, and of course the camera operators couldn't pull away—we were practically fucking with our mouths for everyone to see.

But I didn't care. The only thing that mattered in that moment was his mouth against mine and the way his hands were gripping me like he owned me, as if he wanted to take a piece of me and keep it forever. If we'd been alone, in private, my hands would have automatically tried to remove his shirt, I would have been in his lap, and it didn't matter one bit that I'd just met him or that he'd literally just broken up with his girlfriend not fifteen minutes before. All that mattered was his mouth and the way he was using it on me.

But it did end eventually, to the dismay of everyone in the arena. He pulled away, but just his mouth; his hands remained on me and mine on him. We were just panting, staring at one another, and the entire crowd started with a round of thunderous applause. But I might as well have been deaf, because all I could see and feel was him.

"You have an extraordinary mouth," he whispered, his eyes darting down to my lips.

"Ditto," I breathed, unable to utter any other words. He'd kissed me stupid. He smirked at me, but then pulled away fully, leaving me wobbly and unsteady. He moved back into his seat and I into mine, both of us resuming our normal basketball-watching positions, but there could have been any number of things going on down on the court and I wouldn't have been able to process any of it.

"Hey," Hadley whispered, nudging me with her elbow. I turned to look at her. "Did that kiss feel as sexy as it looked?"

I blinked at her. She cracked up laughing. I turned back to the court and in my periphery I saw Camden's hand slyly come up to swipe across his lips, and every man within arm's reach gave him a pat on the back. Meanwhile, multiple women surrounding us squirmed in their seats. It was, quite honestly, ridiculous.

Finally, after a few dazed moments, my faculties returned, along with a normal heart rhythm. I leaned just to my right a little, keeping my face forward, and whispered to him, "Where did you learn to kiss like that?"

I felt his shoulders shake with a chuckle, and then he leaned into me, whispering his response. "I don't think

11

I've ever kissed anyone that way. I must have been inspired."

"Basketball really does it for you, huh?"

He let out a real laugh that time. "I told you, it's like foreplay."

"Right." My eyes rolled but my lips smiled. The lights in the arena started flashing and the Renegades returned to the court. The most epic halftime of my life had come to an end and, truthfully, I was a little glad. I didn't know what to do with the man I'd had mouth sex with, who was still sitting next to me. How do you just *go on* after something so damn arousing? So, when the game started back up, and I had something to pretend to be interested in, I was happy for the distraction. That did not, however, mean I wasn't acutely aware of him. Conscious all the time of how far away he was, or how close, where his hands were, whether he was looking at me. I caught him a few times, eyes not on the game but on me instead. I only caught him because I was stealing glances at him too. But as the game continued, the tension eased. I was able to enjoy the last quarter of the game, finding that he and I had very similar complaints and suggestions for the team, agreeing when fouls were ridiculous, when players were being dumbasses, and that was something else my brain grabbed hold of and tucked away, surely to be brought out again late at night when I couldn't sleep.

After much yelling, the players finally saw it our way and decided to win their game, making my night even more exciting. It would have sucked to spend all that money on celebratory tickets only to watch the Renegades lose—kiss or no.

But the kiss was a perk, right? And that's all it was. A silly halftime game that got way out of control and way too hot for anyone's good.

The buzzer sounded, the crowd erupted in yells and applause, and the great migration out of the arena began. Hadley and I stood up and turned to shuffle down the narrow aisle that led to the stairs. I tried not to notice if Camden was behind me or not, but somehow my body knew he was following. We moved onto the stairs but then were stalled as all the people above us slowly filed out.

"So," I heard Camden's voice say, but also felt against my ear, his breath feathering over the shell of it. "If I asked for your phone number, would you give it to me?"

"What would you need my phone number for?"

"First you didn't understand kissing, and now you're confused as to why I'd want your number?"

My cheeks pinked at his words. "I *know* why you'd want it, I guess I'm just confused by this whole situation."

"It's not rocket science, Riley. That was an amazing kiss. I'd like to do it again sometime. Possibly after a meal. Or a drink."

"You want to go out on a date?"

"Even I can tell he wants to take you out," groaned Hadley from in front of me, giving me an epic eye roll.

"Thanks, Had," Camden said, as if he knew her well enough to use her nickname.

"No problem, Cam," she replied sweetly.

"What the hell is going on?" I was terribly confused. "Do you guys know each other? Is this some sort of poor man's *punk'd*?" They both started laughing, but I was still looking between the two of them.

"Is she always this hard to date?"

Hadley shrugged before climbing the few empty steps ahead of her. "She doesn't date much."

"Okay, don't talk about me like I'm not standing right between you." I turned to Camden, a fierce look in my eyes to tell him I meant business. I was thwarted, however, by the way his eyes were moving up and down my body—appreciatively. I swallowed hard and wished I still had some beer left; my throat was like the Sahara.

"Then give me your number," he said, his voice lower and deeper somehow. "You already kissed me," he argued.

I followed Hadley up the stairs, trying to get as far away from Camden Rogers as possible. He made me nervous, and he made me feel like it was okay to just date guys I kissed at basketball games. He wasn't having any of it, though. He was hot on my heels when we exited into the giant hallway that was the perimeter of the arena, and then he fell into step right next to me.

Hadley, who was on the other side of me, leaned closer and whispered, "He's persistent."

"Yeah, no shit."

"You ladies are forgetting that I'm a lawyer. I can argue my point until we all die or you give up." He said the words with a smile, and something gnawed at my insides, telling me he was being truthful—he was going to pester me to death. That was as good a reason as any to keep denying him.

"Listen, it's nothing personal, I'm just not looking to date anyone."

I felt a warm hand on my elbow and then I was being turned to face him. People kept walking right past us, a few grumbling about us blocking the walkway.

"Riley, you can't tell me you aren't even a little interested, given how much you participated in that kiss." He raised an eyebrow, and fuck me if it wasn't sexy.

"So, because I kissed you, now I have to date you?"

"I like your mouth, Riley. I like the way you use it and the words that come out of it. I've only spent one half of a basketball game talking to you, and I know with near perfect certainty that I would never tire of hearing you speak."

I couldn't help but smile at his response. "Not like Sophia the princess?" I batted my eyelashes at him.

"Come on," he urged quietly. "Give me your number."

Something about Camden Rogers felt dangerous. Not serial-killer dangerous, but the kind of dangerous that made me want to keep my heart safe right inside my chest and not offer it to fantastic kissers who could argue their way out of anything.

"I'm really just not looking to date anyone. Sorry." I gave a sincere smile and shrugged. Then I turned back to Hadley. I could tell by her expression she was annoyed with me.

He followed us out of the arena, down the steps at the street entrance, and all the way across the street to the MAX station. We were surrounded by hundreds of people who'd also taken the light rail train to the arena, and I wasn't looking forward to cramming myself inside the small train car with all of them, but I couldn't help but pray the train came quickly.

"Just one date," he said from behind me.

"He's literally begging," Hadley said to me, clearly taking his side.

I heard the train coming from the west and watched it cross the bridge and come to a slow stop at our station.

"Come on," he pleaded. "At least give me your last name."

I managed a laugh and tried to ignore the part of me that wanted to see where a date with him would lead, but the circumstances were just too strange.

"Have a good rest of your night," I called through the doors as I grabbed the pole above my head to keep myself steady. He was smiling at me, but it was more of a challenging smile, as if he couldn't believe I would leave him hanging. The doors started to close and I held my breath.

"SMITH!" Hadley yelled just before the doors closed. I turned to her, mouth gaping open, shocked she'd give some stranger my name. "Her last name is Smith!"

The doors closed and the train started slowly making its way up the hill to the Park and Ride lot.

"You sneaky bitch," I said, shooting Hadley with the imaginary laser beams that came from my eyes.

She smiled and then blew me a kiss. I rolled my eyes and made a mental note to post embarrassing pictures of her on Instagram.

Chapter Two

Camden

There were approximately one fucking million Riley Smiths on Facebook.

The morning after our impromptu kiss at halftime, I sat in my office staring at my computer, trying to locate her online. Facebook was my first stop, but it was looking like a bad option. I didn't have time to sift through all the women on my screen.

Well, that wasn't entirely accurate. I had the time and I was normally a patient guy. I could spend my evenings looking for her if that's what it took—I wasn't above Facebook stalking. But for some reason, I wasn't feeling very patient with Riley. I didn't know anything about her except her name and how fantastic her lips felt pressed against mine, and I wanted to know more. Much more.

So my next stop was good old Google. I typed in "Riley Smith Event Planner" and a few results came back. I clicked on the top return, but didn't find any pertinent information. I clicked on the second and third links, and neither one of those led me anywhere either. But the fourth link for a company called Rose City Event Coordinators brought me the information I was looking for. At the bottom of the page there were headshots of all the coordinators and I was immediately drawn to the photo of Riley. She looked a little different in her photo—dressed professionally, her smile more forced than natural, but beautiful nonetheless. Her hair still sported the new trend of darker on top, fading into a honey blonde toward the ends. The night before she'd been wearing Chucks and a pleather jacket, but in her photo she was wearing a blouse that looked like appropriate work attire.

It didn't matter what she wore, I still found myself picturing what she had on underneath it all.

Right under her picture was a link to send her an e-mail. Perfect.

Just as I clicked on the link a knock came on my door. It opened and Justin's face appeared.

"I'm headed to get some coffee from Case Study. Want me to bring you something?"

I leaned back in my chair and my hand absently ran through my hair. "Mind if I come along? I could use some air to clear my head."

He gave me a puzzled look, but then said, "Sure."

Justin had been a good friend of mine since we both started at the firm around the same time. He was just a year older than me and we had similar backgrounds. When I wasn't taking insane women to basketball games, it was to him I usually gave my extra ticket. We'd just made it out of the door of our building when he asked about my date.

"How'd it go with Sophia last night?" His question was probably supposed to sound innocently curious, but I could hear the contempt in his voice. He had met Sophia briefly when she'd stopped by the office unannounced, and when I told him I was taking her to the game last night, instead of him, I'd seen him try very hard not to roll his eyes.

I groaned before I could stop myself.

"That well, huh?"

"We're finished. I'm not sure why I let it get all the way to a third date. She got bent out of shape because I wouldn't skip my grandma's birthday party for her. I let her walk."

Justin clapped his hand on my back, saying, "Good man." We walked in silence for about half a block before he spoke again. "She's not why you're upset, is she? I mean, I'm sorry you're taking the breakup badly, but man, come on. She wasn't right for you."

"No, it's nothing like that. I couldn't care less about her. In fact, after she left the game last night, I met someone."

"You move fast," he replied with a laugh.

"She was sitting right next to me and sort of heard the whole breakup, then watched Sophia stomp away." I paused, remembering the way Riley was saying all the things I was thinking in my head, how she seemed to think Sophia was just as ridiculous as I did, how she just seemed to get me. "She was cute and funny, and an incredible kisser."

"You kissed her? The same night you broke up with someone else?"

"Well, yeah, I guess so. It was that stupid Kiss Cam they do at halftime. The camera was on us, and people were yelling at us from all around, trying to get us to kiss. Finally, I just kind of grabbed her and kissed her. But it was amazing."

"Dude, seriously? Amazing?" Justin asked, his voice skeptical.

"I don't know. It was different, I guess."

We approached the door to Case Study and Justin opened it, letting me go in first. "So, are you going to see her again?"

I let out a big sigh. "That's up to her. I was just about to send her an e-mail when you knocked on my door."

"An e-mail? Who are you? Tom Hanks? Is this the year 2000?"

"She didn't give me her number, and her friend shouted her last name just before they took off on the MAX."

"And you never considered the fact that if she didn't give you her number, maybe she just wasn't into you?" Justin ordered our drinks, paying for mine before I could stop him, and we walked to the end of the counter to wait.

"I don't know, man. There was just something different about her. She was fun. And witty. She just kept saying the funniest shit. She wasn't doing that annoying thing where women try to flirt with you but it just comes across as desperate. She just was having a good time at a basketball game, and I had a good time with her. She was refreshing."

The barista slid our drinks over to us and we took them and started walking back to the office.

"So you're going to e-mail her?"

"I think so. I'm just not sure what I'm going to say."

"You'll figure it out," he said, slapping his hand down on my shoulder. "And if she's as cool as you say she is, then she'll probably say yes regardless."

I lifted my coffee to my mouth. "Here's hoping."

To: rsmith@rosecityevents.com

From: camden.rogers@gmail.com

Subject: Not a stalker

Is this, by chance, the Riley Smith I met at the Renegades game last night who liked the disturbingly disgusting combination of cotton candy and Hefeweizen beer? She ran off last night without giving me her phone number (obviously a side effect of the previously mentioned strange combination of foods), so I'm looking for her. I came across this e-mail address and was hoping you were her. If this isn't the cute and funny woman I met at the game last night, please disregard. But if it's you, please respond. I'm not done talking to you yet.

> *Cam*

I stared at the e-mail for a good ten minutes before I finally just hit the Send button. I knew there would be no way to get any work done until I sent it, and then I knew there would be no work getting done until she replied.

"Dude, you've got to get yourself under control," I said to myself as I scrubbed my hands down my face. *She's just a girl. Just an awesome girl you met at a basketball game. Who is cute as fuck and knows how to kiss.* "Goddamn it."

Luckily, there was a meeting I had to attend that gave me a reason to stop refreshing my in-box every ten seconds. It was long and painfully boring, just as one would imagine a lawyer meeting to be, and when it finally ended I nearly sprinted back to my office. Electricity shot through me when I saw a response in my in-box.

From: rsmith@rosecityevents.com

To: camden.rogers@gmail.com

Subject: Pretty Stalkery

I can't decide if I'm flattered or totally creeped out that you found me in one day. But, then again, you are a lawyer and seemed pretty determined. And don't dis the cotton candy and beer combo; it's delicious.

Since I assume now that you've found me, it would be impossible to shake you, let's move this conversation to text. I'm sure my boss doesn't want to read about how you're obsessed with me. My number is 503-555-8574.

—Riley

Holy shit, she gave me her phone number. Ignoring the fact that it would probably be best to wait a while to text her if I didn't want to seem too eager, I started tapping out a message. Screw societally expected wait times between messages. I couldn't care less if I seemed too anxious. I *was* anxious. And excited. And nervous. Something about Riley had gotten under my skin.

I hope I don't get you in trouble with your boss. But I'd like to remind you this could have all been avoided had you just given me your number last night.

I hit Send and then put my phone in my desk drawer, hoping it would give me enough distance to focus on my work for a while. When it buzzed ten minutes later I couldn't reach into my drawer fast enough.

**She loves me, it'll be fine. And if I'd given you my number last night, this wouldn't be as much fun. I like thinking about you scouring the Internet for any piece of

information about me you could get. I hope you didn't find anything terrible. *

She was flirting with me. This was good.

* *Nothing too terrible. I promise to keep all your secrets safe if you agree to see me again.* *

* *Are you blackmailing me?* *

* *I like to call it being extremely persuasive.* *

After a few minutes of torture, the phone buzzed again.

* *I'll be at The Tank on Hawthorne tonight after work. 6pm. Maybe I'll see you there.* *

Chapter Three

Riley

I had no idea why I told him to meet me here. The Tank was a bar from my younger years. I'd always loved it there, but forgotten until I'd walked in how out of place I would be in my black slacks and button-down blouse. I didn't let the hipsters faze me though. I walked straight to the bar, glad to see my favorite bartender was still working there.

"Riley," George said with a great big smile. "Long time, no see."

"Same to you," I said, returning his smile. "I decided to stop by and make sure the place was still standing."

He grabbed a rag and wiped down the wooden bar top. "We're still here, just waiting for you." He winked and my smile broadened. "What can I get you? Hef, like always?"

"Like always," I replied with a nod. I hauled myself onto a barstool and smiled at George as he passed me my beer. "What's new?" I asked before taking a sip of the ice-cold beer.

"Annalise is pregnant." His wide smile turned proud, and I could have sworn his shoulders pushed back too.

"What? No way. That's amazing, George. Congratulations."

His smile beamed as he used a rag to dry off a glass and place it on the shelf behind him. "Due in February."

"That's amazing." A few years ago, before I'd started adulting regularly, I'd come down to Tank with my college friends. The beer was cheap during happy hour, and they were always playing some awesome movie on the big screen or doing a fun trivia night. I watched George and Annalise start dating and fall in love. She was a Portland transplant, and he was a very doting tour guide. She'd come in on the nights he was working and do her homework at the bar, making lovey eyes at him. She was a doll and he was a lucky man.

"When are you gonna settle down? You look pretty sophisticated in your fancy work clothes. You growing up on me?"

"Never," I gasped.

"Oh, good. I'm not the only one overdressed for this place." I heard his voice and my insides grew warmer; every part of me was heating up. I swiveled on my stool only to see Camden's perfect body wrapped up in a three-piece-suit bow. He'd looked fantastic casual the night before, but standing before me looking all Armani model, it was a low blow.

"Camden," I breathed, then chided myself for letting him have such an effect on me. I took a drink of my beer, then said with more conviction, "You found me."

"What kind of a stalker would I be if I couldn't find you?" He sat on the barstool next to me, winked at me, then ordered a Hef for himself.

"You like Hef?" I asked, hopeful for some reason.

"Never had it. I usually drink darker beers. But it's your favorite, so I might as well give it a try." The idea that he was going to drink something completely opposite of what he liked, just to see if he liked it, for me, was cuter than I wanted to give him credit for.

"You drink that and I'll try one of your favorites," I offered.

He tilted his head a little and narrowed his eyes at me, then said, "You've got yourself a deal." He stuck his hand out, I placed my palm in his, and we shook on it. Just then, George slid Cam's beer over to him. I watched with rapt attention as he put the rim of the glass to his stupidly luscious lips and took a sip. His eyebrows shot up and the corners of his mouth turned down as he nodded his head. "Not bad, Smith."

"It's the best ever," I said, rolling my eyes for dramatic effect. Just then, a loud group of people entered the bar, all of them wearing either too much black or too much plaid. It was a toss-up in Portland: lumberjack hipsters or emo hipsters. "You're right. We're totally overdressed for this place."

"But there's two of us, so we're not completely out of place." His eyes wandered over my body and he didn't even try to hide it. "This is a far cry from Chucks and jeans."

"The day job pays the bills and it requires a certain dress code." I shrugged one shoulder.

"You like your job?"

"Most days. Party planning is always fun, it's dealing with the uptight parents or bridezillas that gets old. But at the end of the day, when that same bride is dancing with her new husband, and she's not worried about one single thing, that's the real reward; watching people enjoy the big moments of their lives instead of worrying about whether there's enough food or if the cake has arrived. It's a good job." I sighed a little then took a drink of my beer. "And you like your job?"

"My job is pretty boring." He laughed.

"It can't be all bad, though. An entertainment lawyer, right? So, you've worked with some celebrities and stuff?"

"Not many you would have heard of. Mostly local actors and recording artists. It's not glamorous or anything though. It's just contracts."

"Well, I'm sorry, but your stock just drastically declined." I tried to keep a straight face, but when he seemed to be taking my comment seriously, his brow furrowing and lips parting slightly, I realized he hadn't picked up on my sarcasm. "Cam," I said, resting my hand on his forearm, "I'm only kidding. I'm sorry. That was a terrible joke."

I watched as the tension left his face and a smile replaced it. "Damn, Riley. For a minute I thought you were just like all the others."

"The others?"

"The ones like Sophia, who only date me because of my name or my connections." He was smiling when he said the words, but I could tell the idea bothered him. It only made me feel worse.

"I'm sorry, truly. I would never want you to think that was why I was here. I couldn't care less about all that."

"It's fine," he said with a sincere smile. "I'm just going to have to get used to talking to someone with a personality." He winked at me and my heart started waving a white flag, tripping over itself. "So," he continued, unaware of the way my heart was thumping in my chest, "is this your normal hangout?"

"I came here a lot in college, when I was young and carefree. It's close to my apartment, and, the best part—there's Skee-Ball." I gave a nod over my shoulder toward the back of the bar and watched as Cam's eyes followed.

"Ohhh." He laughed, drawing the one tiny word out over a few chuckles. "You're going down, Smith." The smile on his face was blinding, and for a moment, it was all I could see.

Pushing all the stupid feelings he was causing away, I managed to retort, "You like Skee-Ball?"

"I'm a Skee-Ball master." He was completely serious.

"Them's fightin' words," I said, hopping down from my barstool. "Care to make a wager on your Skee-Ball skills?"

"You wanna bet? On Skee-Ball?" His eyebrows rose, but he looked intrigued.

I shrugged. "Why not? Afraid you'll lose?"

He smiled. "No, sweetheart. I'm not afraid I'll lose." The look he was giving me was so intense, it made the hair on my arms stand up and the bottom of my stomach drop out. "What's up for grabs?" And there went the shiver along my spine.

"If I win, you have to take me to a Renegades game, Mr. Season Ticket Holder."

He laughed again, this time rougher and under his breath. "And if I win, you have to come back to my place tonight to try one of my favorite beers."

I weighed my confidence in winning against possibly being roped into going back to his place. I liked him, more than I'd liked someone in a long time, but I didn't want to give him the wrong impression. I wasn't going to sleep with him. "Listen, I'm going to win—there's no doubt. But in the event that there's a major earthquake during my turn and I end up losing, I'm not going back to your place to have sex. I'm not that kind of girl."

He held up both his hands like he was surrendering. "The thought never even crossed my mind." His eyes never left mine and he looked sincere.

"Liar." I laughed.

"Okay, honestly? You've crossed my mind a lot in the last twenty-four hours, but I'm not interested in a one-night stand. It just so happens that my favorite beer is back at my place, and I'd love to share it with you."

I held his gaze for a moment, believing his words even though my heart was throwing up caution flags. "Lead the way," I finally said, waving my hand to the back of the bar where the Skee-Ball was located. He grabbed his beer and walked toward the game, reaching in his pocket and pulling out a few quarters. There was only one lane, so we'd have to take turns. He held out his hand to me, dropping two quarters into my palm when I opened it for him. "Ladies first," he said with another wink. Damn him.

I deposited the two quarters and then smiled when I heard the familiar rumbling of the balls rolling down the track. That sound brought back a million memories. Most of them hazy. I reached for a ball, rolling it around in my hand. "I swear I've put $500 worth of quarters in this machine."

"But you mainly played when you were drunk, right?"

I shot him a halfhearted glare. "I wasn't *always* drunk."

He laughed. "I'm just saying, maybe we should get a few more drinks in you to make it fair."

I narrowed my eyes at him, but then turned and concentrated on my game. I let out an exhale, lined my right shoulder up with the track, stepped forward with my right foot, then my left, and then sent the wooden ball soaring down the lane toward the backboard. It rolled up the track and landed directly in the fifty-point bucket at the top. I resisted the urge to turn back to Camden and stick my tongue out at him.

"Nice shot," he said.

"Thanks," I said as I turned my head back to look at him, catching him staring directly at my ass. "No wonder you wanted me to go first." I laughed, shaking my head.

"Can you blame me?"

I didn't even bother answering him, I just lined up my next shot. Each ball got progressively harder, if only because I could feel his hot gaze on me. I wished I hadn't turned to look at him because after that first shot, I was completely distracted. I managed a decent score of 540 points. Not my best, but not too shabby by any means. "You're up," I said with a smile. I picked my beer up off the floor next to the game and walked to stand next to him. I took a long drink, trying not to stare as he removed his suit jacket and laid it gently over the back of a nearby chair.

Next, he unbuttoned his cuffs and rolled his shirtsleeves up to his elbows. The muscle in his forearms bulged and twisted with his movements and my eyes were completely glued to them. I'd even given up my ruse of drinking my beer. All eyes were on that man.

"Like what you see?" My eyes snapped up to meet his, which were gleaming with amusement at having caught me ogling him.

I shrugged, feigning indifference. I knew I'd been busted, but I didn't need to feed his ego any more. Although, egotistical wasn't the right word to describe him. He knew he was sexy as hell, and he knew I was into him, but he wasn't all bravado. It was more like he enjoyed the fact that I was attracted to him and wanted to use it to his advantage. I got the impression he wasn't that forward with all women. He laughed at my brush-off, but then he reached up and loosened his tie and I couldn't watch any longer, for self-preservation's sake.

"Just so we're clear, when I win, you come home with me for a drink."

"A deal's a deal," I said with a smile. How good at Skee-Ball could he possibly be? *Renegades game, here I come.*

He lined his shots up in the same manner I did, concentration high, one knee bent slightly, but when he lobbed the ball down the lane, it veered left wildly, ricocheted off the side and careened to the right exactly at the perfect moment to leap at the lip and land directly in the one-hundred-point bucket in the top corner.

That son of a bitch.

"You're a Skee-Ball shark! I can't believe you!" My words were a mixture of laughter, rage, and disbelief. "What the hell is wrong with you?"

He turned, a new gleam in his eye, one of pride and amusement. "I had a Skee-Ball game in my basement as a kid. I'm very good at it."

"You're a cheater," I accused.

"No, I very clearly stated I was a Skee-Ball master. You asked for a competition."

I narrowed my eyes at him. "You realize this makes you look like a jackass, right?"

"Are you a sore loser?" He reached down and grabbed another wooden ball, forearms rippling, causing my breath to catch.

"No," I snapped, still watching his arms move, his hand palming the ball. It was suddenly sweltering in the bar. "I just don't like being taken advantage of, or lied to."

Keeping the ball in his hand, he walked over to me, stopping with barely inches between us. I had no choice but to look up at him, my eyelids nearly fluttering when the forefinger of his free hand came to pull my chin up a little, forcing our eyes to meet. He still wore a slight grin, which was annoyingly cute, but he looked mostly contrite.

"I'm sorry. I've never met a woman who gets as excited over Skee-Ball as I do. I couldn't help myself. Forgive me?" His thumb took a gentle swipe under my bottom lip and I held in a whimper. Without permission, my hands came to rest on his hips and my fingers gripped him just tight enough to tell him I didn't want him backing away.

32

"I suppose," I whispered, my eyes locking on to his lips.

"I'm still going to try and win," he whispered.

"I'd do the same."

He leaned forward and his lips met my forehead. I exhaled while he kissed me, both excited for the contact, but irritated he was neglecting my lips. Then he stepped away, my hands fell back to my sides, and I watched as he played a perfect game. A whopping 900 points to the man in the three-piece suit, which showed off his fantastic ass, as he lobbed each ball into the hundred-point bucket in the top right-hand corner.

"The game will never be the same again," I joked.

"Indeed," he said, rolling his sleeves down again, much to my dismay. "Do you want another drink here, or shall we head back to my place?"

"Might as well get the inevitable over with." I shrugged, trying to appear as if the idea of being alone with him in his home didn't excite me.

He smiled, then said, "Don't pretend like you aren't dying to try my beer."

"I'm abuzz with anticipation." He gave me a beautiful smile, then headed toward the bar and settled the tab with George.

"Don't be a stranger, Riley," George called out as we walked toward the door.

"I won't be. Tell Annalise I said hi. And congrats on the baby. That's awesome." He waved, and I waved back before walking out onto the sidewalk. The sun was beginning to set, the sky turning a pinkish-orange color. "I love it when the sky is any color besides blue," I mused.

"Even gray?" His question sounded completely serious, as if we were discussing our opinions on politics or religion, yet we were only speaking of the sunset.

"Especially gray. Storms are the best."

"What's so great about storms?"

"I dunno. Something about the unpredictability and the electricity in the air. The thunder. The lightning. It's exciting."

"Hmmm," he responded, not giving away his own opinion on storms.

"What? You don't like a good storm?"

"I like you, and you remind me of a little storm." His compliment caught me off guard, which only made my cheeks pink faster. "Oh, look," he said, gently gripping my elbow and effectively turning me toward him. "Your cheeks match the sky."

I had no words, so I didn't even try to speak.

"My car's just over there," he said, pointing over my shoulder. I turned and watched as a sleek sports car's lights flashed and the horn beeped. I'd never really been a car girl—sports cars didn't do it for me, per se. But, good Lord, watching Camden walk up to the passenger side of the tiny black car and open the door was more than I could take. I couldn't help but giggle as I approached him.

"What's so funny?"

"I can't figure you out. I can't tell if you're the rich lawyer guy who wears amazing suits and drinks impressive beer, or if you're the guy who likes to go to basketball games and play Skee-Ball."

"Perhaps you shouldn't try to fit me in a box, Riley." He said the words with a smile, but his tone was serious. "Maybe I'm all of that."

Maybe he's everything.

I swallowed, trying to tamp down all the emotions rising inside of me, and brushed past him to climb into his tiny car. The inside was just as impressive as the outside, and I spent a few seconds simply marveling at all the buttons and screens the manufacturer managed to fit in the small space. I also purposefully didn't look over at Camden until he was seated. I knew watching him settle in the car would be a great show, but I was done torturing myself for the evening.

"This is just a car, right? It can't, like, fly or anything, can it?"

He chuckled. "Welcome to the Batmobile."

"You're not joking," I agreed. "It's pretty impressive, but how long did it take you to remember what all the buttons did?"

"I'm still not sure and I've had it a year," he said, giving me an honest smile. "As long as I can turn it on, listen to the radio, and drive it, that's all I care about."

"Then why did you buy it?" I laughed. "You could have paid a fifth of what this car probably cost and gotten a perfectly capable vehicle."

"Because, Riley, it's sexy as fuck." The car rumbled loudly as he pressed down on the accelerator. His gaze was on me and I felt it everywhere. My heart thumped wildly, my breath was uneven, and my thighs squeezed together, trying desperately to relieve the ache growing between them.

The list of sexy things about Camden Rogers was growing rapidly: kisses, thighs, mouth, three-piece suits, Skee-Ball skills, and now his driving abilities. Hot men handling hot cars was, apparently, something I was into. Huh. Who'd have thought?

"You lure a lot of women into your Batmobile?" I was trying with everything I had not to react to him the way my body wanted to. I didn't lean toward him, I didn't try and catch his scent, and I definitely tried not to look at him driving around Portland in his tiny black sex machine.

"I don't date that often."

"Sophia was an anomaly?"

"Sophia was a disaster."

I couldn't help but laugh; he was totally right.

He drove smoothly through the streets of Portland, taking me to the west side, and I knew instantly I would be impressed with his place, and also that it would be just as fancy as his car and his suit. Minute by minute I was feeling more and more out of place. The night before, sitting next to him at the Renegades game, we'd seemed so similar—or at least comparable.

We continued to talk about our jobs and other inconsequential drivel until he slowed, pulling into the underground parking lot beneath a tall building right on the Willamette river. He pulled into a numbered spot and shut off the ignition. He gave me his brilliant smile, then turned and climbed out of the car. I tried to look away, but I couldn't. I saw his ass as he climbed out and it would go down in the history of me as one of the best moments of my life. He shut his door and I took in a deep breath, trying to steel myself for what I knew was coming; more confirmation that we were worlds apart.

I reminded myself that after the next hour I could go back to my own little apartment, the one I loved that was over a tiny thrift store, and Camden could go back to his high-rise life. The thought saddened me more than I hoped it would, and that surprised me, but like everything else, I pushed those feelings down. I'd drink a beer, I'd joke around with him, appreciate his impressive body in that deadly suit, his beautiful eyes, and his fantastic sense of humor, but then I'd go back to real life.

Chapter Four

Camden

The small heels of her shoes echoed through the parking garage as we made our way toward the elevator. I was having high school flashbacks as I contemplated holding her hand, but I was nervous she'd shake me off, find a reason to shrug away from me, and I didn't think I could handle the rejection just yet.

The last hour I'd spent with Riley was more fun than any date I'd ever been on. She was hilarious, laid-back, witty, and her sarcasm was on point. And she was gorgeous. A spitfire little thing, and a large part of me wanted to feel exactly how small she was by holding her against me, by wrapping my arms around her, but her signals were less than clear. I could literally see the moments where she seemed really into me and then suddenly pulled herself back, almost as if she were talking herself out of it.

She followed me to the elevator and I punched in my security code. The doors opened and I motioned for her to enter first. It was a glass elevator, and after I'd pushed the button for the ninth floor, she watched the skyline as we rose.

"When my brother was little he used to call it Ice Mountain," she said with a sweet smile.

"What?" I asked, confused but still staring at her, taking in her beauty with the city behind her.

"Mt. Hood," she said as she gestured out of the elevator to the mountain in the east.

"Older or younger?"

"He's three years younger than me." She turned back to me and her smile was different, more loving, warmer. It looked as though she had a lot of affection for her younger brother.

"Does he live near here?"

"He's still in school down in Eugene." A flash of sadness moved over her face, but she looked happy again in an instant. "He's working on his master's degree. Wants to be a music teacher."

"That's a gamble in today's society."

She shrugged and held up her hands. "I tried to warn him. People are far more concerned with their next event than the musical education of our nation's youth. Which is why my career choice is much better."

I laughed as the elevator came to a stop on my floor. I led her down the hallway to my door, and for some reason I was nervous. I unlocked the door, stepped in, flipped on the lights, and then watched as she took in my space. A weird new part of me wanted her to like my apartment, wanted her to feel at home there. This thought had never occurred to me when I'd brought other women home. I'd never given a thought as to whether the woman I was entertaining would approve of my home, but for some reason, with Riley, I did.

I wondered if the dark colors and bare walls made me appear cold, or if the sharp lines and leather furniture made me seem hard. For a strange and unfamiliar reason, I needed her to see me as approachable, likable, touchable even. But I was afraid my home wasn't a good representation of that.

She walked slowly through the entryway and moved straight to the large window in the living area. It had the same view as from the elevator, just a wider window. The river was a stone's throw away, the bridges, the eastern skyline, the trees, the mountain. It didn't include Portland's impressive skyscrapers, but those weren't what made Portland famous anyway. It was the way the strange big little town was nestled between nearly every kind of nature you could imagine. Beaches, mountains, deserts, rivers, lakes—they were all within a few hours' drive.

"Ice Mountain looks gorgeous from your living room," she said, tossing a sexy smile over her shoulder at me.

"There are a few things that look gorgeous from my point of view," I said, surprised at my own level of cheese. I could almost hear her rolling her eyes at me, and I couldn't blame her. It sounded like a line, but it wasn't. I was so stupidly nervous to have her in my house, the words were coming out of my mouth without passing through the filter I normally employed.

When she finally turned back around, her eyes were friendly and she was still smiling. "So, where's this fancy beer you've promised me."

I walked back toward the kitchen, saying, "I never said it was fancy."

"No?"

"No. I simply said it was dark and it was my favorite." I reached into the refrigerator and pulled out two cans of Guinness.

"Guinness is your favorite beer?" she asked, eyebrows high in surprise.

"All others pale in comparison, quite literally."

"My first legal St. Patrick's Day, I got totally smashed on Irish car bombs. Guinness and I do not get along."

"A deal's a deal," I said, holding a can out for her. She took it with a huff, placed it on the counter, snapped it open, and then held it out toward me. "Here's to getting your ass handed to you by a Skee-Ball shark."

I opened my own can and tapped it against hers, my smile pulling on my cheeks. "Cheers." We both took our drinks, but hers ended in a pinched face along with a groan.

"Nope. I can't," she said, placing the can on the counter again. I couldn't help but laugh at the sour face she was making. She gave me a wry look, but then surprised me by hopping up onto my kitchen counter, making herself at home, and folding her hands in her lap. "So, you're the mayor's son, you're an entertainment lawyer, you kick ass at Skee-Ball, you live in a palace in the sky, and you drive the Batmobile. What else do I need to know about you, Camden Rogers?"

I didn't like the implication of her question, the idea that I was *more*, or in some sort of league that was above her. I could practically feel her building a wall between us. I stood across from her, leaning back against the island in the kitchen, and brought my beer to my lips, taking a long pull while keeping my eyes on her. "How about we ask each other questions. You first, then me. Totally honest answers, no matter the question."

"Like truth or dare without the dare aspect? Where's the fun in that?"

"I'm not interested in stunts or pranks."

"Just the truth?"

"Just you." Her eyes widened at my words and her breath caught. I watched as she tried to rein in her reaction, tried to brush it off as if it hadn't affected her at all.

"Fine. You're on. How old were you when you lost your virginity?"

"Sixteen," I answered immediately. "Couldn't start with something less personal, like favorite food?"

"Your tongue's been in my mouth," she said, rolling her eyes.

"Trust me," I said, letting my eyes roam her entire body, hoping to make her squirm, "I remember." When I saw her shift her weight from one side to the other and her cheeks pink up again, I considered it a job well done. "When did you lose your virginity?"

"Seventeen. He'd been my boyfriend for three years. He dumped me two weeks later."

"Well, he sounds like an asshole."

"I'd drink to that if I didn't hate your favorite beer." She smiled at me playfully. "Okay, um, worst way you ever dumped a girl?"

"You can't be serious. I plead the fifth. There's no way to answer that question without incriminating myself or making myself look like a jerk."

Her eyes narrowed and she nodded slowly. "I see. You're a bad breaker-upper. I probably should have seen this coming. I did witness the Sophia debacle."

I rolled my eyes. "Can we not talk about Sophia? Using her as an example is like, I don't know, claiming watermelon Jolly Ranchers actually taste like watermelon."

"What are you saying? Sophia didn't taste right?" She asked the question with a smile, playfully, so I took that cue from her and moved to close the distance between us. I pushed off the counter and my hands went right to her knees, sliding up her thighs a little, my hips fitting between her legs.

"I know you tasted better."

She sucked in a quick breath and her eyes darted from my eyes to my lips, but she didn't pull back. She didn't close herself off or push me away; in fact, she leaned into me, just barely.

"You tasted like cotton candy," I said softly, my gaze unable to stay off her lips. "And Hefeweizen."

"That sounds gross," she whispered.

"It was fucking amazing." I reached up slowly and thumbed her bottom lip, loving the way she sucked in another breath when I touched her. "And I imagine if I were to kiss you right now, you might taste like Guinness." I watched as her lips pulled up into a smile.

"You'd like that, wouldn't you?" She laughed.

I nodded and moved my gaze from her lips to her eyes, glad to see her smile extended to them. "May I? In the name of kissing and research?"

She rolled her eyes playfully, shrugged, then said, "I guess. But only for the sake of science."

"Right," I whispered, leaning in. "Science."

One thing became clear the moment our mouths connected: the only time in the last twenty-four hours Riley was being completely honest with me was when we were

43

kissing. Her kisses were real, and the way she moved her mouth against mine left me feeling as though she felt just as connected as I did, not as if we were too different or too wrong for each other. The way she kissed me only cemented the fact that together we were perfect.

Just like the first kiss, this one was effortlessly spectacular. Her lips fit perfectly against mine, moved in rhythm with mine, tasted perfect, like Guinness and Riley and lip gloss. Her face was the perfect shape to fit right into the palms of my hands, and her legs were made to wrap around my waist, just like they did that instant.

I knew she'd feel amazing in my arms, that the smallness of her would be the biggest turn-on I'd ever experienced. I wrapped my arms around her, pulling her body closer to mine so that she was barely balancing on the edge of the counter. My mouth moved over hers and her fingers twined in my hair as she let out a small moan.

The smooth fabric of her blouse glided underneath my fingers as I brought my hands around her waist, finding the tiny pearl buttons along the front. I absentmindedly played with the bottom one, then pulled my mouth just far enough from hers to ask, "May I?"

Her breaths panted out quickly, but her response took a few moments, my heart thundering a thousand beats with every passing second. I didn't want her to pull away, but I also didn't want her to feel pressured. Fuck, I wanted her to be on the same page as me; I wanted her to want this as much as I did. Finally she nodded, and then immediately pressed her mouth against mine again. I'd never been so good at unbuttoning blouses as I was in that moment, each one sliding through my fingers and falling open, obviously on my side.

When her blouse slid off her shoulders and caught in the crook of her elbows, I managed to pull away, wanting to see her.

Fuck me twice.

"You can't be real," I whispered, unsure why I let the words slip out, but meaning them even so. Her perfect breasts sat in a sexy-as-fuck white lace bra. No deceiving pillows or pads, no pushing up, just her perfect fucking tits beautifully displayed. Through the delicate lace, her pert pink nipples were hard and looked as though they might ache from want.

My hand cupped her over the lace, bringing the gorgeous mound to my mouth so I could taste the top swell, my thumb teasing the hard nub.

She moaned again, her back arching into me, offering me more, asking me to take so much more. My fingers slipped beneath both straps and slowly slid them over her soft shoulders, the lace peeling away, both of her breasts rising and falling with the quickness of her breathing. Her arms were trapped by her shirt and the straps of her bra, but her eyes were begging me to continue. Her palms rested on the counter and she offered herself to me.

I bent and lowered my mouth to hers, my tongue tracing her lips, her teeth, tentatively tangling with hers as my hands moved to cup her breasts. The warm, soft flesh fit perfectly in my hands, as I'd expected, because everything about Riley was perfect for me. I pulled my mouth from hers, but only to taste her nipple. I sucked one in and the sound she made, the moan mixed with a whimper, went straight to my dick.

"Oh, God," she whispered as I drew her farther into my mouth, my other hand still palming and teasing her. "This is crazy," she continued, her neck bent back, chest still

45

open and waiting for me. My mouth moved from her breast to leave openmouthed kisses all along her chest, up and over her collarbone, and up her neck, focusing then on the soft skin right below her ear.

"Please," I said between kisses, "please tell me I can take you to bed." My hands still worked her breasts, but I wanted to feel all of her against all of me. I wanted to lay her out and focus on every part of her.

"We can't," she panted. I groaned, torn between respecting her wishes and begging like a teenage boy. "I'm sorry," she said immediately.

"No," I replied, pulling away from her, trying to keep my eyes north. I would respect her but that didn't mean I would torture myself with the sight of her perfect naked breasts. "Don't apologize." I let out a large breath and pulled the straps of her bra up, watching the lace cover her again, hoping to fucking God I'd get a chance to taste them again.

"It's just, well, we only met last night." I looked in her eyes as she pulled her shirt closed, now looking embarrassed and ashamed.

"Hey." I moved into her again, my hips forcing her knees to open wider, and brought my hands to each side of her neck. "There's nothing to be sorry for, nothing to be ashamed of. I understand, and I'm glad you stopped me." I leaned in, hoping she wouldn't stop me, and pressed a gentle kiss against her lips. "Don't hate me for saying this," I said, then kissed her again. "But you have fantastic tits." Lucky for me, she laughed.

"Thanks," she said, laughing and blushing at the same time.

"I should be the one thanking you," I said, watching as she shyly buttoned her shirt back up. I watched her beautiful skin disappear with every button, silently mourning each one. I didn't miss it when her eyes darted down to my crotch, or the way her eyes widened when she saw the bulge of my erection there.

"Um, no. I think you're in worse shape than me."

I shrugged, trying to play off the uncomfortable way my cock was being strangled by my pants. "Nothing a cold shower won't take care of." Lies. As soon as I was alone, I'd be rubbing one out. Not even cold water would tame that erection.

All put back together, she hopped off my counter, straightening her shirt, trying to erase the evidence that I'd been thoroughly in there just moments before. I reached out for her hand and pulled her against me. "Hey," I said, tucking some hair behind her ear, "you all right?"

She smiled up at me, perfect white teeth shining. "I'm fine. I'm just not used to everything moving so quickly."

"Me, either," I said, letting my thumb move over her chin, liking the way her eyelids fluttered slightly as it did. "Can I see you again this week? Take you out for dinner?"

The light faded from her eyes and the smile fell from her lips. "Um, I'm not sure, I'll have to check my schedule." She said the words and then she pulled away from me and suddenly everything felt different. "This week's not really good for me."

"Okay," I said, confused at the way she transformed from pliant in my hands to awkwardly trying to wiggle out of the conversation. "How about this weekend? I know you lost at Skee-Ball, but I'd still love to take you to a game." I hoped a little joke would reel her back in.

"This weekend's no good either." She was fidgeting and looked around until she spotted her purse on the coffee table in the living room. She beelined for it and I turned, watching her. "You know what? How about I e-mail you when I get some free time?"

"You'll e-mail me when you get some free time? Riley, come on...." My words trailed off as I was left utterly confused by the abrupt change in her.

"It's really bad timing right now. I just got my promotion, work is crazy." She gave me a weak smile and headed for the door. She was literally rushing to get away from me.

"Riley, wait. I'll drive you home."

"No, it's fine. I'll Uber it."

"Jesus, you were just topless in my kitchen. I'll fucking drive you home." I didn't mean to swear, but she was acting like she couldn't get away from me fast enough, like nothing had happened between us.

"Cam, it's fine. I promise. I use Uber all the time."

"Can we talk about this?" I stepped toward her, trying to come between her and the door.

"There's nothing to talk about," she replied, giving me a fake smile.

"Riley," I pleaded, "I'm sorry. If I pushed you too far, or made you feel like we needed to—"

"No, Cam, really. Everything's fine. I need to go."

I realized in that moment, even though it was the last thing I wanted to do, I had to let her go. No matter how much more I wanted from her, I wasn't going to keep a woman in my home against her will. I pushed my hands into my pockets and took a step back from the door. She moved to open it and I watched her go, feeling helpless and confused. Just before the door closed, she turned and looked back at me. I wanted to ask her to wait, to stay, to talk to me and explain what I'd done wrong, what she was running from, give me a chance to apologize at least. But I said nothing and she didn't either. She closed the door with something that looked like regret written across her face, and I wondered if I'd ever see her again.

Chapter Five

Riley

It had been over a week since the evening I'd spent with Camden. A week and two days, actually. But who was counting? I hadn't reached out to him, hadn't e-mailed him, texted, or called. And sometimes it had been necessary to hide my phone from myself in order to keep it that way. He'd sent me one text the morning after I'd run from his condo.

I hope you'll give me a chance to apologize for whatever I did to make you run from me last night. I don't know what happened, but I do know I'd hate to never see you again. Please, just text me or something this week.

That had been the only message I'd gotten from him, and even though I appreciated the fact that he was giving me the space I'd asked for, I couldn't ignore the large part of me that wished he'd find me again, find a way to make me see him, to force me to explain everything to him. Because maybe he'd be able to convince my brain that it was being ridiculous.

It was Sunday morning and I'd been lying in bed avoiding the day. When my phone pinged on my nightstand, my heart thumped rapidly, both hoping for and dreading a text from Camden.

Hey, you've been avoiding me all week. Meet me for brunch, bitch.

I smiled at Hadley's demand, and couldn't think of a better way to spend my afternoon than brunching with my best friend. I was in desperate need of a mimosa.

I'll meet you at French Toast in an hour.

See you then!

French Toast was always terribly busy, especially since they were only open for brunch on the weekends, but Hadley had hooked up with one of the waiters a few times in college, and he always gave us the first spot in line. It was one of the few times in life when her previously wild ways had some long-term benefits. As I sipped my mimosa, I silently toasted Hadley's choice in sexual partners during college.

"So," she said before she popped a piece of her brioche French toast in her mouth, "why've you been so quiet this week?"

I shrugged. "Just trying to stay on top of work. I can't disappoint everyone now that I've got this promotion."

"Uh-huh," she said, nodding and chewing. "Great, thanks for the bullshit answer, now tell me the truth."

I laughed, always appreciative of the way Hadley never minced words. "That is the truth."

"That's half the truth, and you know it. You can't fool me. You went on that date with Camden on Friday and then you went into communication blackout. I was this close to sending up smoke signals." She held her thumb and forefinger up. I considered myself lucky she didn't end the gesture with the middle one. I decided to give in to her because, honestly, I knew that's what would happen when I agreed to meet her. I knew she'd ask and I'd tell. That's how our relationship worked.

I let out a large sigh, placing my napkin on the table and leaning back in my chair. "The date was perfect. He was funny, smart, polite, and he wasn't doing that stupid thing guys do where they try to seem uninterested. I could tell he was excited to see me and that made me feel great," I said, my mind wandering back to how wanted Camden made me feel. "But I realized early on it wouldn't ever work with us. There was too much about us that was different."

"Mmm hmmm, like what?" she asked before lifting her champagne flute to her mouth, sipping like she was at a tea party and not a brunch on her third drink, pinky high, right up there with her nose, making me smile.

"You should have seen his car, Hadley. He called it the Batmobile and he wasn't joking. It probably cost more than my undergrad degree."

"And?"

"And he lives in a condo on the river in a sky rise."

She blinked at me, waiting for me to continue.

"He's the mayor's son, he's a lawyer, he's smart and funny and sexy and perfect, and it just wouldn't work."

Hadley finished her mimosa, used her napkin to wipe the corners of her mouth, and she cleared her throat. Then she narrowed her gaze at me. "There are a few things about your statements that bother me. Let's go over them, shall we?" She didn't wait for me to agree before she plowed forward with her argument. "You're sexy and funny and smart and perfect, so you can't base your decision to not see him anymore on the fact that you're too different because that, my friend, is a load of bullshit. I imagine the difference you're alluding to is the fact that he has money and you don't. So, I ask you this, did he ever make you feel like your lack of money was a problem?" She didn't give me a chance to answer. "Of course he didn't, because one of the very first things you said about him today was that he *wanted* you, Riley."

"Yeah, wanted me, but being physically attracted to someone doesn't mean anything."

"Come on, Riley. Give yourself a little more credit than that. I saw you guys at that game. Sure, he thought you were gorgeous, because you are, but it was more than that. You guys clicked."

"We kissed," I corrected.

"Yeah," she agreed with a little more enthusiasm than I expected, "and how'd that go?"

My mind wandered back to that first kiss in the arena. The one that started out of obligation and pressure from the crowd, but grew from heat and need. I shook the memory from my head. "A kiss doesn't automatically mean we have to be together."

"Well, I think you're being ridiculous."

"I've never been with anyone like him before, Had. I don't go to fancy parties with socialites, I *plan* those parties. He's upper-class, and I'm just...."

"Classy," she supplied, her voice softer than it had been.

I shook my head. "I'm fun, and I'm sassy, and I'm clever, but I wouldn't fit into his world."

She sighed and fell back into her chair. "Well, best friend, I think you're making a mistake, but I'll stop harassing you about it. But, I have a feeling, if you gave him a chance, he'd make you his whole world."

I didn't respond, mostly because a part of me was pretty sure she was right. And that was terrifying.

When our food had been eaten and all the mimosas had been drunk, Hadley left me with a knowing look that told me to reach out to Camden. I wasn't sure, yet, what my next move was, but I knew I wasn't ready to go back home and mope. So I took an Uber to my favorite bookstore and wandered the aisles. Sunday was a busy day in Portland proper, so I liked to hang out on the outskirts. There was still plenty to do on the east side of the city, and far less people.

I found a little corner in the bookstore with an armchair next to a window, took a seat, and read half a book. It was the most relaxed I'd been all week. The three mimosas had helped, and so had the reading therapy, but after I'd bought a month's worth of books and a coffee to go, I still didn't know what I was going to do about Camden.

I thought about it all the way to my apartment but was still confused as I climbed the stairs over the thrift store that was already closed for the evening. I pulled my keys out of my purse but stopped halfway to the top when I heard his voice.

"Your stairs aren't very comfortable." He stood slowly, grimacing as he did, one hand rubbing his ass and the other gripping a beautiful bouquet of peonies. "I've been sitting here for hours waiting for you to get home. Next time I decide to stake out your apartment, I'm bringing a folding chair or something."

"What are you...." I turned around and looked down the narrow stairwell, for a moment confused about where I was. "How did you...."

54

"Hadley found me on Facebook. Sent me a message. Told me your address. It didn't take much convincing either. She's either a really great friend or a terrible one."

I let out an annoyed sigh. "Ugh, both."

"Well, I think she's great," he said with a nervous smile, still standing right in front of my door. I was suddenly very aware of the way I probably looked. I'd rolled out of bed, gone to brunch, then sat in a bookstore all day. Inwardly I was chastising myself for not being prepared for a mutiny by my best friend. I should have seen it coming.

I continued up the stairs, still surprised to see Camden there. "What are you doing here?"

"You've been avoiding me, so I thought I'd take matters into my own hands." He looked down at the bouquet. "These are for you. I guessed on the flowers. Roses seemed a little too ordinary. Peonies are so, I don't know, classy." He held them out to me and I could see the fear in his eyes, feel it radiating off him. He was afraid I was going to turn him down again. But I looked at the flowers and took in his words, and the last thread of resistance I'd been clinging to simply snapped.

"They're beautiful," I said, taking the flowers from him. "Thank you." I brought them closer to my face and took in their beautiful scent. "I love peonies."

"I thought you might," he said with a smile, more relaxed, but still a little hesitant.

"I wasn't expecting company, but you're more than welcome to come in," I said, giving him a hopeful look. I wasn't ready to watch him walk away again. He smiled widely and his shoulders relaxed a little, settling back, like a weight had been lifted off him. I brushed past him to get to the door and just being near him made everything inside light up again. Hummingbird wings flittered in my stomach, and my heart thumped harder in my chest.

I opened the door and stepped inside, watching as he followed me. I closed the door and took in the image of Camden standing in my shabby apartment. None of the guys I'd brought back to my place before had taken the time to check out my place; it'd been more of a beeline straight to the bedroom and then a sneaky exit in the middle of the night. But Camden strolled around leisurely, making himself at home, taking the time to examine the little things about my apartment that made it less of a "place" and more of a "home."

I let the silence hang over us for a few moments, but then decided someone had to say something.

"I would have picked up, but I wasn't expecting my stalker to show up tonight." Keeping the smile from my face turned out to be impossible, so I spun and walked into the kitchen so he couldn't see my goofy grin, and found a vase for my beautiful flowers.

"I think stalker is a strong word. Real stalkers don't just e-mail you and wait at your door—they're stealthier than that."

"You better work on your ninja," I said, laughing, as I filled the vase with water and placed it on the counter.

His next words were whispered into my ear, startling me. "Noted." I jumped and he chuckled, but it definitely broke the ice. "But seriously," he said, his voice gentle and full of apology, as he reached for my hand, turning me, "I'm sorry about last weekend. I got carried away and I shouldn't have let things move so quickly—"

"No," I said, my free hand covering his mouth before I'd thought the move through. "You don't have anything to apologize for. If anyone should be sorry, it's me. I totally flipped out and then bailed, and it wasn't cool." I watched as a grin appeared behind my fingers, so I dropped my hand, only to have him catch it. He twined all his fingers through all of mine, and pulled me in a little closer.

"So, we're both sorry."

I laughed. "I guess so."

"Now what?"

"I'm not really sure."

He held my gaze, neither one of us smiling or frowning, just taking each other in. Then, suddenly, he was pulling me closer, his hands—which were still holding mine—moving to the small of my back, pressing me into him.

"I think maybe we should start over. Neutral ground. A real date. No public coercion to make out, no Skee-Ball championship, just a regular date. Dinner. I'll pick you up. *I'll take you home*," he said, narrowing his eyes at me while still smiling.

I blushed, remembering the way I'd run away from his condo the last time we were together. The idea of him driving me back to my crappy apartment in his fancy car had made me nervous. I let out a sigh, trying to let go of all the negativity. My apartment wasn't crappy. It was homey and small and cozy. And Camden looked anything but out of place there. In fact, he looked right at home.

"I'd love to go on a real date with you."

The smile he wore changed to something that radiated happiness. Teeth gleaming, eyes crinkling, cheeks bunching—all of it was adorable. Then, much to my delight, he leaned in closer and kissed me. All our previous kisses had been somewhat explosive and while, internally, I was still feeling all kinds of rockets going off and bells ringing, outwardly, this kiss was slow and sweet. Almost reverent, as though he were cherishing the kiss.

When he pulled away, the same adorable smile graced his face. "Can you be ready in an hour?"

I pulled back, a little shocked, but smiling still. "Tonight?"

"Why not?" he asked, shrugging, then he brought the back of my hand to his mouth, kissing it softly. I was a goner.

My eyes darted between his, thinking and plotting. Finally, I answered. "Can you give me two?"

Two hours later there was a soft knock at my door, and the birds were flying in exhilarating circles in my belly. My heart thought we were in the middle of a marathon. And my lungs, well, they were holding on to my last breath, hoping it wouldn't be the end. I'd showered and changed, picking out a white lace dress with cap sleeves I'd never had a chance to wear before. It came down just short of my knees and looked cute with my merlot-colored ankle boots. My hair was curled into soft and loose ringlets, with one side pinned back. I'd put in some dangly pearl earrings and a delicate silver chain bracelet.

I opened the door smiling, knowing my smile probably wouldn't leave for the rest of the evening.

Camden looked nervous, like I imagined a high school boy would look picking up his date, but excited at the same time. I watched his eyes flow down my body, taking everything about me in, appreciating what he saw, then meet my gaze again. "You look amazing," he breathed.

"I needed that extra hour," I joked, but then I let myself examine him. If I looked amazing, he looked like perfection. He hadn't shaved and was sporting some serious designer stubble, which only did wonderful things for his sharp jaw. And who in the world ever had a sexy Adam's apple? Camden did. All those beautiful things led to his open-collar button-down in a light blue color, which was contrasted by the dark blue of his jeans. Those fucking thigh-hugging jeans. He came in perfectly between casual and dressy and, of course, was still sexy as hell. "You're looking pretty handsome yourself." My smile only grew wider.

He grinned, held his hand out, and pulled me to him as he leaned down and pressed a chaste kiss against my cheek. More flutters.

I closed and locked my door, then smiled as he twined his fingers with mine, leading me down the stairs. The Batmobile was parked at the curb, and I slid in more gracefully than I thought possible after he opened the door for me.

When we zoomed into traffic my body was still all aflutter. There was soft music playing on the radio and his hand was gently resting on my knee. There was a part of my brain that thought his hand on my bare leg was presumptuous, that normally I'd need to know a man for more than ten days to feel comfortable with that much contact. But I couldn't deny the majority of my body liked feeling his skin against mine, longed for his hands to claim me in that way, to make me feel like he wanted me. Plus, the man's mouth had been on my breast the week before. This was tame in comparison.

"Where are we headed?"

"Ever been to The Melting Pot?"

"No, but I've always wanted to go. Melted cheese is the way to my heart."

He laughed and gave my knee a squeeze, causing all the butterflies in my stomach that had landed to swarm up again, like running through a flock of birds.

He drove into downtown Portland and parked in a garage, then led me across the street, all the while holding my hand. We came to a staircase leading underground and I gave him a confused look as he pulled me down the stairs.

"It's underground?"

"Don't worry. It's legit."

And he was right. The restaurant was completely underground but it made the atmosphere more intimate. There were no windows, only dim lighting and sconces on the wall with one fixture hanging above every table.

A waiter led us to a booth and I was surprised when Camden slid in next to me. We both ordered drinks and when the waiter left I felt the warmth of Cam's hand on my leg again.

"It was probably a bad idea for you to wear this dress, babe." His whispered words feathered over my neck, causing all kinds of shivers and clenching. "I've got a million indecent thoughts running through my mind."

Smiling, I slid my hand over his. "You're going to have to save the indecent for later. I'm here for some bread covered in melted cheese." I was trying to deflect the arousal caused by his words, the pulsing happening in very private places, places I wanted parts of him to invade. Humor—that was my best defense at this point. Otherwise I foresaw us finding a private bathroom. No, not happening. I wanted a normal dinner with Camden. I wanted the anticipation of what would happen after dinner. I did not want his hand to creep up my thigh. I mean, I did and I didn't. Just to make my point, I pressed my legs together, squeezing our fingers between my thighs. He only squeezed my leg right back, so I rolled my eyes.

"So," he said as the waiter brought our fixings for the bread and cheese I'd been waiting for all my life. "There's a game this Thursday. Wanna go with me?"

"To the Renegades game?" I asked, dipping a tiny square piece of bread in the cheesy pot. I wanted to open a restaurant where people could just dip giant chunks of bread in troughs of cheese. These tiny pieces simply wouldn't do. "Don't you usually take your friend?"

He shrugged. "Justin's cool. He knows there's someone I'm trying to impress." He winked at me, the bastard.

"Oh, well, impress away. I'll have to make it up to him though. I feel bad taking his ticket."

"You'll do nothing of the sort," he said, suddenly sounding possessive. His rumbly voice sent even more shivers down my spine. "Save all your favors for me."

The meal that followed the cheese was fantastic, and I couldn't remember a date I'd had where it felt so effortless and comfortable to sit next to someone and just talk. We talked about everything and anything, we laughed, we kissed, and we touched. By the time dessert was served, Camden's arm was around me and I was curled into his side, and we cracked up as we fed each other tiny bites of cakes and fruit dipped in chocolate.

His kisses were sweet, but it wasn't just the chocolate. It was him. I could see he was trying hard to be respectful, to get to know me while still dancing around the weird yet invigorating sexual buzz that floated around us ever since that first kiss. I'd be the first to admit I'd tried to deny it, to tamp down the raging attraction I felt for him, but every moment we spent together that night chipped away at my resolve.

He paid the bill and led me up the staircase, his hand wrapped around mine, and we walked unhurriedly back to his car.

"That was the perfect dinner," I said, feeling nervous all of a sudden. I didn't want the evening to be over, I didn't want to watch him walk down my stairs, away from me again. He didn't answer; instead, he drew light circles on the back of my hand with his thumb.

We were both relatively quiet as he crossed the river back to the east side of the city, but he held my hand the entire way. As we neared my neighborhood my heart started fluttering, the nerves taking over. The closer he got to my apartment, the more I wanted the night to extend. There was an open spot right in front of my building and he pulled in quickly. He put the car in park, but didn't turn off the ignition. My eyes were glued to his hand in my lap.

"Hey," he said, using a gentle finger to pull my chin in his direction. "That was a great date."

"Yeah" was my breathy agreement. He moved in and pressed his mouth again mine, a soft kiss that felt too much like a good-bye. With his lips barely pressed against mine, I said, "Come upstairs." We were paused, noses touching, breaths intermingling, and my request hanging in the air between us. His finger moved down my chin and trailed a soft path down the side of my neck, and then I felt the warmth of his entire palm at my cheek.

"I want to, Riley. So badly. But every other time we've been together, I've taken things too far and you've run from me." He let out a large and heavy sigh. "I don't want to push you away again."

I brought my hand to cover his, which was still resting against my cheek. "You won't. You can't. I want this. I want you." He pulled back slightly, his eyes darting between mine, then pulled his hand from my face, opened his car door, and climbed out. I watched him walk around the front, come to my door, open it, and hold a hand out to me.

I took his hand and let him lead me out of the car and toward the door that opened up to my narrow stairwell. When we reached the top, he let me go to allow me to open my door, but I fumbled with the keys as I felt his hand gently move my hair from my shoulder. The tinkling of the keys in my shaking hand was all I heard before I felt his lips right on the curve where my neck and shoulder met. I gasped as the sensation sent rockets of pleasure throughout my body, my eyes fluttering, but I still managed to get the key in the door and open it.

The door swung in and suddenly I was weightless. Camden's arms wrapped around me from behind—one around my waist while the other was around my shoulders—and he held me close to him, walking me into my apartment, his mouth still doing wonderfully arousing things to my neck. I felt him kick the door shut and somewhere in my mind I registered my purse falling to the floor, but I didn't care about anything except his mouth and the way it had my whole body igniting.

"Bedroom," he rasped against my skin, the stubble along his jaw completely undoing me.

"Down the hall," I whispered, unable to use my voice at all. "Second door on the right."

He wasted no time moving me to the bedroom, my body still completely in his arms, lost to the feeling of finally letting myself have this man.

The room was dark, only moonlight shining through the window, but it was enough to see by. He stopped just in front of my bed and gently placed my feet back on the ground and unwrapped his arms from me slowly, dragging his hands over my body as if he didn't want to lose contact for even a moment. His hand smoothed over my chest, the swell of my breasts tingling at the feeling of his fingers there, even over the material of my dress. I was absolutely a goner for him and my body wanted nothing more than to simply connect with his, to feel him, press against him, be filled by him.

The warmth of his hands moved down the sides of me, over my ribcage, past the curve of my waist and the swell of my hips, until I felt him grasp the hem of my dress.

"All you have to do is tell me to stop, and I will," he said softly, pausing, my dress still in his grip.

"I don't want you to stop," I managed to whimper.

His hands moved up slowly, peeling the dress away, removing the last layer of resistance between us. I lifted my arms as the dress moved over my head, the ends of my hair falling back onto my oversensitive skin, causing new goose bumps to break out. I heard the fabric of my dress hit the floor somewhere in the corner, but was brought back to Camden when his fingers unclasped my bra. I felt it unsnap and fall forward, so I let it drift to the ground at my feet, but then gasped when I felt his lips at my spine. He trailed soft kisses down my back, slowly moving all the way down to the edge of my panties, all while my breath was caught in my lungs and my heart was tripping over itself. He pulled the back zipper down on my little-heeled booties and slipped my shoes off, tossing them in the same direction as my dress. Then his hands came to my hips and gently turned me to face him.

To see him kneeling before me, moonlight highlighting every beautiful feature of his face—his jawbone, his mostly perfect nose with just the slightest knot on the bridge, and that gorgeous stubble I wanted to feel grazing over every inch of my body—it made everything seem perfect, even the crazy way we met. In that moment I regretted nothing because I knew, had we taken any other path, that moment would never have occurred. And I'd have given up a lot to see those eyes staring up at me with nothing but adoration and lust.

Without breaking eye contact, Camden slid my panties down my legs, and I gently stepped out of them, waiting for his eyes to leave mine and take in my body. I was nervous, but only a little. There was that normal nagging voice in the back of my mind, worried he wouldn't like something about me, but it was quieter than it usually was in moments like this. Sure, I wanted him to like my body and find me attractive, but there was something about the way he was looking into my eyes that told me it wasn't my body he was after and he'd take me any way he could get me, that my body was something he craved just as a vehicle to something else, something more.

When his gaze finally drifted down my body, I watched as the sexiest grin spread over his face.

"Fuck me," he said softly, "you're perfect." His hands slid up the back of my calves, pulling me forward ever so slightly. They continued up my thighs and stopped when each of his hands was palming my ass. My hands wound in his hair at just the same moment as he pressed the lightest of kisses just above the strip of curls between my legs. His mouth continued upward along the path between my breasts, his hands following, gliding over every part of me. When his lips finally connected with mine, the fire had become an inferno. Long gone were the slow and sultry kisses; we'd moved on to the deep, passionate, frantic kisses that stoked the flames.

He pulled me into him, and my hands got busy unbuttoning his shirt, pushing it off his shoulders and throwing it to the floor, all while his tongue swept through my mouth and his hands pawed at my naked body. I had never tried to unbutton a shirt without looking before, but it turned out I was pretty good at it. With even more haste, I pulled off his undershirt and then started working on his belt. I managed to get his pants unzipped and down his legs, and while he kicked them off I slid my fingers into the waistband of his boxer briefs. I pulled away from him, wanting to give him the same image of me kneeling before him, so I looked him in the eye and then slid down to the floor, taking his underwear with me.

There was so much to look at, so much to take in, but I held his gaze, loving the way heat and lust crept into his eyes as I rested back on my ankles. But I could only keep my eyes from his body for so long before I broke down and let myself take all of him in. His cock was magnificent, long and thick, slightly intimidating but not big enough to make me hesitate. It was just big enough to allow for a small pep talk. *I know this dick is the biggest dick you've ever seen, Vagina, but you've got to take this one for the team.*

And then there were his thighs. Good God. Clad in denim they'd been my undoing, like blocks of muscle just defined enough to make me want to sit on his lap for all kinds of various reasons—both sex related and not. But bare, those thighs were begging to be handled. I reached

66

forward, my hands coming to rest on the mound of muscle above his knees, and they felt amazing.

"Ever since I saw you sitting next to me at that Renegades game," I said, my voice barely above a whisper, "I've wanted to get my hands on these." Feeling more confident and brave than I ever remembered, I leaned forward and pressed a kiss to his massive thigh, letting my hands move around to his ass. I knelt up, pressing kisses up his leg, letting his cock brush against my breast, trying not to seem too much like a tease but enjoying the way his muscles tensed beneath my touch.

Before I could take any more action, I was suddenly lifted from the floor and tossed onto my bed. I bounced a little, but all momentum was stopped when Camden's hard and heavy body pressed me into the mattress.

"One day, I'll let you take the lead. I'll lie back and let you do whatever you want, let you have your wicked way with me." I let out short little puffs of air, my lungs apparently forgetting their one and only job, as Camden's mouth moved to my neck and his nose moved gently up the side of my throat, stopping just at my ear. "But tonight, I'm in control." He kissed me just below my ear, and then he moved south. Lips, tongue, and teeth all moved along my throat, along my shoulder, down my chest, and in between my breasts. He palmed one of them, bringing the other to his mouth, greedily sucking my nipple in and hungrily using his teeth and tongue on it.

He stayed there for just a moment, but moved on once I'd gotten accustomed to his mouth around my nipple. His large, strong hands followed his mouth and he left more open kisses down my belly. His fingers gripped my sides and I didn't know if he was holding me down or just holding me. His hands felt purposeful and possessive. This was no sloppy hookup, this wasn't some booty call; this was intentional and thoughtful.

He finally settled himself between my thighs, staring at me, spread open and bared to him, with so much intensity I almost couldn't watch. But the idea of missing the show, of not watching Camden Rogers use his mouth on me, wasn't an option in my book. His arms wrapped under my knees, hands coming to rest on top of my thighs, both holding me open and pinning me down. His eyes flicked up to meet my gaze, and without breaking it, I watched as his tongue moved against my opening.

My eyes fluttered, nearly closing, but I forced them open, forced myself to enjoy every aspect of what he was doing to me. I wanted to watch him, to feel him, smell him—everything. His tongue swiped over my clit, making my hips jump toward him, and I saw his eyes smile even though his mouth was occupied. He alternated between circling with his tongue and sucking with his mouth, all the while he used his chin and stubble to grind into me, causing my hips to move to a rhythm I'd never found in the past. I was circling my hips, my fingers had found their way to his stupidly soft hair, and my cries were getting louder and more insistent. Before I knew what was happening, I found myself on the cusp of a fantastic orgasm.

"Cam," I whisper-cried. He only hummed in response, the sensation against my clit sending me over the edge of sanity and into the crevasse of ecstasy. My back arched off the bed, my head rolled back, my mouth gaped open, and I prayed—absolutely begged inside my mind—that he would do that to me a million times before he got tired of it. All the while he still held me down, his strong hands gripping my thighs, his mouth not letting up one bit.

When I'd finally stopped convulsing beneath him, his hands loosened up and he pressed soft kisses to the insides of both my thighs while I caught my breath. Then he moved north again, splaying kisses up my center, making his way back to my mouth. When his mouth came back to mine, the kiss was gentle and sated, almost as if he'd gotten as much out of my orgasm as I had. Never had a man gone down on me and then kissed me on the mouth, and for a reason I couldn't completely grasp, it was the sexiest fucking thing. I tasted a mixture of him and me, tasted the arousal he'd given me, and I was lost in the way the entire experience was making me feel.

He kissed me for ages, it seemed. His hands moved all over me, lightly caressing me, forcefully palming me; each moment it was something different, something better. Each passing second with Camden was better than the last.

I wrapped my legs around his waist and could instantly feel his erection at my core, the length of it fitting perfectly against me. We both realized the connection at the same time, both our bodies going still. His forehead rested against mine, both of us panting, eyes closed, and then he ever so slowly slid his length over me, his cock cradled by me, his head applying the perfect amount of pressure to my clit, and we both groaned at the same time.

"Fuck, Riley, I'm not even in you yet, and I can tell you're made for me." His voice was low and raspy, like each word was a chore to get out.

"Please," I said, my hands fisting the sheets at my sides, worrying my bottom lip between my teeth. "I need more." The sensation of his cock moving over my clit was deliciously agonizing. I loved it and hated it simultaneously. It was everything, but it wasn't enough.

He thrust against me a few more times, his breathy grunts only pushing me past a sane level of arousal, when he finally pulled away and hopped off the bed. It occurred to me instantly what he was searching for, so I rolled toward my side table and pulled a condom out of the drawer.

"Here," I said, holding it out to him, watching his mouth turn up into a smile. He stood at the edge of my bed, rolling the condom down his shaft, and it was possibly the most erotic thing I'd ever seen. The image was just so *male* and he was so entirely beautiful. He finished and then climbed back on the bed, crawling toward me, his eyes starting at my waist and then moving up until they met mine.

When he was over me, he paused for a moment, just looking at me, both his hands pressed into the mattress on either side of my face, my legs spread to accommodate him. When his lips met mine, it was the fucking sweetest kiss, and if I hadn't been so turned on, I would have simply melted into it.

"You okay?" he asked, his face just a hair's breadth from mine.

"Yes," I breathed, squirming beneath him, aching for contact.

He kissed me again, but this time, as his tongue swept through my mouth, his pelvis tipped and he slowly slid into me, inch by fucking inch.

I moaned into his mouth, not even caring, just feeling. My pep talk to my vagina hadn't been enough; I hadn't warned her that she'd be ruined for all other penises. Because in that moment, when Camden was buried in me, pushed so far into me I never wanted him to leave, I knew it would never be the same with anyone else. I was a goner.

And then he pulled out.

And then he thrust back in.

Fuck.

Me.

He slowly built a rhythm, finding a pace that was both punishing and wild. He fucked me and kissed me at the same time, and I couldn't keep up. He was always one step ahead of me and I was lost to sensation, completely and utterly useless. But I think he liked that about me. I think he got off on the sight of my eyes fluttering, of my fingers gripping the pillow behind my head, and my voice spewing unintelligible words. He was grunting and biting and saying small words like "yes," and "fuck," and "goddamn."

When he grabbed my ass and pulled me higher onto his cock, I knew he had to be close. His momentum changed, his urgency. Suddenly he was chasing something. He thrust quicker and quicker, and every time he moved inside of me it was like tiny sexual fireworks detonating within me. Then the bastard moved one hand to my clit, rubbing circles around it with his thumb, and that was officially the end of me.

I exploded into a million tiny fractals, scattering, pulsing, electrified.

And then Camden's hands gripped me, collected me, and pulled me back together, holding me close to his body.

He thrust wildly and then, with a groan, finally came.

"Oh, fuck," he said, moments later, before I could even fathom putting together a two-word sentence. "Oh, fuck," he repeated, with a little more enthusiasm. This was the moment I was used to the men rolling off me and making an excuse as to why they had to leave. But Camden simply pulled his face far enough away from mine so that I could see his clear eyes and said, "We're doing that again. All the fucking time."

I couldn't help the laugh that broke from me, shot out of me like a cannon, then turned into a fit of giggles. He'd rendered me stupefied.

"Jesus," he whispered, his hand brushing my crazy hair from my face as he smiled at me with such sincerity. "Where the hell have you been all this time?"

I managed to shrug, not finding any words suitable for the emotional whirlwind inside my body.

"Well, it doesn't matter anymore. From now on, you're with me, yeah?" I nodded, holding my breath, knowing that committing to a man while he was still inside of me for the first time wasn't the smartest move. "You're gonna go to the game with me later this week. We're gonna find the guy who operates the Kiss Cam, and I'm gonna buy him a beer."

I smiled at the thought, the idea that there was actually a real person out there responsible for all this.

"Just so long as it's a Hef," I said with wink.

Chapter Six

Camden

My internal alarm clock woke me well before sunrise and before I even opened my eyes all the way I was thinking about running. I ran every morning and my groggy mind was wondering about the weather and how long I had until I inevitably had to move my morning jogs indoors because of Portland's rainy season.

All thoughts of jogging faded away when the fantastic scent of woman and sex made me remember where I was and who was tucked up against me.

Riley.

She was pressed up against my side, one of her arms draped over my chest and a leg thrown over my thigh. She had absolutely nothing on and every bit of her incredible body was hugging mine.

Suddenly a morning run was the last thing on my mind.

Rolling toward her, I pressed my nose into the crook of her neck, smelling her and the faint floral scent that still lingered there from the night before, while I moved my hand down her back and over her ass. She slowly woke and I could feel her body having the same slow realization mine had. After a few moments her hands slid lazily up my back and her knees shifted, opening for me, and I smiled against her skin between kisses on her neck.

"Morning," she whispered, her voice both hazy from sleep and raspy from arousal.

"Mmmm, indeed," I replied, not so subtly pressing my erection against her, loving the way she gasped as the head grazed her opening.

"I'm not usually a morning sex kind of girl," she said, but moaned in my ear afterward when I thrust against her.

"No?" I asked, moving my mouth down her chest and taking one of her gorgeous breasts into my mouth, sucking and gently biting her nipple.

"I could probably give it a try." Her fingers threaded through my hair as she spoke and her back arched, giving me unobstructed access to those perfect breasts.

"I wouldn't want to put you out." I mocked a concerned face, then watched her eyes roll back into her head as I slipped a finger into her.

Her hips tilted up toward me and her eyes opened, finding mine as she said, "I very much want to put you *in*."

Something that sounded like a growl rumbled out of me and I leaned over to her nightstand, pulling out a condom. Then I broke the world record for fastest condom application. My fingers had never been so coordinated. The condom was on, I was back over her, and then I sunk into her and fuck if it wasn't better than the night before.

I buried my face in her neck again and pinned her knee at my hip, trying to get as deep as I could, slowly inching my way to a point where our connection was so blurred I couldn't tell where the end of me met the end of her.

"Oh, God," she moaned, her hands gripping me. One on my shoulder, the other firmly on my ass, holding me to her, probably trying to achieve the same goal as me.

"It's not supposed to feel this good every time." Her words were breathy, but their meaning felt heavy. I knew exactly what she meant. Every time our bodies connected, whether it just be our hands pressed together, or our entire bodies, it was electric. Something about being with her was perfection.

"Don't question it," I said with a slow thrust. "Just trust it."

We were quiet from then on, aside from moans and curse words said in ecstasy. We weren't hurried, but we were frantic. I simply could not touch all of her fast enough, couldn't find enough ways to bury myself in her, or explore all the ways I could touch her to set her off. She came around me as I circled her clit with my thumb, and just the sight of her orgasm was enough to send me over the edge. We were both a jumble of arms and legs, all quivering and sweaty, lying in a heap on her bed, coming down from our high.

"I suppose I could consider being a 'morning sex' convert." She looked over at me with a straight face, but then couldn't hold it in any longer and covered her mouth when a giggle escaped.

"How do you feel about afternoon sex?" I asked as I pushed her crazy hair behind her ear, loving the way her smile was bright and wild.

"I have no ill feelings toward it," she answered, shrugging one shoulder. "I might need some convincing. You know, someone to point out all the pros and make me a firm believer."

"I love it when you talk dirty."

She giggled again and I turned into a complete tool because nothing ever sounded as good to me as Riley's laughter. It was the kind of laugh that was contagious and instantly I was laughing along with her, pulling her closer, loving the way she let me, the way she curled in closer as if being next to me was what she wanted too.

"What does your week look like?" I asked after a few minutes, hating the fact that soon I'd have to climb out of her bed and leave to get ready for work.

She sighed and then pulled back, but I didn't release her entirely, leaving my arms draped around her back. "Pretty busy. I've taken on a few more accounts since my promotion, and I'm still feeling out the new position."

"Got time for a Renegades game on Thursday?"

"Ugh," she groaned. "I'd love to go, but I've got a rehearsal dinner I have to attend."

"Someone hired an event planner for their rehearsal dinner?"

"It's kind of the whole package. If there's an event that has to do with the wedding, I'm expected to be there to make sure it runs smoothly."

"Ah ha."

"I'm sorry," she said, cringing.

"Don't worry about it. I'm sure Justin will be happy to go with me. I just want to know when I'll get to see you next."

"I could do lunch on Friday, or even happy hour that evening."

"How about both?"

"Both?"

"Yeah, if I have to wait until Friday then I want two dates."

"Hmm. That could probably be arranged."

"Pencil me in," I said, then rolled over her once more and kissed her until we both had to get ready for work.

The next few days were crazy, but I found myself smiling even when I was by myself. I was stupidly happy and I couldn't have wiped the emotion from my face if I'd tried. Thinking about Riley during the day made it go by faster, but in the evenings when things settled down and she'd text me, that was the best feeling in the world. I'd never found myself eager to hear from a woman before. Sure, I'd been excited for booty calls every now and again, but I'd never been so enthralled by a woman to the point where I was checking my phone every few minutes just waiting to hear from her.

I had it bad.

Obviously.

On Wednesday when Justin asked me to grab a beer after work, I happily agreed if only to give me a distraction.

"Hey, you down to go to the game tomorrow night?" I asked as I took a drink from my Guinness. We'd walked to the bar down the street from our office and our favorite booth was available.

"You're not taking the new girl?"

"Nah, man, she's busy."

"I'm not above taking her leftovers," he said with a laugh.

"All I'm saying is, if she's free for a game, she's got dibs."

Justin let out a sigh and shook his head, then brought his beer bottle up to take a pull. "Bros before hos, man."

"I agree," I said, tapping my beer against his. "We're not talking about hos though. We're talking about Riley."

"I get it."

"No hard feelings."

"It's cool. Free Renegades tickets couldn't last forever." He shrugged and watched as a woman in a short skirt passed by. After giving her a few seconds of appreciation he turned back to me. "So, this thing with Riley, is it serious?"

"About as serious as it could be after one real date. I mean, she's different. I don't really know how to explain it. It's never been like this before."

"Dude," he said, laughing and shaking his head. "I'm never going to get my tickets back."

I laughed with him and felt my phone vibrate in my pocket.

I have thirty spare minutes. What are you doing right now?

It was stupid how much my heart rate spiked at only the thought of seeing her, even if for just a few moments.

I'm at a bar having drinks with my friend from work. I just got here though, and he's giving me crap about Renegades tickets and bros before hos. I don't think he'd like it much if I bailed.

Which bar?

I sent her the name of the bar, but didn't get a response. We both got a second beer and got into a heated debate about the Renegades defending the pick and roll better. Suddenly there was a presence beside me and I looked over to see Riley's smiling face. She wasted no time scooting into my side of the booth, reaching her hand out to Justin.

"Hi, I'm Riley. Nice to meet you."

"Hey. Justin," he replied, not unkindly, a smile on his face. Then Riley turned back to me.

"Hey, you." Her eyes were darting all over my face and I was still blinking at her, trying to figure out if she was really there or if my mind was playing a cruel trick on me.

"Hey," I said, finally coming to my senses. I leaned forward and kissed her lightly. When she pulled away, obviously thinking I was only trying to give her a chaste hello kiss, my hand cupped the back of her neck, holding her mouth against mine, and I moved in, bringing her as close to me as possible in a booth at a bar. My tongue swiped across her lips and when she opened for me I nearly sighed. My tongue swept in, swallowing her slight moan, and she gripped the lapels of my suit jacket.

My mouth simply plundered hers. There was nothing I could do about it, nor did I want to. What I wanted was her mouth up against mine, and I would have challenged anyone who said anything about it in that moment. After a few lengthy moments, and one epic and incredibly inappropriate kiss, I finally let her go.

"I missed your lips" were the brilliant words I had for her next.

"Everyone in this bar can tell," an unfamiliar voice said, and I looked up to see Hadley standing at the end of our booth, two beers in her hands. She was smiling though, obviously pleased with herself.

"Hadley, I feel like I should be buying you beer for eternity, what with all the help I got from you with this one," I said as I wrapped my arm around Riley and hugged her close.

She shrugged with a smile. "It was so obvious she wanted you."

"Hey, you're supposed to be on my team," Riley whined.

"Sit down," I said to Hadley, motioning toward Justin, who was gawking open-mouthed at her.

"Justin," I said, then used my hand to indicate he had drool on his chin. When he wiped at his jaw and blushed, I couldn't help the laugh that escaped. "This is Hadley. Let her in." Finally picking up on what was going on, he moved over and made room for her. "Had, this is my friend, Justin. Justin, this is Riley's friend, Hadley."

"Best friend," Hadley corrected. She reached her hand out to Justin and he took it and they engaged in the most awkward handshake ever. She'd completely obliterated his game; he had turned into a bumbling fool.

"What are you doing here?" I asked Riley, loving the way her eyes were sparkling up at me.

"I have a few spare minutes and I wanted to see you." Hadley passed a beer across the table to Riley and the girls took healthy pulls. "Oh my goodness, that's so good. You would not believe my day so far."

"What's going on?" I asked as I pushed a lock of hair behind her ear.

"You know that wedding I'm working on? The one whose rehearsal dinner is tomorrow? Well, last minute the bride decides she wants to change the venue of the dinner. So, guess how easy it is to book a party of *sixty* on twenty-four hours' notice?" She rolled her eyes and took another drink of her very blonde beer. "So, I was supposed to spend this evening setting up for the rehearsal dinner, but instead I was looking for a new venue to fit her *vision*." Another eye roll. "Now I get to spend tonight setting up."

"But you found a place?"

"Luckily."

"Do you need help?" I didn't know the first thing about decorating, but I could follow directions.

"No, thank you. Hadley is going to help. Plus, it's going to be a long night. No need for you to be tired too." She sighed. "I can't wait until this wedding is over. Part of my promotion means fewer weddings and more corporate events." She let out another sigh, seemingly shaking away her irritation. "How are you?" Her voice was softer and sincere, her eyes searching mine.

"Good," I said, smiling down at her. "Really fucking glad to see you," I said, kissing her again. She laughed through the kiss, her hand cupping my cheek.

Somewhere in the back of my mind I heard Hadley and Justin talking, but I was trying to ignore them and focus on Riley and her mouth.

She wasn't joking when she said she only had a little bit of time because after only ten minutes she was edging her way out of the booth.

"I'll walk you out," I said, following behind her. "I'll be right back," I said to Justin as I stood.

"See you later," Hadley said to him, giving him a finger wave and a sly smile.

"Later," he said, giving her a nod. "It was nice to meet you, Riley. Enjoy my seat at the Renegades games." I knew he was joking, and luckily Riley laughed.

"See you around," she said with a smile. I took her by the hand and walked her out. It had rained while we were inside and the pavement was wet, shining in the neon lights of the bar.

"It was good to see you, Cam," Hadley said, giving me a brief kiss on the cheek. "I'm going to pull the car around." She gave Riley a not so sly wink and then disappeared around the corner.

It wasn't late, but it was dark out and the street was unusually empty of traffic. As soon as Hadley was gone, Riley wrapped her arms around my waist inside my suit jacket.

"Sorry to crash your bro night." She was looking up at me and her hair was falling against my hands where they gripped the small of her back. I wanted to run my fingers through her hair, to take a few minutes just to look at her.

"You didn't crash anything. And I am really glad you came."

She bit her bottom lip, then pressed in closer, whispering, "I've missed you." Her eyes met mine, but then she looked away again. "I know it's only been a few days, and I know I probably sound like a stage-five clinger, but I wanted to see you, even if it was only for five minutes."

I looked around and didn't see Hadley in a car yet, so I grabbed Riley's hand and pulled her around the side of the building into the alley. Pressing her back up against the wall, I cupped her face in my hands.

"I haven't stopped thinking about you since that first night at the game, and I definitely spent more than a reasonable amount of time thinking about what it was like to have you in my arms for an entire night."

"So you're saying the stage-five clinginess is mutual?" she asked, gripping my lapels again and pulling me in closer. Instead of answering her with words, I kissed her. She yelped in surprise, but then melted into me when my hands slid down her neck, over her breasts, and ended on her ass. I hauled her as close to me as I could, then walked us back until I had her pressed against the wall again, but this time her feet were off the ground and her legs wrapped around my waist. I moved my lips down the column of her throat, smiling against her skin when she tilted her head to give me full access. "This is crazy," she said on a breathy whisper.

"This is fucking fantastic," I mumbled against her, moving my lips farther down until I was stopped by the silky fabric of her blouse. "God, you're so sexy." I wanted badly to be back in a bed with her and have her beautiful body laid out before me and bare, but I had to admit the way the silk shirt molded over her breasts was almost enough to undo me. "I want to touch you everywhere."

"I want that more than anything," she replied.

A loud car horn broke us apart and I quickly turned my back to the street, trying to protect Riley from the eyes of anyone but me. Riley giggled, her face pressed into my chest, and said, "It's just Hadley."

I let out a sigh of relief and set Riley down, but I didn't let go of her.

"I'm glad you came tonight. Even if it was for just a few minutes."

"Me too," she said shyly. "On Saturday, after the wedding, it might be kind of late, but I can stop by your house if you want." She blinked up at me and it was adorable. It drove me crazy how one minute she was a sex kitten and the next she was shy and reserved. I liked the idea of sending her to either end of the spectrum, of making her feel both sexy and shy. Lord knew she was making me feel a thousand different things; it was only fair she was too.

"I don't care how late it is, come over. Even if all you do is climb into my bed and fall asleep. We'll make up for lost time on Sunday. Do you have to work?"

"I'm free as a bird." She smiled and tipped up on her toes, touching her lips to mine. "But right now I should probably go. Hadley will honk again. And if I know her she'll probably lay on the horn until I give in."

"Okay. Don't work too hard."

She gave me another quick kiss and then made her way to the car. As she was rounding the hood, Hadley rolled down her window.

"I thought you were better than a quickie in an alley, Cam. At least take my best girl to a bathroom or something."

I laughed and said, "I'll remember that for next time."

Hadley winked, rolled up her window, and then drove off. I saw Riley's hand above the roof of the car, waving as they pulled away.

Once they were out of sight, I let out a big sigh. That girl had the potential to ruin me in the best way. I ran my hand through my hair, letting my body calm a little, and then I made my way back into the bar and to my seat. Justin was wearing the biggest shit-eating grin I'd ever seen, and I tried to keep a straight face.

"Man, you've got it so bad." Justin's voice was full of laughter, obviously finding a lot of joy in my situation.

"You should talk. Your eyes about fell out of your head when Hadley sat down next to you." I took another pull of my beer, but it had gone warm and didn't taste nearly as good as Riley's mouth.

"That woman is on another level of hot."

My hackles rose almost immediately. "Justin, man, you don't get to talk about Riley and how hot she is."

"No. Not Riley. Although, yeah, she's hot too. I'm talking about Hadley."

My shoulders fell with relief. "Ah. Well, it was obvious to everyone in the room how you felt about her. But you're not wrong. She's pretty good-looking."

"And these two girls just happened to sit next to you at a Renegades game?"

"Pretty fucking epic, right?"

"Yeah. It's no wonder Sophia dumped your ass that night. You probably couldn't keep your eyes off them."

His words made me think about how differently everything could have turned out. If Sophia hadn't dumped me, or even if Justin had gone to the game with me instead, Riley and I might not have ever even spoken that night. And if I hadn't broken up with Sophia, there was no way I would have kissed her when the Kiss Cam hit us. I didn't really like Sophia, but I wouldn't have ever cheated on her.

"I guess it is pretty unbelievable how it all turned out."

"I've never seen you like this over a woman." Justin's tone was more serious, the humor gone from his eyes.

"She's different, I think. I hope. I don't know. It's only been a few days since we've officially started dating, but she's all I can think about. It's maddening. And exciting. And scary as hell."

"Well, if it's any consolation, she looked just as smitten with you as you did her. It seemed like you were both on the same page."

"Thanks, man. That does make me feel a little better." We were quiet for a moment before I braved the question that was blaring in my mind. "You want me to put in a good word for you with Hadley?"

"Nah. I can work my own magic."

"Okay," I said, laughing. "You never know. Maybe at the game tomorrow they'll put you up on the Kiss Cam with someone equally as hot."

"Lightning that good never strikes twice in the same spot, man. Don't worry about me though. I'm not looking to drop my anchor anytime soon."

"Drop your anchor?" I scoffed. "That's the best euphemism you could come up with?"

Chapter Seven

Riley

The only thing that got me through the rehearsal dinner Thursday night was the thought of seeing Camden the following evening.

The bride wasn't particularly terrible, just in love with her vision and naïve about how difficult it would actually be to change a venue last minute. Luckily, it seemed as though the rehearsal dinner would be the biggest and hopefully last speed bump of that particular event.

Camden had a last-minute lunch meeting pop up Friday, so happy hour was the only time he was able to meet me. It made me smile when he suggested we go back to the Tank for our little mini date.

When I walked in I was treated to the three-piece-suit look from the back as he stood at the bar, making conversation with George like they were old friends. I came up behind him, letting my hand on his back tell him I'd arrived. He turned at my touch, smile already on his face, and looked down at me with eyes sparkling.

"Hey." He leaned down and kissed me sweetly, causing all sorts of butterflies to take flight in my belly. He pulled away saying, "I'm sorry about this afternoon."

"It's okay."

"I see you decided to make me stick out like a sore thumb in my business attire." His gaze slid down my body as he spoke, taking in my casual outfit.

"After this I head to the wedding site to set up. No clients will be there, so jeans and a T-shirt are a must."

"You won't be there by yourself, will you?"

"Oh, no," I say, waving away his concern. "There will be a whole team of people plus vendors. I will most definitely not be alone."

Camden nodded, seeming satisfied with my answer, then turned back to the bar, getting George's attention. "Can I get a Hef for my girl?"

George smiled at me and I gave him a shy wave. Something about Camden calling me his girl turned me into putty.

"How's Annalise doing?" I asked when he put my beer down on the bar and placed a lemon wedge on the edge of the glass.

"She's really tired of being pregnant. Can't see her feet anymore."

"Poor girl. Make sure you give her a hug for me, and a foot rub."

"Will do," he said, laughing.

"Come on," Camden said, taking my hand and gently leading me to the back of the bar. It was much busier than it had been the first time we'd met there. He guided us through the crowd, finding a single high-top table free in the far corner. I couldn't help but smile when the Skee-Ball game came into view, remembering the way he'd sharked me.

We both settled into our high stools and I watched as he took a drink of his beer, loving the way his Adam's apple bobbed as he swallowed. He still had stubble covering his face and throat, and I wondered if he was trying to grow it out or if designer stubble was just a look he was going for. He totally rocked it, so I wasn't complaining.

"How's work been?" I asked instead of jumping over the table and licking his throat like I wanted to.

He shrugged. "It's work. Nothing terribly exciting. Sounds like your job is pretty hectic."

"It can be," I said, nodding. "Hopefully that will change next week though."

"Right, your promotion. Working less weddings, right?"

"Yeah. Clients who hire event planners for weddings usually aren't return customers. They'll drop a lot of money for a wedding, but nothing else in their life really calls for professional event planning services. Corporations though, especially non-profits, will use event planners repeatedly for putting on galas and fundraisers. Since they are higher profile events and have the potential to be returning clients, my boss usually only gives those jobs to people who've proven themselves. So, it's something I've been working toward for a while."

"Sounds like you're very good at your job."

"I had no idea what I wanted to be when I was younger, but I always loved throwing parties. It didn't occur to me until I was already in college that I could parlay that into a job, or even a career. There's something extremely rewarding about throwing a great event, especially if it's for a good cause."

"So you like the non-profit work?"

"There are definitely certain organizations that I enjoy working with more than others."

"My job doesn't have one ounce of philanthropy to it. It is, quite literally, laden with greed."

"That's not uncommon. Capitalism is what drives our economy. And I'm sure your job has its moments. You're about protecting your artists, right? That's not all greed and gloom. Artists deserve fair pay and compensation."

"Maybe *you* should have been a lawyer too," he said with a smile.

"Nah, lawyers are assholes." I gave him a wink and laughed when his hand came up to cover his heart.

"You wound me."

"If it makes you feel any better, you're my favorite lawyer."

"Hey, that's cool, 'cause you're my favorite party planner."

"I bet you say that to all the girls."

"Just you, babe."

"God," I said on a rushed breath. "I love flirting with you." The words came out and I instantly regretted them, worried I'd said too much too soon, but his immediate smile made me feel a little better. "I mean, I don't love *you*.... I mean, you're great... oh, shit." My head fell into my hands and I let out a groan. I heard Camden's deep, throaty laughter from across the table, but didn't dare to look up at him. "I swear I'm not as creepy as I always come off."

His laugh started again, only louder, and then he tugged on my hand, forcing me to look up at him. Instead of letting my hand go, he laced his fingers through mine. "You're not creepy. Promise. What you are is funny and cute, which is sexy as hell."

I was grateful he wasn't making me feel worse about what I'd said, but I wasn't surprised. He'd proven to be a class act since the day I met him. The blush spread across my face in a wave of warmth, and I decided we needed a change of subject.

"Justin seemed like a really great guy. You guys are good friends?"

"Yeah," he answered, still holding my hand on top of the table. "We both started at the firm at the same time and we're about the same age. Most of my friends from my childhood moved away around college, but I still see them occasionally. My best friend, Greg, lives on the east coast, but we don't see each other too often. His wife just had their second baby, so he's pretty much stationary. Traveling across the country with two children apparently is every parent's worst nightmare."

"I can only imagine."

"I think Justin was pretty enamored by Hadley, though."

"Yeah," I said with a laugh. "She has that effect on guys sometimes."

"I thought he was going to lose the ability to form words."

"Wouldn't be the first time."

"Have you been friends long?"

"A while. Hadley and I were assigned to be dorm roommates back in college our freshman year. It was totally random that we were paired together, and now she's one of my best friends."

"And what about your family? Do they live nearby?"

"My mom lives in Arizona now. We lived in Oregon until I was about fourteen, but then my parents divorced and my mom moved my brother and me to Arizona with her. I went to high school there, but moved back as soon as I was old enough." I hated talking about Arizona and my time there, and I hoped my voice didn't give away my discomfort. Besides my mom and my brother, who lived through those four years with me, only Hadley knew what had happened there and why I loathed it so much.

"And it's only you and your brother? No other siblings or family nearby?"

"Just us two. But he's pretty busy, so I don't see him often. My aunt, my mom's sister, lives in Arizona as well. But that's it."

"And what about your father?" His tone was so soft and careful, as though he were afraid he'd break me with his question.

"My father left one day and never looked back. Haven't heard from him in about ten years." I pushed the words out quickly, wanting to get the conversation over with, looking for any way to steer the conversation in another direction. I took a drink, trying to steel myself to ask him about his family. His family, and their wealth and status, was still a source of anxiety for me. He'd proved himself different than I thought he'd be, but that didn't mean I'd feel differently about the staggering economic and social differences between us. "Your parents have to be pretty local, your father being the mayor and all."

"Stepfather," he corrected right before taking a pull of his own beer. "And he and my mother live on the west side in the hills."

I tried not to let my reaction show on my face. The West Hills was a notoriously wealthy part of town, filled with mansions and expensive cars. In fact, I would put money on the idea that Camden's parents were neighbors to at least one of the Renegades players. Portland didn't have many professional athletes, but you could bet some of them live in The West Hills.

"Can I ask about your biological father? Is that a sore subject?"

"You can ask me anything," he said with a staggering amount of honesty in his voice. "My father died when I was six. Car accident."

"I'm so sorry. That's terrible."

"It is what it is," he said with a shrug. "I only have a few vivid memories of him. That's either a blessing or a curse—I haven't decided which and I probably never will. It was only me and my mom until I was twelve. I'd gotten used to being the man of the house and taking care of my mom, which is why my stepdad and I didn't get along. He kind of bulldozed his way into our lives. I know for my mom it was sort of a fairy tale, swept her off her feet situation. She was a lonely single mother, and he was a rich, single man with a good standing in a large city, on track to carry a political office.

"He wasn't necessarily a bad guy, he just wasn't taking any of my shit, and I was operating under a similar MO." He shrugged with that final statement and I wanted to know so much more, to understand his seemingly deep-seated resentment toward the man, but I didn't want to push the topic or turn our quick date into a tense situation.

"What's the craziest place you've ever had sex?"

Camden choked on his beer, covering his mouth as he coughed, then chuckled, smiling at me as he wiped his mouth with a napkin from the dispenser on top of our table.

"Jesus, Riley. That's a pretty sharp change in the direction of conversation."

"Hey, I need to know these kinds of things."

"Okay," he said as he laughed and shook his head. "I think I'm going to go with the bleachers at my high school."

I raised my eyebrows in surprise.

"No one was there. It's not like a football game was going on. There was a pep rally inside and my girlfriend and I snuck away to make out, but things got a little out of control." He said the words with a laugh, but a blush crept over his face, glowing bright red under his stubble.

"Ah, young love," I teased, batting my eyelashes at him.

"What about you?"

"I have never had sex in a crazy place. Unless you count, like, the living room. You and me in the alley the other night was possibly the most risqué thing I've ever done in the sexy department."

"The fact that our first kiss was broadcasted to twenty thousand people is really starting to seem like fate to me." His thumb traced a circle over the back of my hand and goose bumps spread all over my arms.

"No wonder you wouldn't let me walk away," I said with a teasing laugh.

"Hmmm." His stare was intense. "So you've never had sex outside of your own home?"

"Nope. The opportunity never presented itself." I watched as his expression steeled, and if I didn't know any better, I would have thought he took my last statement as a challenge. "Plus, I don't feel as though the majority of people have."

"Oh, I think you're wrong," he said with a laugh.

"Have there been more instances than just the bleachers?" I asked, leaning in, intrigued by the idea of Camden having exhibitionistic tendencies. He leaned back in his chair, smirking at me. "There *have* been," I practically squealed. The thought both surprised and excited me. Suddenly all I could see in my mind was Camden laying me down on the Skee-Ball game and tearing my clothes off, giving everyone in the bar a show. Of course, in real life I would never allow that to happen, but fantasy Riley? She very much enjoyed scoring on the Skee-Ball table. "Interesting," I said, giving him a knowing smile.

"There's nothing wrong with a little excitement now and then."

"This is a regular occurrence?"

"No," he said, laughing. "It's happened a few times. It's not like I need an audience to get off. Clearly I proved that earlier this week," he said, lowering his voice and leaning toward me. Images of Camden over me, naked and sweaty, firm body against mine, made me blush. It also made my thighs press together under the table. I needed to change the subject again. I didn't want to go to work all wound up, especially since I knew I wouldn't be seeing Cam again until the next day.

"And when's the last time you attended church?" His laugh was immediate and loud. "You should probably know I'm not a religious person. Spiritual is a better word to describe me."

After he'd finished laughing, he responded. "I think technically I'm Baptist, but I haven't been to church in a long while."

One more thing to tick off on the compatibility checklist.

I smiled at him as I pulled my phone out of my pocket.

"Shit," I said, looking at the time. "I should probably get going." I drank the last of my beer and hopped off my stool. "I'm sorry it was so short."

"Hey, don't worry about it. Work gets in the way sometimes." He smiled at me and then finished his own beer. "Let me pay the tab and then I'll walk you out."

He took my hand and we walked through the bar, even more crowded than it was when we arrived. I said good-bye to George, loving the way Camden pulled me to his side as he paid the bill. We'd only been dating for a week, but it was clear he felt comfortable enough to claim me in a crowded bar, making it clear to everyone that we were together. And I didn't mind it one bit. Quite the opposite, in fact. Even though it had been scary in the beginning, his obvious and blatant *want* for me was stupidly attractive. It had never occurred to me how sexy it would be to feel wanted. Or even needed. When his hand tightened around my waist, pulling me closer still, my breath caught. And when he leaned down and pressed a small kiss against the side of my neck, well, everything inside me bloomed.

Damn him.

We didn't talk as we left, just held hands and walked in comfortable silence. But when we came to my car, I suddenly found myself pushed up against it and Camden's arms caging me in.

"You certainly like to push me up against any vertical surface you can find," I said, letting my hands rest on his waist.

"I like kissing you, and other things. And I like it when I'm sure you can't get away. You've run from me a few times, and I'm just taking advantage of my surroundings."

I knew he was joking, but I also knew the humor was coming from some sort of truth. I had run from him and I had pushed him away. So, I let my hands slip around his body, pulling him in to me, doing the exact opposite of what he was afraid of.

"You don't have to worry about me running anymore. Now that I've slept with you, I'm not going anywhere." I winked at him and lucky for me, he smiled at my attempt of a joke. But he also leaned down and kissed me. Suddenly, nothing was funny anymore.

His tongue swept into my mouth as his hands came to rest on the sides of my neck, thumbs gently moving up and down along the sensitive skin there. I pulled him closer, my hands spread out across his shoulder blades between the cotton of his shirt and the satin of the lining of his suit jacket. I could feel the muscle there. I wanted time to map his body, to use my hands to run over every inch, making notes of all the valleys and hills, letting my fingers and mouth scout the terrain.

I'd never been with someone I had so much sexual chemistry with, and I was surprised to learn that being attracted to him brought out something new in me. I'd never *felt* this way before. Sure, I'd wanted to sleep with men before, and had—thank you very much—but I'd never loved the way I felt with anyone the way I did with Camden. Kissing him was hot, but him kissing me was scorching. I loved the way he made me laugh, the way he was open with me, and how his book had been open since day one. So even though we were making out in a parking lot, his hands moving up to the base of my head and positioning me at exactly the right angle so he could absolutely plunder my mouth, it wasn't just the sex I was falling for—it was the man, too.

I wanted to stay there all night and let him kiss me silly, but I had to go.

"I'll come to you tomorrow night," I whispered after pulling away from him, missing his lips against mine already.

"I'll be waiting."

Chapter Eight

Riley

Even though I was glad to be moving on from weddings, I was going to miss them. Maybe. But just a little bit. Sure, weddings were stressful, but they were beautiful, too. Watching a bride nervously wait to walk down the aisle, seeing the groom lose his shit and cry tears of happiness as his partner walked toward him, the love radiating between a newly wed couple—it was impossible to walk away from a wedding and not feel a little lovey-dovey.

In addition, this was the first wedding I'd worked while being in my own relationship. It was all I could do not to daydream about Camden. Sure, they were fantasies set in the distant future, but fantasies nonetheless. What if we ended up getting married one day? Would he look at me like that as I walked down the aisle? Would he hold me that close as we danced our first dance? Would he kiss me tenderly every time someone clinked their knife on their champagne glass?

I'd always figured I'd get married someday, but the groom always had a blurry face in all my imaginings. Unless you counted the times I imagined myself marrying Justin Timberlake. In that case, his gorgeous face was very defined. But aside from that, marriage and the happily ever after was just a thought bubble, something out of reach and floating above me. But watching that wedding all day only had me thinking of Camden and imagining his face at the altar.

It was scary admitting to yourself that you might have actually caught the love bug. And also that you might have come down with the sickness in record time.

I was tired when I left the wedding, but not tired enough to convince myself to go anywhere but Camden's condo. He'd texted me early that morning to wish me good luck and then I hadn't heard from him all day—which I kind of appreciated. I had a crazy job and the last thing I needed was someone begging for attention when I didn't have the time to give it to them. The fact that he knew I was busy and let me work only made me want to see him more. Reverse psychology at its finest.

When I walked into the lobby of his building I was a little intimidated, remembering how fancy it was and worrying I wouldn't know how to get to his condo. I was greeted by the same doorman who'd been there before, only this time he spoke.

"Good evening, miss. How can I help you?"

"I'm here to see Camden Rogers," I said with false confidence as I adjusted my obvious overnight bag on my shoulder.

"Perfect," he replied with practiced politeness. "I'll need to make a copy of your driver's license."

"Oh," I replied, surprised. I watched him make a copy of my license and then hand it back to me.

"This elevator will take you to his suite. Just select the ninth floor."

"Thank you." I gave him a smile and then followed his directions. I let out a sigh when the elevator doors closed behind me, taking one last moment to calm myself before seeing Camden. The deep breath didn't help because with every floor the elevator rose, so did my nervousness. Something about Camden was overwhelming, and I was practically shaking with anticipation. The elevator slowed to a halt and the doors slid open effortlessly.

Camden's condo was mostly dark with a few dim lights on throughout the open floorplan. My eyes were drawn to the big picture window. It was a rare cloudless fall night and the moon illuminated everything in the east. The mountain looked as though it were almost glowing. There weren't many stars—too many lights for that—but there were all the bridges Portland was famous for, lit, sparkling, and reflected in the river as though it were glass.

"Hey, you." I turned toward the sound of his voice, watching as he emerged from the shadows of the hallway. A hallway I'd never been down because the last time I was at his place we'd only made it as far as the kitchen.

"Hey." My voice was softer than I anticipated. I wasn't usually a quiet girl.

The closer he got the more I could see of him. He was wearing a well-worn pair of light gray sweatpants and a plain white T-shirt. No shoes and stupidly sexy bare feet. I watched his feet, listened to the way they slapped against his hardwood floors until they were only an inch from mine. His naked feet looked silly next to the pointy toes of my high heels. His finger hooked me gently under my chin and I let him pull my face up and met his gaze.

"I'm glad you're here."

"Me too."

He leaned in and feathered his lips over mine. It could have very well been the lightest, gentlest, tiniest whisper of a kiss I'd ever had, but it lit me up from head to toe. I wanted that featherlight touch all over my body, wanted those lips to brush against every part of me, multiple times. When he pulled away I was not ready and had to hold back a groan.

"You must be exhausted," he said, slipping my bag from my shoulder and then threading his fingers through mine and leading me down the darkened hallway.

I was until I got here.

"Do you want to shower or anything before bed?" he asked, taking me into an enormous bedroom. All I could do was gape as I looked around the room, trying to take everything in. His bed was huge, definitely bigger than my full-size mattress, but bigger still because of the massive frame. An incredibly masculine footboard matched the headboard that had big vertical slats. The wood was stained black and the plush bedding was a satiny gray. The bed looked sexy and inviting—a troublesome combination. I wanted to let him do sexy things to me in it, but I also wanted to throw on some comfy pj's and curl that soft blanket around me, and drift to sleep on a cloud. I'd let him share my cloud too.

"I don't think I have enough energy for a shower," I said, making the final decision; sleep's call was too loud. Sex would have to wait.

He put my bag down on his bed, letting my hand go, and pulled out my pajamas.

Even though his wonderful bed called for comfy pj's, that wasn't what I'd been thinking when I packed. Camden held up a tiny, pink, lacy nightgown. Truthfully, when it was on, it hardly covered anything. He eyed it and I watched as his breath pulled in and hissed out. He closed his eyes and clenched his fist around my nightie, then slowly put it back in the bag. Confusion pulled at my face as I watched him walk into what I assumed was either a closet or a bathroom. He came out a few seconds later with a piece of clothing in his hand, holding it out to me.

"There's no way I'll be able to sleep next to you in that tiny lace thing. Wear this, yeah?"

I took it from him and held it up.

"Lewis and Clark Law School, huh?" The T-shirt was worn, soft, and exactly what I needed. In fact, I was considering not giving it back.

"I went to Willamette University for my undergrad, then earned my law degree at Lewis and Clark." He told me this while he pulled me closer and started stripping off my clothes. I wasn't incapable, but I definitely didn't mind the help either.

"I went to Portland State." My statement was simple, but I couldn't help but think about everything it implied. I attended a state school while he earned two degrees from very private and very expensive colleges.

"I applied there," he said nonchalantly as he pulled my blouse over my head.

"You're a few years older. I don't think we would have overlapped."

He unbuttoned my trousers, pulled the zipper down, and let them pool at my feet, all while looking into my eyes.

"Good thing, too. I would not have been able to concentrate on school if you'd been around." He pressed a kiss to my lips, but it was a new kind of kiss, not like all the others we'd shared. The kiss was content. It felt as though he was kissing me because he was grateful I was with him, not expecting it to lead to anything or move forward in any way. A kiss just because.

He broke from me and leaned down to pull off my heels and my pants.

"How in the world do you walk around all day in these?"

"That's a secret known only by women and drag queens," I said, smiling down at him. I rested a hand on his shoulder for balance as he lifted my feet, one by one, removing my shoes and pants. "If I told you, I'd have to kill you."

He stood and walked behind me. I felt his fingers at my back as he unhooked my bra. The light brush of his skin against mine caused all kinds of goose bumps to appear. I rolled my shoulders forward, letting my bra fall to the floor with the rest of my clothes. He pressed a tender kiss to the top of my shoulder right before he slipped the shirt over my head. It was all I could do to keep myself from gathering the material between my hands, bringing it to my nose, and inhaling deeply. I could smell him, his scent woven into the fabric from years of use.

Nope.

I was keeping the shirt.

And never washing it.

"Come on," he said quietly, taking my hand again and leading me through the other door. The en suite bathroom was beautiful. Well, as beautiful as a bathroom could be. It was all white marble and porcelain, and again with the gray accents. He stepped up to the counter and pulled open a drawer, producing a brand-new toothbrush. He held it out to me and I took it, smiling.

"I brought my own toothbrush," I said with a laugh.

"That's nice," he said, pulling toothpaste from the same drawer and applying it to his own toothbrush. "But now you can leave that one here and you'll always have one."

Always?

My heart could not take promises of eternity and dental hygiene equipment. I was too tired for that.

I took the package and opened it, tossing the trash in the garbage, and brushed my teeth standing next to Camden, our eyes meeting in the mirror. It was weird and intimate and wonderful all at the same time. I couldn't think of another time when I'd brushed my teeth with someone. Not since high school slumber parties.

It was also educational as I learned that Camden was a spitter. It had never occurred to me that there were people who spit every ten seconds while brushing their teeth, but he did. And he grinned at me every time.

"You sure spit a lot," I said as we rinsed our mouths.

"And I couldn't help but notice you didn't."

I caught the smile creeping across his face, like a teenage boy saying something dirty and hoping his mother didn't catch on. Well, I was nobody's mother.

"Don't let that give you any ideas," I teased.

He laughed and pressed a kiss to my forehead. "Babe, I wouldn't be a man if I didn't get extremely vivid and detailed ideas after that." He bent down and gave me a minty kiss, then said, "You finish up in here and I'll meet you in bed."

I watched him leave, my tired body not immune to the way his ass looked in sweatpants. He closed the door behind him and I let out a sigh.

"Riley, what in the world have you gotten yourself into?" I asked the question of my own reflection, but I didn't have an answer to give.

A few minutes later I headed back into the bedroom and walked toward the huge bed that now had a shirtless Camden lounging in it.

"Do you work out?" I asked, my filter obviously equally as tired as I was. Okay, I'll admit, I don't really have a filter.

He laughed at my forward question. "I do, in fact. There's a gym downstairs. I can take you down there tomorrow if you'd like."

"Gyms aren't really my thing," I said with half a shrug as I climbed into the bed. "I don't want to assume I'll be spending a lot of time here or anything, but if this becomes a normal, regular thing, I'm going to have to request one of those sets of stairs for small dogs. Climbing into this bed is like scaling a mountain." I slid between the silky sheets and satiny blanket, wondering how something that felt so luxurious and smooth kept anybody warm at night.

I didn't even wait for an invitation, I simply slid right over to Camden and snuggled myself in the little crook made in men's sides for women. My hand draped over his abdomen, my cheek rested on his chest, and I was comfortable as hell.

"I also hope that you having an enormous bed didn't mean you wanted me on the other side of it. I'm kind of a snuggler."

He laughed, and the sound vibrated through his chest and into my ear. His arm tightened around me, pressing me even closer to him, and a content sigh slipped out of me. I felt his mouth against the top of my head and smiled sleepily as he kissed my hair.

"I missed you," he whispered. "And it's crazy because I hardly know you. But I do know I want you here, in my bed, and right next to me."

"Same goes." My words were slurred, everything fading away. "Sleepy time now." He laughed again, but that time it sounded softer.

The next thing I heard were the telltale sounds of raindrops slamming into window panes. But the sound was different than I was used to. Waking up to rain wasn't uncommon in Portland, but I usually heard it on my roof, above me. This sound was coming from another room and sounded farther away. I stretched before I peeped my eyes open and my hands ran into warm flesh.

I looked over and saw Camden's muscular back facing me, stretching every few moments with his even breaths. Even asleep he was perfect.

I rolled toward him until my face was right between his shoulder blades, and rested my forehead against him for a moment, loving the way the heat of his body warmed me.

"Morning." His voice was groggy from sleep, but sexy too, all raspy and deep.

"Morning," I replied, kissing his back and sliding a hand over his hip. I felt him still at my touch, and my still-sleepy mind couldn't comprehend if he was going still in a good or bad way, so I pulled back. In hindsight, this might have been a stupid move, but I'd always argue that point because mere seconds later I was flat on my back and Camden was over me, his too-long hair crazy and falling over his eyes.

"Sleep well?"

I nodded.

"Good." His eyes wandered down my body, which was mostly covered, but I couldn't help but think of what my face looked like. I was so tired the night before I hadn't washed my makeup off, and I was sure there were raccoon eyes happening all over the place. "I think I want you wearing my T-shirt all the time."

Warmth bloomed in my chest at his words, and my hands came to rest on either side of his waist.

"I was thinking of stealing it and taking it home with me. But if I have your permission to take it, I'll have to swipe something else."

He narrowed his eyes at me. "Are you a kleptomaniac?"

"No?" I tried to keep a straight face, but when the sides of his mouth curled into a grin, I broke and laughed. My laughter slowed when his hand slipped under the hem of my shirt, his hands warm against my skin. Without taking his eyes from mine he inches my shirt up higher, taking his time, building the anticipation. When his thumb skimmed the sensitive flesh right below my nipple, I gasped, my back arching without permission, willing me closer.

His eyes were steady on mine, never wavering as his thumb swept closer and closer to the peak of my breast, teasing me in the best way possible. I panted, holding my breath every time he inched closer, then exhaling as he retreated.

"Please," I heard myself beg. A new smirk formed on his lips as he contemplated my request. Slowly his eyes disappeared as he lowered his face to my chest. He used his mouth the same way he'd been using his thumb—to tease me. He pressed openmouthed kisses all over my breast, except for the one place that was aching for attention. He kissed, nibbled, and even bit, making me gasp. His mouth worshiped my breast as his hand came to cup the underside, holding it to his mouth, obliterating my senses and holding my pleasure captive, not giving me what I wanted.

Finally, his mouth latched on to my nipple and he sucked ravenously, all the while using his hand to squeeze my breast with just enough pressure to completely undo me.

Surely I couldn't have an orgasm from breast play, right?

I was beginning to think it was altogether possible, and felt myself creeping closer and closer, when both his mouth and hand abandoned me, leaving the skin of my breast chilled as the air hit my wet flesh. My eyes snapped open, wondering what he would do next, and I was surprised to see him climbing off the bed. It was then I noticed a faint tune in the background.

"What's wrong?" I asked, when I really wanted to ask him why he'd stopped and demand he return his talented mouth to my nipple at once.

"It's my phone," he answered distractedly.

"Let it go to voice mail," I whined, taking the opportunity to whip my shirt over my head and slide my panties down my legs, fully preparing to let him do whatever he wanted to me if he'd only get back in the damn bed.

"Camden, this could be considered torture in a few countries. Come back." I wasn't against begging. Obviously.

He disappeared out the door of his bedroom and I flopped back down on the bed with a huff.

Fine.

I'd continue without him.

Almost on autopilot, one hand went to my abandoned breast while the other slid between my legs. I was still buzzing from what Cam had done to me, and even though my hand wasn't my choice as a replacement, it would have to do. I heard him returning to the bedroom, and I imagined his face when he walked in and saw me touching myself. I pictured his eyes zeroing in on my hand between my legs, watching as I used my fingers to get myself off. I envisioned him completely enraptured by the sight of me, unable to take his eyes from my body, but fully capable of taking himself in his own hand, stroking himself to the sight of me.

Instead, I heard him say—with a smile in his voice— "Hey, Mom."

Instinct kicked in—along with my old high school fear of being discovered by mothers—and I grabbed the silky gray blanket to cover myself immediately. I whipped the blanket over my head, effectively cocooning myself, but the fabric wasn't enough of a barrier to stop the sound of Camden's laugh hitting my ears.

"No, it's not a bad time," he said, trying to muffle his laughter. I felt the mattress dip and I fought the urge to kick him right onto the floor. "Just lounging around."

I stayed under the covers listening to Camden have a normal, rational conversation with his mother while I lay naked just feet from him. I tried not to eavesdrop, but honestly, if he didn't want me to hear what he was saying, he probably should have taken the call in another room. Or, oh I don't know, *not answered the phone!*

"I don't really have any solid plans for the day, no." He paused, and I could hear the Charlie Brown teacher voice of his mother through the phone *and* the comforter. "Sure, brunch sounds great. Give me an hour. Actually, make it two." I opened my mouth in a silent gasp. "Okay, see you then. Bye, Mom."

I held perfectly still, hoping he had forgotten I was there. But when the top of the comforter was peeled away from my face I saw him looking down at me.

"Where were we?" he said in a sultry voice.

"Oh, no," I said, sitting up and tucking the blanket around my body so tight not even light could get through. "There will be no nookie *now*. I cannot believe you just sat there talking to your mother!"

He had the nerve to laugh.

"Listen, Riley...." He laughed. *Again.* "My mom has her own ringtone, so I knew it was her. I also knew she'd call endlessly on a Sunday until I picked up. It's kind of her thing."

I didn't want to accept his excuse. "It's a little weird that you'd rather talk to your mother than *do things* with a woman."

"Babe," he said softly. "The instant I hear my mother's ringtone, nothing good happens downstairs. You think it's weird to stop when my mom calls? How about

112

being able to continue knowing my mom is calling?" He raised a knowing eyebrow at me, and I had to admit, he had a point.

"You could have said something. You just bolted."

He stuck his bottom lip out a little and tugged at the top of the blanket, silently asking for permission to enter. I gave the blanket a little slack, but he overpowered me and pulled it away fully, climbing in with me, not even trying to hide the fact that he was checking out my naked body.

"I'm sorry. I should have said something, but my brain was scrambled. Now," he said, cupping my breast again and kissing the top swell, never breaking eye contact. "Where were we?"

"You were about to give me a fabulous orgasm."

"Ah, yes."

And then he did.

Twice.

It was an hour later and all was forgiven. It was hard to stay angry at a man who spent more time making you come than any man you'd ever been with. The sex was fantastic, and then we'd spent a few minutes cuddling and catching our breath. He asked me about the wedding, and I gave him the CliffsNotes version, all while totally blissed out.

Eventually I knew I had to get up and make my way home.

"Do you mind if I shower here?" I asked against his chest, still lazing against him.

"Of course not. I might join you." He said the words against my hair while his hand gently ran up and down my arm.

"I can wait if you're in a hurry. I know you've got to go soon." His hand stilled.

"You're not coming with me?"

Shock and confusion registered at the same time. "Going with you? To brunch? With your mom?"

"Well, Not only my mom. My stepdad will be there too."

"The *mayor*?"

"Shit, I'm sorry. I should have asked you before I accepted."

"Wait, you assumed I was going with you?" My heart rate was rapidly approaching detonation. "I thought you were making plans. Like, I'm going home to water my plants, and you're going to brunch with your parents."

"I thought we were spending the day together."

"I thought so too."

"Damn it." He ran his hands down his face. "Riley, I'm sorry. My mom asked if I'd come to brunch and you and I hadn't made any plans, so I thought we'd go there. You were sitting right here when I made the plans. I thought you were cool with it."

"Oh, my God," I squeaked, panic taking over. I sat up, holding the blanket to my chest. "I can't go have brunch with the mayor and his wife."

Camden narrowed his eyes at me. "It's my mom and stepdad."

"Yeah, to you. To me it's the mayor and the first lady of Portland!"

"They're just like any other people. And I know they're going to love you."

"I brought over my weekend jeans and a slouchy sweater. I don't have brunch-with-the-mayor clothes in my bag."

His hands dropped back to his face. I watched, still panicked, as he took a few deep breaths and let them out. Then his hands fell away and his eyes met mine. "I'm sorry. I pushed you again. I should have thought about how comfortable you would be meeting my parents, and I know we've only been seeing each other for a couple weeks. This was a hasty decision. All I wanted was to spend the day with you and for you to meet my mom, for her to see how happy I am when I'm with you."

His words were so honest and heartfelt, something inside me crumbled a little. Even though I felt 100 percent in the right, a tiny part of me could see his point as well.

"You should have asked me first." I poked his chest with a finger.

"I know. I'm sorry. I'll take you home. I didn't mean to ruin the day."

"The day isn't ruined, Camden." I let out a dramatic sigh. "Can we at least go to my apartment to let me pick out some more appropriate clothes?"

"You'll come?" He smiled his sweet smile and any resistance I'd built up melted away.

"I will. But you owe me. And I intend to collect."

"Sounds interesting," he said with a snicker.

"Oh, it'll be more than interesting."

He laughed like I was being ridiculous, and suddenly it became my mission to surprise him. But first, I had to meet his parents.

Chapter Nine

Camden

I loved the Batmobile. But the car had never felt sexier than when Riley was in the passenger seat.

I'd showered at my place and I pretended not to notice when she took the opportunity to look through my medicine cabinet. She thought she was sneaky, but in reality, I was extraordinarily aware of her. When she came into the bathroom, asking me to tell her about my mom and stepdad, to give her a little background, I had to laugh when she pried open the cabinet.

I followed her back to her apartment and waited while she got herself ready.

In truth, she could have worn a paper sack to my parents' house and it wouldn't have mattered to me. I didn't care what they thought about her, but only because I knew they'd love her. I knew my mom would be able to see past whatever she wore, down to the things that actually mattered. Like how I felt about her. My mom would be able to see what she meant to me.

But when she emerged from her bedroom in a beautiful and soft-looking sundress, I was torn between admiring how gorgeous she was and demanding she go back in the bedroom and put something less arousing on. The dress, which was white with pink and blue flowers, came down to midthigh, allowing so much leg to show between the hem and the little brown ankle boots she wore. I wanted to run my hands all over the smooth expanse of skin, let my fingers linger at the especially soft place behind her knees. The dress had no sleeves so her arms were bare all the way down to her graceful hands. Hands I wanted to feel on me right that instant. Riley, in that dress, was too much. Too

117

much beauty. Too much grace. Too much sexiness. I couldn't handle it.

"You look beautiful," I managed to say even though my voice was strained. "Won't you be cold?" That was my non-caveman way of asking her to cover herself up.

"Oh," she said, flipping her freshly curled hair over her shoulder, "I have a cardigan." She said the words as though a cardigan was a chastity belt, like it would keep wandering eyes away from all of her.

"Babe, it's like, fifty degrees out there." I hitched a thumb toward the window and sure enough, it was gray and drizzly, a typical Oregon fall day. Surely she would listen to reason.

"Your car has a heater, right?" she asked with a smile. "And we're just walking from the car to your parents' house. It's not like we're going hiking."

All her points were valid.

I watched as she slipped a baby blue cardigan over her arms and flipped her hair out of the collar. I wanted to walk her back into her bedroom and peel the cardigan off her, watch her dress float to the floor as I took it off her body, but I knew we had to go. I held my hand out to her, giving it a squeeze when she placed it in mine. I used it to tug her close to me, making sure I had her gaze before I spoke.

"You really do look beautiful."

"Thanks," she said as a blush crept over her cheeks. I wanted to see that blush all over her body. She tilted up on her toes and pressed her lips against mine. "I want to make a good impression."

"You will," I said, pressing another small kiss against her neck.

I held her hand until we'd made it to my car and I closed the passenger door behind her. The entire ride I watched as her eyes panned the scenery. When we pulled into my parents' neighborhood, I noticed her mouth gaped open slightly, and her leg started bouncing. Gently, I placed my hand on her thigh, noticing the way it stopped bouncing at my touch.

"Everything's going to be fine. It's just brunch."

"Brunch with the mayor." She gave me an exasperated look but added a smile.

"I know, but he's not the mayor at home. Besides, he'll probably eat with us and then disappear into his study. On Sundays, he likes to read the newspaper from front to back."

She nodded, and I gave her thigh a squeeze. When we pulled up to the house, her eyes widened.

"Did you grow up here?" she asked, her voice breathy as she stared at the house.

"Nope. When they got married they bought a house a little farther west, and that's where they lived until I moved out for college. They bought this house a few years ago."

"Empty nesters are supposed to downsize."

I laughed. "Well, I guess they didn't get that memo."

"Apparently not."

"Come on," I said as I put the car in park in the circular driveway. "It'll be fine." I hopped out and walked to her door, opening it and offering her a hand. She took it with a smile and we made our way to the front door. Even though I'd never lived there, I didn't bother knocking. My mother had a fit the few times I knocked, so I'd made it a habit not to. I opened the door and called out. "Mom, we're here."

"In the kitchen," my mother called.

"I brought a guest," I replied.

"Oh, fantastic," she replied, her voice excited. "I made too much bacon anyway."

"See?" I whispered. "She made too much bacon."

"I feel much better now," Riley replied sarcastically.

I led her into the kitchen and my mother turned toward us as soon as we entered. The initial shock that registered on her face when she saw us didn't escape me, and it probably didn't escape Riley either, but my mother was married to a politician and recovered quickly. She put on her perfect smile and walked around the island to greet us.

She lifted up on her toes to kiss my cheek, giving my shoulder a squeeze as she did, then pulled back with an expectant smile on her face.

"Mom, this is Riley, my girlfriend. Riley, this is my mother."

"It's nice to meet you, Mrs. Rogers." Riley held her hand out for a polite handshake, but my mother pulled her into a hug instead.

"No handshakes for the girl my son brings home and introduces as his girlfriend." My mother held her captive for an appropriate amount of time and then released her. "And call me Meg."

"Thank you, Meg, for having me over."

Mom gave her another sparkling smile and then said, "I'll go find out what's keeping your father." I tried to hide the immediate tensing in my body that happened whenever my mother called Andrew my father, but it was interrupted by the man himself.

"I hear Camden brought a guest," he said, rounding the corner. Andrew was not nearly as good at hiding his disappointment in seeing Riley as my mother was. "Who's this?" he asked, unkindly. I felt Riley stiffen next to me and my arm wrapped around her shoulders, turning her in to my side.

"This is Riley. My girlfriend."

"What about Sophia?"

My eyebrows drew together in confusion and my heart started to pound in my chest.

"What *about* Sophia?" I retorted.

"I thought you were dating Senator Greenway's daughter." Andrew had the audacity to look at me as though I were the one being rude, and that made my blood boil even more. I used my arm to move Riley behind me, shielding her. There was no reason to think she was in any danger, but I didn't want him even looking at her.

"I went on a few dates with her, but it ended. I'm dating Riley now."

"Andrew, please," my mother quietly begged, whispering as though she were ashamed of the situation. Then she turned to me and said, "Obviously, we were expecting to see you with someone different. I'd love to get to know Riley and have a nice brunch, all four of us."

"No offense meant to your friend here, Camden, but I was counting on you to see things through with the Greenway girl."

"See things through?" I scoffed.

"Andrew!" My mother was done whispering at that point. "You cannot dictate who Camden decides to date."

My stepfather had the nerve to look put out by my mother's interference, but he relented.

"I can go." The small voice came from Riley, and I turned around immediately to see her with her shoulders caved, looking humiliated. My hands immediately wrapped around her neck and brought her eyes up to look at mine.

"Don't worry, we don't have to stay. I'll take you home. Or back to my place. Whichever you prefer."

"No. No one's leaving," my mother interjected. My body turned to see my mother and with it came Riley. I tucked her back into my side, not willing to let go of her. "Riley, I am sorry for my husband's behavior, but I am sure you have known some men who sometimes put their foot in their mouths. Andrew is a good man and only trying to look out for Camden. He might look like an ass right now," she said, shooting him the death glare I'd been exceedingly familiar with during my teenage years, "but I assure you it is nothing personal, and he'd love to have brunch with you."

"With all due respect, Mrs. Rogers," Riley said in a small voice I'd never heard from her before, "your husband absolutely does *not* want to have brunch with me."

"He wouldn't know what to wear every morning if I didn't put it out for him. And I'll be honest with you right now, after the last five minutes, if he doesn't want to be sleeping in the guest bedroom for a week, brunch with you is exactly what he wants." My mom gave Riley a genuine smile, and I felt her relax against me a fraction.

"Listen," Andrew started, taking a few cautious steps toward us. "I'm sorry. I wasn't trying to make you feel unwelcome, I was just surprised. Please accept my apology and stay."

I used my free hand to pull her chin toward me. "It's okay if you don't want to stay. I'll take you wherever you want to go." She pulled her bottom lip between her teeth, seeming to contemplate her next move carefully. Without another word she pulled herself from my embrace and walked toward Andrew. When she was a few steps away, she put her hand out to him.

"My name is Riley Smith, and I am not the daughter of a senator, but I am Camden's girlfriend."

I couldn't help the cloud of pride that expanded in my chest at her words. She wasn't backing down from him and that was impressive and sexy at the same time. After all the worries she'd voiced to me about the differences in our families and our backgrounds, in our socioeconomic status, Andrew's rant was the very last thing she needed to hear. She already thought we were too different, and now he was basically saying that Sophia was perfect for me only because she was the Senator's daughter. Never mind she was a vapid Barbie doll with no personality. Sophia had absolutely nothing on Riley.

Andrew reached out and shook her hand politely and he seemed sincere, but I couldn't tell if he was putting on a good show for us or not. Truth be told, it didn't matter to me. As long as he was decent and polite to Riley, we wouldn't have a problem. He didn't have to approve of her; the only person whose opinion mattered in that room was Riley's.

"Fantastic," my mother said on a sigh, a strained smile on her face. "Let's all head to the dining room and get to know each other a little better."

Riley gave another small smile to my mother but then came to my side, her hand finding a place on my stomach right above my navel.

"Can you show me where the restroom is really quick?"

I nodded and steered her toward the guest bathroom down the hall from the front door. As soon as we were out of earshot and alone, I stopped her, pressing her up against the wall in the hallway.

"I'm sorry about all that," I whispered, spreading my legs wide so that I was eye level with her.

"That was fucked-up." She looked down at her hands between us, which were fidgeting. "I knew this was a bad idea."

"Hey," I said as I tipped her chin up, wanting to see her eyes as we spoke. "Just because Andrew is being a dick doesn't mean anything, and it definitely doesn't have a bearing on our relationship. Sure, he wanted me to date Sophia because it would be good for him and his political career, but that doesn't mean shit to me, Riley. You do."

"He didn't want you to just date her. He wanted you to 'see it through.' He wants you to marry someone on your level, and that's definitely not me."

"Are you proposing?" I asked, trying to make her smile. Luckily for me, it worked.

"No, I'm just saying, the person he envisions you with and the person I am are not on the same level, Camden. It will be really awkward if your parents hate me. This," she said as she motioned between us, "doesn't have to be super serious, but it would be easier if your parents didn't think I was pond scum."

I wasn't sure what bothered me more—that she was lumping my mother in with Andrew, or that she didn't think we had to be serious. I was nothing but serious about her and wanted serious things with her. It was stupid how serious it was. Seriously stupid.

"Andrew's a tool, but my mom is really looking forward to getting to know you. I can tell. Don't push her aside with him, trust me. She'll love you. Andrew will warm up to the idea of you, but it doesn't matter if he does or not, not to me anyway. Say you'll stay."

She looked up at me with eyes that appeared sadder than I'd ever seen, and I wanted more than anything to make it go away. But all I could do was try to make her see my mother wasn't as bad as the last five minutes might have painted her to be.

"I'll stay," she finally said, her voice soft and unsure.

"Thank you," I said, before pressing a kiss to her forehead. "I'll meet you back out there, all right?"

"Okay."

I watched her walk into the bathroom and then headed back into the dining room where Andrew had already taken his seat at the head of the table, and my mother was setting down a platter full of scrambled eggs.

"Andrew, that was completely uncalled for and I won't stand for you making Riley feel uncomfortable. She was nervous enough to meet you both and now you've scared her out of her mind. When she comes out here, you will treat her with respect or I will walk out of here and it will be a long while before I come back."

"Listen, I apologized and I meant it. I'll treat her like I would any other guest, but I won't be threatened by you in my own house. Besides, I am only looking out for your future, Camden. Sophia would have been a good match for you."

I saw red instantly.

"No, Sophia would have been a good match *for you.* I am not basing my life decisions on how to further your career. And for the record, Riley is a perfect match for me. I've never met anyone so full of life, witty, smart, independent, and *good.*"

"You really like her." The soft tone of my mother's voice was in stark opposition to the emotions running through the room.

"What?" I asked gruffly, turning to her.

"You like her. A lot. I can tell."

I let out a sigh it felt like I'd been holding for hours. "Yes, I like her. More than I think I've ever *liked* anyone. Like isn't even a good word to describe it, Mom. She's.... I don't know.... She's it."

My mother drew in a slow breath and pressed a hand to her chest. Her eyes welled and her breath shuddered out.

"Camden," she whispered.

"Mom, don't go getting all sentimental on me. It won't matter how much I care about her if you and Andrew make her feel uncomfortable. She's scared. I don't fully understand why, but if she feels unwelcome or unwanted, she will run. It's already happened once before. So, please, I need you both to be on my side right now."

My mom shot Andrew another death stare. He held his hands up in surrender.

I took a seat at the table, making sure there was an empty seat next to me, as far from Andrew as possible. When Riley finally reappeared, she looked stiff and had an obviously forced polite smile on her face. I stood and pulled out her chair, thanking the universe that she'd decided to come back and hadn't slipped out the door when I wasn't looking.

"You have a lovely home," Riley said to my mother, her voice so much smaller than I was used to.

"Thank you very much. It's more work than I'd like, but really comes in handy when we have parties for holidays and such."

"It wouldn't be too much work if you'd hire a housekeeper, like I've been telling you for years," Andrew said, not unkindly, as he spooned eggs onto his plate.

"I'll hire a housekeeper when I'm old," she replied with a shrug. "If I am able, I'll clean my own house."

"I'd kill for someone to clean my bathroom every once and a while," Riley said as she absently passed a platter of food to me.

"Bathrooms are the worst, aren't they?" My mother laughed as she said the words. "So, Riley, what do you do?"

"I work for Rose City Event Coordinators."

"She just got a promotion," I said proudly, placing my hand on the back of her neck, giving her a squeeze.

"That's wonderful," Mom said with enthusiasm. "What exactly do you do there?"

"I work directly with clients and plan high-profile events. My new position allows me to work with more corporations and non-profits."

"That's so fantastic," Mom replied.

"Meg is always planning events for all her projects." My stepfather said the words as he cut through his food, and they sounded slightly patronizing, but I knew he didn't mean them that way.

"I'm on the board for a few organizations and I try to have a few fundraisers each year. It's a lot of work. I find it fascinating that you do it for a living."

"It's a relatively new concept for employment. Twenty years ago there weren't professional party planners, so sometimes my job takes people by surprise. But Rose City is groundbreaking in that they combine the actual planning and promotion. We have in-house PR that clients can utilize as well. So, not only will we plan your event, but we'll also get the word out about it, maximizing visibility and profits. Of course, PR isn't always needed for events, but non-profits especially like that feature. They're trying to raise funds, after all. The more people who know about the event, the more money they will raise."

"That's fantastic."

"You should use her for your Angel House event next month," Andrew said, using his fork to gesticulate toward Riley.

"That's a wonderful idea!" Mom was practically bouncing in her chair.

Riley, on the other hand, looked as though she might be sick.

"Mom, can you pass the bacon?" I asked, trying to redirect in any way I could. Mom hardly acknowledged me as she handed the platter over, her eyes trained on Riley.

"I have an annual event for my favorite non-profit, Angel House. This year I'm trying to put together a black-tie dinner gala. I've got the location booked, and invitations out, but that's it. Do you think you could help?"

Riley swallowed a bite of food, wincing slightly. She took a sip of her orange juice and then finally spoke. "Angel House? The shelter for victims of domestic abuse?"

"That's the one. You've heard of them?"

"Yeah, I've worked on a few events for them. Small ones. I was always on the team, never the lead on those projects though."

"Will you help me?"

"Uh," Riley stalled. I reached under the table and grabbed her hand, threading my fingers through hers.

"Mom, this isn't really good brunch conversation."

"Oh, I'm sorry, Riley. I'm not trying to put you on the spot. You just got me all excited over the possibility of making the gala spectacular."

"I could point you in a few directions, but other than that my hands are sort of tied. I have a non-compete agreement in my employment contract with Rose City, so I can't offer my services outside of their company." Riley paused for a moment, still looking as though she might lose the small amount of food she'd eaten. "I'm sorry."

"Oh, don't be silly," my mom said, waving her worries away. "Of course I want to hire you. I didn't expect you to work for free. Can I contact Rose City directly?"

"Um, yeah. I can leave you a card."

"Splendid."

I looked at Riley and noticed her face was a little green. I leaned over to her and whispered, "Are you all right?"

Her lips thinned, but she tried to give me a smile. Then she managed a feeble nod. This was not going well.

"So, how did you two meet?"

I heard Riley choke on her juice after Andrew asked the question, and I reached over to rub her back until she'd calmed down, but the sputtering lasted a while.

"Riley and I were next to each other at a Renegades game a couple weeks ago." I was definitely not about to tell them all the details.

"Oh, are you a Renegades fan?" my mother asked with a little too much enthusiasm. I had to smile. I loved my mother for trying to make Riley feel comfortable.

"I love the Renegades. I usually watch the games from a bar down the street from my apartment, but I bought tickets that night as a splurge to celebrate my promotion." Riley's demeanor loosened as she spoke, and I could see her relaxing as she told the story. "I sat next to Camden and I couldn't take my eyes off him." She blushed, looking down for only a moment, then continued. "After the game, he basically stalked me until he got my number. And the rest is history."

"That's sweet," my mom gushed. "Isn't it sweet, Andrew?"

"Indeed," he said, before taking another bite.

Brunch continued without any more stressful situations. The more my mother talked to Riley, the more she relaxed. My mom regaled her with stories of my childhood, especially the embarrassing ones. It didn't bother me though; I was too caught up in watching Riley laugh at my misfortune.

Riley was open and answered any of the questions my mom and stepdad had for her, talking about her college experience, where she grew up, her family—all the necessary information for new girlfriend examination.

After we ate, my mom took Riley into the kitchen for coffee, Andrew disappeared into his office to read his paper, and I sat in the breakfast nook watching and listening to my mom and my girlfriend talk about all kinds of girly shit. It was cute, but it wasn't interesting.

Finally, I made enough noises that my mom caught on.

"I think Camden is ready to go," she said with a laugh.

"Are you willing to let her go?" I asked her, standing and wrapping an arm around Riley's shoulders, pulling her to my side. My gaze drifted to the slight cleavage her dress revealed from my vantage point, and it became my mission to get her out of my parents' house as soon as possible.

"It's been a pleasure, Riley. I do hope you'll come back soon. And bring Camden with you. And I'll get in touch with your boss this week."

"Oh, let me give you her card."

Riley fished a business card out of her purse and then we slowly made our way to the door, she and my mom making a bunch of tentative and vague plans. My mom was saying, "we should do lunch one afternoon." And Riley was answering with, "Yeah, that'd be great."

Why couldn't girls just say "See ya later?"

We waved to my mother as I opened the passenger door for Riley, and again as we pulled around the driveway.

"That wasn't too bad," Riley said after we'd been on the road a few minutes. "Well, the beginning sucked, but it got better. Your mom is wonderful." She looked at me and smiled, the warmth of it radiating toward me.

"I think she really liked you."

"That's good." Her voice was quiet and she relaxed down into the bucket seat even further, making the hem of her dress slide up her thighs. I reached over and rested my hand on her bare skin, smiling when she threaded her fingers through mine, holding my hand there. We didn't talk the rest of the way home, and when I pulled into my parking spot in the garage I looked over and realized she'd fallen asleep.

Suddenly a midday nap with Riley sounded fantastic.

"Riley," I whispered, gently shaking her knee, trying to rouse her enough to get her back upstairs where I could put her in one of my T-shirts and fall asleep with her in my arms. "Wake up, baby. We're home." Her eyes fluttered open and she looked around, trying to figure out her surroundings, and when they finally landed on me she gave me a smile, but it wasn't as brilliant as it usually was.

"You look like you're far away," I said softly, sweeping some loose hair behind her ear. "Everything all right?"

"Can I tell you something I've never told anyone before?" Her words were rushed, as if she were afraid she'd change her mind before she got them all out.

"Of course. I'll listen to anything you want to tell me."

She took in a deep breath and then let it out in a rush. Her eyes dropped down to her lap and she laced her fingers together.

"When my father left, my mom had to find a job for the first time in over ten years. She had little education and no experience, so her choices were limited. My aunt worked as a maid in Arizona and told her there was a job waiting for her, and that's when we moved. My mom, thankfully, was given a job as a live-in maid and babysitter for an exceptionally wealthy family, the Waldens. It was a perfect setup for us because my mom, brother, and I were able to live, rent-free, in a little house at the back of their property, and because of our address we went to very good schools.

"The problem was, since the first day we were there, we were treated like second-class citizens. Mr. and Mrs. Walden didn't let their kids talk or play with us, and their kids were so jaded that when school started, they made sure everyone knew we were *the help*. For four years I was friendless and constantly reminded of the differences between me and everyone around me."

I tried to imagine Riley lonely, and it didn't compute. Riley was bright and enthusiastically magnetizing. Just being around her was enough to want to know more about her, to spend more time with her, to soak up as much of her as you could. But I also knew kids in high school were assholes.

"I think it was easier for my brother because he found a niche. He played football and performed in the competition choir, but I didn't have anything to distract me from how miserable I was."

"I'm sorry," I said, placing a hand on her knee. "That sounds horrible."

She nodded but didn't look up at me.

"I'm not sure how much you know about teenage girls, but a bad day is the end of the world, and I'd had four years of bad days. As soon as I could, I left. I moved back to Oregon for college and haven't been back since. I've never felt more alone or worthless than when I lived with the Waldens. And they're the ones responsible for making my life miserable."

"And that's why my family's money and status is a problem for you."

"*Was* a problem for me. Well, I'm trying not to let it be a problem anymore. It's obvious that your mom is too sweet to be evil, and you're clearly not an asshole. I need you to know that I have an extremely low tolerance for being treated poorly, and I don't know if I'll be able to handle it if people treat me like I'm less than."

I knew she was talking about Andrew, and I didn't blame her. "Hey," I said, bringing my hand to her cheek and leaning over so I could look her in the eyes. "Trust me enough to protect you from all that. Andrew will come around, and I can guarantee his reaction to you had very little to do with you at all. He didn't know anything about you before today. But I also need you to understand that no matter what Andrew says, I'm not going anywhere and there's no way I could ever think you were less than. You're more than anything I've ever imagined."

Chapter Ten

Riley

I'd never had to run to work before. And to be completely honest, I didn't run all the way to work, but I definitely sprinted to my office once I'd reached my floor. Some mornings I opted to take the stairs all eight floors, just to get some exercise, but that morning there was no time.

Waking up with Camden on a work morning was going to prove to be problematic. The man had a thing for morning sex, and it turned out that I simply had a thing for him. It was, as far as I could tell, impossible to tell him no. So we'd had sex. Ahem, *amazing* sex. And then I had to rush to my apartment to grab work clothes and by that time I was running behind for work. Any normal day I'd take the MAX, but being late to work so soon after a promotion was never a good look, so I drove and paid a fortune for parking, then practically ran into the elevator.

It didn't seem like a good sign that my phone was ringing as I power-walked into my office, or that I was out of breath when I answered.

"Riley Smith's office. How can I help you?"

"Riley. My office. Now."

It was the voice of Rose, the owner of the company. She hadn't waited for a response before she hung up, which was good because I didn't have one. I took a good ten seconds to let the shock sink in. Rose McAllister was *the* head honcho. Before my promotion I'd had a meeting with her, but it felt as though it had been a formality. My immediate supervisor had pretty much indicated that the promotion was mine and that Rose had only wanted to give her stamp of approval.

She terrified me. I didn't know why, though. It was probably because she was a strong, powerful, successful woman and I admired her. It could have also been the fact that she was like stone. She never smiled. Never laughed. Never even was nice, per se. She was all business, all the time. Which was probably why her company did so well.

But I was a sucker for recognition and it killed me not to know if Rose thought I was doing a good job or not. And the fact that she'd called me personally to meet her in her office, well, I couldn't think of a single good reason for it.

I looked at the clock.

Shit.

I was three minutes late.

She was definitely going to fire me.

My phone rang again, startling me. I picked it up and sputtered out, "Hello?"

"Bring a notebook." Rose abruptly hung up again.

I grabbed a legal pad on top of my desk and hurried out of my office and through the open-concept floor. There were a few rows of long tables filled with other employees, and only a few offices along the perimeter. I had been at those tables up until a couple weeks prior, and I missed them—to some degree. I passed my old spot and my old neighbor, Rachel. She smiled up at me, but must have noticed the panicked look on my face because her eyes grew wide.

"What's up?" she asked as I zoomed past her.

"Rose," I silently mouthed and pointed to Rose's office at the back of the room. I wouldn't have thought it possible, but Rachel's eyes grew wider.

"Good luck!" she called, winning the annoyed gazes of a few people around her.

Rose's office was made of four glass walls. It was intimidating that she could always see you.

I peeked into Alison's office, my immediate supervisor, and nearly cried when I saw she was on the phone and probably not attending this little meeting with Rose.

My stomach turned and my entire body was going into fight or flight mode, reacting to the adrenaline I was obviously high on. My hands shook and my head was woozy. The closer I got to the door to Rose's office, the harder it was to take a full and deep breath.

As I approached the door I noticed her tall chair was turned away, facing the beautiful skyline behind her, and I felt a small wave of relief roll over me. I used the opportunity to calm myself, trying to take a few breaths and slow the rapid beating of my heart. After a few seconds, I felt calmer and told myself I was only delaying the inevitable. With a sense of determination and bravery I didn't feel, I marched in.

"Riley, please sit down," Rose said in her cool voice, giving nothing away, before I was even fully in the room.

"Rose, I'm so sorry I was late. I pride myself on being punctual and it won't ever happen again."

Her chair had turned around all the way by the time I finished my speech and had taken a seat in one of the chairs opposite her desk. Her blonde hair was perfectly straight and lay picturesquely over one shoulder, contrasting with the black dress she was wearing. Her eyebrows drew together and her head tilted.

"Riley, that's ridiculous. Everyone is late every once in a while. It's statistically impossible that you would never be late again. Don't make promises you can't keep or hold yourself to unrealistic expectations. You will only fail."

"Oh-kay...," I said slowly. "That's not why you wanted to see me?"

"No. It's not."

"Oh," I said, confusion thick in my voice.

"I would like to talk about why the mayor's wife was calling me early this morning to book us for a premium event package, asking specifically to work with you. And more so, I would like to know why I had to hear about this from the mayor's wife and why you didn't tell me or Alison that you were working that particular connection. Furthermore, how in the world do you have a connection to the mayor's wife?"

I swallowed hard.

"Well, I gave Meg your card yesterday afternoon. She asked for my help with an event, but I very clearly told her I couldn't help, you know, because of the non-compete clause, so she said she'd book me through the company."

"Meg?" she asked, exasperation in her voice.

"The mayor's wife," I supplied.

"I know who she is, Riley. I want to know how you're on first-name basis with her and how I'm only now hearing about it."

"Oh! I'm sorry. I just met her yesterday. She's my boyfriend's mother."

"You're dating the mayor's son?"

"Stepson."

"Okay, well, she wants you on this event, and I want it to be perfect. Take whoever you need to build a team and make it happen. She's given us a budget, but it's a generous one, so don't hold back. I'll e-mail you all the details. Until further notice you are off all other projects. I want you focusing on this, and this alone. Understand?"

"Yes," I said, and punctuated it with a swift nod.

"I want frequent and informative updates."

"Of course."

"If you impress her there's a chance we'll keep her business, and she is extremely high profile, Riley. I'm sure I don't have to tell you this. Why aren't you writing any of this down?"

I almost opened my mouth to remind her she'd said she would e-mail me all the details, but decided against it, and instead put pen to paper.

"She's secured a location for the third weekend in December, and that is only six weeks from now, so time is of the essence. She booked the Crystal Ballroom which is, in my opinion, a strange choice for this type of event, but it's not up to me to make those kinds of decisions. You need to check out the venue immediately and make sure it can fit her vision, and if not, you need to find an alternative—which will be difficult on such short notice—and convince her it's the best choice."

"Right," I said, not looking up at her but furiously scribbling notes on my legal pad.

"Normally I wouldn't allow my employees to work so closely with someone they had such a close relationship with, but my hands are tied. She asked for you, and I'm not about to turn her away."

That stopped me cold. "Rose, I didn't suggest to her that she request me. The opposite, in fact. I told her I couldn't help her since I worked here. I was trying to uphold my end of the non-compete."

"And I appreciate that. I'm trying to make it clear that this is an unusual circumstance and that I'm making an exception for the first lady of Portland."

"I understand. I want you to know I would never try to weasel my way into an account."

"Noted." She nodded and then looked at her computer. "I'm e-mailing you the file now. Put your team together and call your client to set up a meeting."

"Will do." I stood up and made my way to the door. When one hand rested on the doorknob, I turned back toward Rose. "I worked hard for my promotion, and I'm going to work really hard on this account. But I want you to know it has nothing to do with the fact that it's for my boyfriend's mother. I'll do a good job because I'm good at my job."

Rose didn't speak for a beat, but then turned to face me again. "Words mean little to me, Riley. Actions. Actions are important. Show me that you mean everything you just said."

I nodded and then turned and left.

When I was positive I was hidden from her view, I let out a huge sigh, letting my shoulders sag and my head loll back.

I needed a drink.

I walked directly to Rachel and sat in the empty seat next to her that I used to occupy.

"Rachel," I said, making her jump in surprise.

"Shit, Riley," she exclaimed, holding her hand to her chest. "You can't sneak up on people like that."

"Sorry, but there's no time to chitchat. I need you to come to my office, like, right now."

"Okay...," she said, a worried tone to her voice. I stood up and walked toward my office, knowing she was behind me, all the while trying to take deeps breaths and calm myself down. When we made it there I collapsed into my chair and heard Rachel close the door behind us.

"What's going on?"

I let out another breath, but then looked up and met her gaze.

"I'm dating the mayor's stepson and his mother just called Rose and hired us to plan her black-tie event in six weeks and asked that I be the point person on the account."

"You're dating the mayor's son?" she practically screamed, a smile stretched across her face.

"Stepson," I corrected.

"I can't believe this, I had no idea you were dating anyone." She fell quiet for a moment but then her eyes lit up in understanding. "Wait, is this the guy you kissed at the Renegades game?"

I nodded while holding my bottom lip captive between my teeth.

"And his mom is the mayor's wife?"

I nodded again, this time a little more frantically.

"All right, you're going to rock this party." Her support was clear and unwavering, which was good, considering my next statement.

"I'm glad you think so because you're going to help me."

"Me?"

"Yes, you. Rose told me to pick anyone I wanted to build my team, and I want you."

"Me?" she asked again, even more doubt in her tone.

"Don't make me say it again, Rachel. Of course you. You're my right-hand woman. I need your help. Please say you'll help me."

"I'll definitely help you," she said without hesitation, which I appreciated. She sat and gave me a wide-eyed look. "Did Rose really tell you to build your own team?"

"Yeah. Got any suggestions? I think we need at least one more person, just to make sure all our bases are covered." I watched as she mentally ticked through the staff, trying to pick the perfect person.

"You know, JasperJasper has been impressing me lately."

"Hipster JasperJasper?" I asked, surprised. Rachel and I had kind of been mocking JasperJasper since he started. He was all skinny jeans and suspenders.

"Yes, hipster JasperJasper." She couldn't say it without smiling. "Since you've moved into this office I've gotten a chance to get to know him, and there's more to him than his mustache."

"Okay, but I'm not picking people based on how I get along with them or how much I like them, I want people who can work hard and not complain. This is going to be a hellish six weeks."

"I totally think he'd be up for it. He loves planning and has a lot of vision. Think of Anthony from *Sex and the City.*"

"The gay wedding planner?"

"Yes! He's just like that guy, only, I don't know... Portlandier."

"Okay, get him in here."

Five minutes later I had Rachel, JasperJasper, and Alison in my office and a hot mocha in my hands. Alison wasn't going to be on my team, but I wanted her there to help me get started if I needed her.

Okay.

Fine.

I wanted her to hold my hand.

"JasperJasper, please close the door and everyone take a seat." I took a sip of my coffee as they settled in. "Whatever you were working on five minutes ago, you're no longer working on it. Per Rose, Rachel and JasperJasper, you are with me until we complete this new project."

"What new project?" JasperJasper asked, confusion so evident on his pretty face. The guy had on his signature skinny jeans and suspenders, but he'd upped the ante today with a red flannel bow tie. It was hard to look away for a number of reasons, the main one being it looked ridiculous. Which probably meant it looked awesome by hipster standards.

"Meg Rogers has hired the company to plan an exclusive event in under seven weeks."

"Who is Meg Rogers?" he asked, looking around as though he couldn't be the only person to not know the name.

"The mayor's wife," Rachel supplied.

"Portland's mayor?" Jasper asked, shock in his voice. "Portland has a mayor?"

"Are you for real?" Alison questioned, only half serious.

"Portland is huge. It seems too big for the term mayor. Mayor is so small town. Shouldn't we have, like, a governor or something?"

"Ah, Jasper." Rachel sighed. "You're pretty."

"*Anyway*, she's secured the Crystal Ballroom, but we're in it for everything else, and it must be stellar, ladies and gentleman. We're talking black-tie fundraiser."

"Who are we raising funds for?" Rachel inquired.

"The Angel House."

"Great cause."

"Yeah, which is one more reason we have to hit it out of the park."

"How about a premium silent auction?" Jasper asked. "High-quality stuff. No vouchers for oil changes. Expensive shit."

"I like it," I said, urging him on.

"We could ask the Heathman to donate a weekend package, and maybe Dosha Salon and Spa could donate a beauty package."

"Jasper, work that angle. Think expensive and exclusive. We want donations that will bring a high dollar bid. Rachel, I need you on catering. We must think outside the box on this one. Until I get to the venue, I don't know if it will house a sit-down dinner, so we have to play it fast and loose for now. We want classic but trendy, all right? Nothing crazy like sushi, but we need gluten-free-friendly options, but it can't taste like it's gluten free, okay?"

"On it," both Jasper and Rachel responded simultaneously.

"All right, let's get to work." As soon as I'd said the words, the two of them stood and walked back to their desks in the main room, but Alison stayed behind. When we were alone, she spoke.

"How in the world did this happen?"

"You mean why is the boss giving me, arguably, the biggest account we've seen all year?"

"Yeah, that."

"Her son is my boyfriend," I said and couldn't help the grimace that crossed my face.

"Don't look so excited by that notion," Alison said with a laugh.

"No, it's not Camden—he's great. I feel icky about how I got this account. I don't feel like I earned it. It was only handed to me because of who I'm dating."

Alison shrugged. "Listen, everyone uses connections at some point in their career. There's nothing wrong with how you got the account, you just have to make sure you do a great job and earn it."

"Okay," I said, letting out a breath, trying to force self-confidence. "I can do this."

"You can totally do this. Plus, if you kill it you'll be Rose's favorite new toy."

"As weird and gross as that sounds, I really want it."

We both laughed and Alison stood and opened the door to my office. "Let me know if you need anything. You're going to do great."

"Thanks."

She gave me a friendly smile and left, shutting the door behind her.

As soon as I was alone, my head plopped down on my desk. Luckily I had one of those padded wrist-resters for my keyboard, so my forehead had a soft landing spot. I took a few moments to softly thump my forehead on it a few times. Then I took a deep breath, breathed it out, and then sat up with determination.

"You can do this," I said to myself with conviction. "You're a badass party planner and Meg Rogers is going to weep when she sees what you deliver. Weep!" I said, pumping my fist in the air.

With renewed and only partly genuine confidence, I picked up the phone and got to work.

It was hours past lunchtime before I came up for air. The only reason I stopped at all was because my stomach was growling loudly and interfering with phone calls. When I stepped out into the main office, I saw the workstations had thinned out and only a few people remained. Usually in the afternoon people in event planning had meetings to see venues or meet with clients. It wasn't unusual to have an empty office in the afternoon, especially not on a Monday, but I smiled when I saw Jasper and Rachel still at their desks, asses to chairs, working hard.

"Hey guys," I said as I came up behind them. "What have we come up with?"

"I've reached out to quite a few vendors about donations and I'm still waiting to hear back from most of them, but Dosha is a go, as is the Heathman. It's funny how you mention the mayor's name and people give you stuff." Jasper laughed as he said the words.

"I think it helps that it's the end of the year. Companies are looking for tax write-offs," I added with a laugh.

"I've got a few catering options, nothing solid though. I'm still looking for the perfect blend of cool versus elegance." Rachel didn't even look at me while she spoke, her eyes were glued to her computer.

"I've got a viewing of the Crystal Ballroom today at four. Mrs. Rogers will meet us there at four thirty to discuss options. We don't have to have all the answers today, but I want to have something to work off, something to show her, something tangible she can take home, even if it's just an idea. We need something she can chew on."

"We're on it," Rachel said brightly, still not looking at me, which I weirdly kind of appreciated. The more she stared at her computer, the more work she was getting done.

"I'll probably take off from the ballroom for the night, so let's meet there at 3:45, okay?"

"Sounds good," Jasper said, a smile on his face.

"I'm gonna go grab something to eat. You guys need anything?"

"Get out of here, Riley. We've got it," Rachel practically yelled.

"Okay, okay."

I grabbed my coat and purse from my office, making sure my phone was in it, and then headed out. It felt good to walk after being in my office all day long. I took the stairs down and made a left out of the building, heading toward the food trucks a few blocks down. The craving for a hot dog had never been stronger.

I paid for my hot dog and a hot chocolate and found a bench. I took a bite, painfully aware of how awkward it is to eat a hot dog in public but not caring, and then let my shoulders sag a little, finding a rare moment in my day to relax. After a few minutes of quiet people watching, I dug my phone from my purse. I had a couple missed texts and read the one from Camden first.

Who can I talk to about getting a repeat performance of this morning again tomorrow?

A smile took over my face as I sipped my hot chocolate. I loved how playful he always was and enjoyed that he brought out a feistiness in me I hadn't ever experienced with anyone else.

I guess that depends on whoever you have in your bed tomorrow morning.

My smile grew as I waited for his reply. I wasn't expecting a quick response, but the butterflies in my stomach took flight when I saw the little moving dots nonetheless.

What makes you think it won't be you?

What makes you think it will?

I added a winky face after the last text just to show him I was being playful.

I think the way you came around my cock might be incentive enough.

They were only words on a screen, but I still felt a little quiver down below. A park bench downtown wasn't an opportune place to get aroused. Before I could respond another text came through.

Coupled with the way you came on my face, surely, will get you back in my bed.

Oh, lord. He was obviously an exceptional sexter. If he didn't stop there'd be a pile-up at my intersection, and

I'd definitely get some sort of ticket for indecent exposure. So I did the first thing that came to mind. I sent him a selfie of me taking a big bite of my hot dog.

That is both horrifying and sexy at the same time. But more horrifying. Are you just now eating lunch?

Yeah, busy day.

Can I see you later?

My wiener biting didn't turn you off of me forever?

It'll take more than a few bites to make me go away. I can take you out to a late dinner. Or hang out. Your place or mine. I'd just really like to see you.

Aw, the guy had it as bad for me as I did him. That was comforting, and completely unusual. I wore a big smile as I texted him back.

Do you like pizza?

Do you like hot dogs?

And he was funny too. Damn it, he was going to steal my heart.

Bring a pizza to my apartment at eight tonight. I'll try to be wearing clothes when you arrive, but I can't guarantee anything.

That's the sexiest thing anyone's ever said to me. Just one question.

Yeah?

I quite nearly forgot to breathe waiting for his response.

What kind of pizza do you like?

I was giggling all the way back to my office. And blushing too.

Chapter Eleven

Riley

The Crystal Ballroom was on the west side of town and not in an optimal location. There wasn't much parking and it was on a busy intersection. But, all that taken into account, I could see the appeal of holding an event there.

It was classic Portland.

What I'd learned from the raven-haired woman named Taryn giving me a tour, was that the room right below the ballroom was also available for events. The Crystal Ballroom was used mainly for concerts, so it felt a little strange to be planning a gala for the space, but Taryn assured me they could make anything work and that we weren't the first people trying to put a square peg in a round hole.

Rachel and Jasper followed us, taking notes so I didn't have to, and whispering between themselves. When a man stepped into the large ballroom and called Taryn's name, she excused herself and left to see what he needed.

"So, what are you guys thinking?" Jasper and Rachel gave each other side-eyes, obviously communicating silently. "I did not get in on the telepathy, so please, use your words, kiddos."

"Well, I didn't want to say anything, because it's kind of a long shot, but...." Jasper looked too scared to finish his sentence and if he could bite any more of his fingernail off he would have.

"What?" I cried. "Tell me before I die of anticipation."

"Jasper thinks he might, and emphasis on the *might* part, be able to get Indigo Ale."

The ballroom was silent as I stared at him, mouth agape.

"Jasper, now is not the time to play with my emotions." My words would have been steel had they been any harder. "Tell me what you mean by this."

"Well," he said meekly, starting to waver. "I've worked with their publicist on a few things before, and they've been back in town from a world tour for a few weeks now. A year or so ago I helped their publicist with an event and she said she owed me, so I called her. She said a fundraiser for the Angel House was something right up their alley, and that she'd reach out to them."

"Are you serious right now?" I asked, stepping close to him. His eyes went wide. My blood pressure was about to skyrocket.

Indigo Ale was a Portland institution. A glittering diamond in the history of a pretty dull city. World-renowned musicians who were pretty fucking cool too. They were classy and fun and fucking *perfect* for this event. They were also completely out of our price range and grasp. There was no situation in my daily life where I ever thought I'd be able to reach out to anyone involved with Indigo Ale and ask for a favor.

"Listen," I whispered harshly to Jasper. "We don't speak a word of this to Meg. We don't mention Indigo Ale unless it's in the bag, got it?" My finger was in his face and I had to pull myself together. I stepped backward and took in a few breaths. "I'm not cut out for this," I said, dragging the air into my lungs.

"Riley." Meg's soft and happy voice filled the empty ballroom and I spun to face her, a smile automatically crossing my face.

"Meg," I said as I walked toward her. "It's good to see you again. Thank you for coming to meet us on such short notice."

"Of course," she said before giving me a polite hug. "I was so grateful you could fit me into your schedule."

"Let me introduce you to my team. Meg, this is Jasper and Rachel. I have full confidence in them and we're excited to make this a successful event."

Meg reached her hand out to both of them, giving them the same warm smile she'd bestowed upon me. "It's so nice to meet you. The next time we all have to get together we should do it at my house. I make an award-winning sangria."

"There's nothing about that I want to say no to," Rachel said with a laugh.

"I love sangria," Jasper added.

"We're very excited to work on this event, Mrs. Rogers," Rachel said, a genuine smile.

"Please, call me Meg."

"Thanks, Meg."

"We've been working all day on preliminary ideas and I think we've got a good starting point."

"That's great. Now that we're here, do you think this venue will work?"

"That depends wholly on what exactly you want. There's a stage, so if you want musical entertainment, this will work."

"I want some sort of music. I'd like there to be dancing. I want people to eat, drink, and be merry. But I also want more than the typical dinner party and dancing."

"How would you feel about a silent auction? We already have a few high-end vendors willing to donate goods and services to the cause."

Meg's eyes lit up and her smile went positively solar.

"What about a bachelor auction?"

My head tilted at her words, not sure I'd heard her correctly.

"A... bachelor auction? Like, people bidding on men? For a date?" The idea seemed a little off-base, seeing as we were trying to raise money to support survivors of domestic abuse. I tried not to sound like it was a bad idea, but it was a bad idea.

"Well, I like the idea of a silent auction, but it's not exciting enough. I want it to be fun and lively. I want people to talk about the event afterward, to remember it, so that perhaps they'll want to come to another. Word spreads, and if I throw another boring gala, soon it'll just be me sitting at a table by myself."

"I hear you completely. You want something different, but still appropriate and refined."

"Yes! That's exactly what I want. What can we do?"

"Excuse me, Meg?" Jasper spoke up from behind us. "What if, instead of auctioning off, uh, men, we auction off experiences *with* men."

My eyes practically fell out of their sockets and Rachel started choking on air. "Jasper," I exclaimed, "we're not selling sex!"

"No! Oh, God, no! That's not what I meant. I'm sorry! Jeez...." He slapped his hand over his eyes. "I swear, that's not what I meant. I meant that we could reach out to some people who could offer unique experiences and see if they could donate their time and access. Like, maybe we could get someone to donate a private dinner for two on the sternwheeler with the captain. Or a box seat at a Renegades game with the owner. Stuff like that."

"Jasper, that sounds fantastic! Do you really think you could get people to donate those kinds of things?"

He shrugged. "I can try."

I was a little peeved he brought this up in front of Meg because if it didn't work out, I'd have to disappoint her, but I did like the way her face lit up with the idea. And it was a good idea, just hard to put together. Would we be able to find enough high-profile people who were willing to donate to make it worthwhile?

"We could do the big auction in this room and have the silent auction for the smaller items in the ballroom downstairs with cocktails and hors d'oeuvres. We can have a dinner upstairs and then clear the tables for dancing and bidding." Rachel's eyes were alight with inspiration.

"Perfect, we can move people downstairs while the tables are being cleared," I said, thinking out loud. "Maybe instead of hors d'oeuvres we can do dessert."

"If there's room downstairs during the dessert hour I could put together some information about the families that the Angel House has helped and display it, give people something to look at, a little incentive to spend their money." Meg looked thoroughly excited by her idea.

"That's actually brilliant. Nothing opens wallets like tugging on heartstrings."

Right as I said the words, Taryn returned.

"Sorry about that, administrative details," she said, waving away the interruption.

"No problem. Meg Rogers, this is Taryn. She's the coordinator here at the Crystal Ballroom."

"Nice to meet you," Meg said, sticking out her hand.

"Likewise. Are there any questions I can answer?"

"If we wanted to do a formal, sit-down dinner in this ballroom, how many people would that seat?"

"We seat six hundred in this ballroom."

"Oh, Riley," Rachel said from behind me. "I just received a text from the owner of Unico downtown and she says she can get you an eight-course tasting on Friday night if you'd consider her restaurant for the event catering."

"Unico? I've never heard of them," Meg said.

"It's a newer restaurant, but it's getting great reviews. It's pretty exclusive though. I heard the reservations are out two months and even then it's dicey. But they're rumored to have the best Italian fusion cuisine ever. It'd be great for the event."

I looked at Meg with raised eyebrows. "Are you free on Friday night? We could go check it out, see if it's what you're looking for."

"Me?" she asked surprised. "I'm sure anything you pick would be fine, Riley. Why don't you take Camden?"

"You don't want to go to the tasting?" Surely she'd want to be involved in picking the food for the event.

She shrugged with a smile. "I think you're more qualified to pick the right kind of cuisine. Obviously you wouldn't make a poor decision, and I love Italian food, so I'd really be no help. You should take Camden." Her smile was so genuine and eyes so caring, it was hard to argue with her. So I didn't.

"I guess tell the owner I will be there with a plus one to audition her restaurant."

When I entered my apartment that evening, the walk to my bedroom seemed like miles, so I slumped back and let myself rest against the door. My feet hurt, my head ached, and my eyes were tired. It had been a stressful day, but a productive one too. We'd accomplished a lot, but I almost dreaded all the work that was to come in the next six weeks. We usually had six months to plan similar events.

I had practically fallen asleep against the door when I heard the soft knocking coming from the other side. I managed to pull myself upright and open the door to see Camden's handsome face smiling at me. The smile dimmed though, as he stepped into my apartment and got a good look at me.

"You look exhausted," he said, concern in his voice.

"Thanks," I said, a tiny bit of sarcasm finding its way into my voice, but mainly I just sounded lethargic. He walked to my dining table and set a pizza box down and then came back to me, wrapping me up in his arms.

"Everything all right?"

I sighed and snuggled closer in to him, taking the strength he was offering and giving him my weight.

"Did you talk to your mom today?" I asked, my words garbled against his chest.

"Um, no." He chuckled. "Why?"

I pulled back far enough to look up at him.

"She called my boss this morning and hired Rose City Event Planners to coordinate her event next month."

"That's good, right?" he said, running his hands along my back. I wished there weren't a few layers of clothes between his hands and my skin, because I really needed a massage.

"It is good. She also insisted I be the lead on the project."

He raised his eyebrows and pursed his lips. "That's good too, right?"

I lifted one shoulder in a shrug. "It's not bad, it's just a big job. There's no way I would have gotten an account that big at this stage in my career on my own. So, my boss gave in and let me have it, but if I screw it up, it could be bad. Not only professionally, but, I mean, I don't want your mom to hate me. We've only just started dating, but I kind of like you and I'd hate for your mom to dislike me."

Camden's eyebrows drew together and I could see him thinking in the way his eyes darted around the room but never landed on anything specific. After a few moments, he suggested, "Why don't I call my mom and ask her to back off a little?"

I shook my head. "I don't want that. I want to do a good job. I'm just afraid it's too much too soon. Plus, I don't want my boss to think I'm afraid of hard work—I'm not. It's a lot of pressure. And I don't want to disappoint you either."

"You want to know what's disappointing?" he asked, his tone deadly serious and eyes trained on mine.

"What?" I asked, afraid to hear the answer.

"Your preference in pizza toppings." He held the stern look for a moment, but then the corner of his mouth tugged up into a grin and I couldn't help but laugh a little, resting my forehead against his chest. "Seriously, Riley. Chicken, pineapple, tomatoes, and green peppers? That's the oddest topping combination I've ever heard of."

"I'm nothing if not original," I mumbled, smiling still as I felt his lips against the top of my head, kissing me gently.

"Which would you prefer first? Food or bed? Pizza tastes just as good, if not better, the morning after." His arms were still around me, holding me to him, prepared to take me wherever I wanted, waiting for my command.

"I think I'd like food, then shower, then bed, if that sequence of events is all right with you."

"I'm nothing if not agreeable."

He took me to the table and made sure I had everything I needed before he sat down to eat. My eyes roamed over him, appreciating the way he looked in a suit. Camden in a suit was like my kryptonite. His tie was pulled loose and the top button of his shirt undone, and my eyes were absolutely drawn to the scruff on his neck over his Adam's apple. He swallowed and I practically let out a moan. I needed to distract myself before I jumped him.

"You made a point to mock my topping choices, but I notice yours are boring and predictable."

"You think pepperoni is boring and predictable?"

"Isn't it?" I replied before taking another bite of my delicious pizza.

"Pepperoni pizza is a staple in American cuisine. It's steady and reliable."

"Oh, my gosh," I laughed, mouth still impolitely full. "You're such a lawyer."

"I've said it before and I'll say it again—I can argue anything for any reason."

"I'd have to be crazy to start a relationship with someone I'll never win an argument against."

"Firstly, it's too late, you already have. And secondly, if I really care about someone I'll let them win sometimes." He winked at me and I had to hold myself back from throwing my pizza at him. I didn't want to ruin his suit.

"You can't *always* win, it's statistically impossible."

"I might not always win, but I always get my point across."

"I'm too tired to be infuriated, but trust me, this would normally infuriate me."

"I like it when you're all feisty."

I narrowed my eyes at him. "How can this be attractive? I don't want it to be, yet, I can't help it. Your arrogance is alluring. Stop it."

"Sure thing, baby." Another wink.

Damn him.

I took another bite and shook my head, trying to seem more irritated than I actually was. Camden's brain and the way it seemed to circle me was extremely attractive. And just as he seemed to like it when I was feisty, I liked it when he was argumentative. On any other man it would have been a repulsive trait. In fact, I'd not gone on second dates with many men who seemed to always want to correct me or tout their opinions. But Camden was different. His arguing was almost like foreplay and I knew it made him hot when I argued back.

It suddenly occurred to me he hadn't brought in an overnight bag and the thought of him not staying over upset me.

"Are you going back to your place tonight?"

"Hadn't planned on it," he replied, focused on his pizza and how much of one piece he could cram in at one time. Camden might have been a fancy lawyer, but he was still just a dude.

"Oh, I didn't see you bring in a bag."

He swallowed and then replied. "I didn't bring one. I don't plan on wearing any clothes to bed, and I don't have any meetings until nine tomorrow, so I was going to go home when you left for work."

"Oh," I repeated, feeling the relief wash over me that he would be staying.

"Don't want to spend a night away from me, do you?" His smile was so big and obnoxious, but it was impossible not to smile back. I decided not to dignify his question with a response, so I continued eating.

For the rest of the meal the electricity between us crackled. The seconds sizzled. Every time my eyes wandered his way he was looking at me, lust darkening his eyes and turning up the corner of his mouth into a sexy grin. He knew he'd gotten to me, that I was practically trembling in anticipation.

When we'd both finished our meals, he wiped his mouth with a napkin and then said in a very lawyerly tone, "I'd like to propose an adjustment to the agenda."

Fuck me. Lawyer talk.

"What is your proposition, counsel?"

"I'd like to strike shower from the schedule and move directly to the bed."

"Motion granted," I said on a breath. It was only a second before he pounced on me.

Chapter Twelve

Camden

Riley's alarm went off way too early the next morning. I felt her move to silence it, but when she tried to roll out of bed, I reached out and brought her back against me with an arm wrapped around her waist.

"Cam," she said with a laugh, her voice gravelly from sleep. "I have to go to work."

"Five minutes," I mumbled, my face buried in her hair. Two words were all I could muster. She made a noise like she was going to argue, but then I felt her relax against me and snuggle back.

Good girl.

I would have loved to drift away to sleep again, but Riley in my arms was distracting.

I'd been with my fair share of women before, some serious and some not, but never had I experienced the type of connection I shared with Riley. Yeah, the sex was amazing, but it was a whole different kind of sex. Normally when I was with someone, I found them attractive and that was arousing. With Riley, it wasn't only her body that turned me on, it was the way I felt privileged to even touch her, the way her body felt precious to me. Being with her was a gift.

As corny and ridiculous as it sounded, being inside of her felt like coming home. And it wasn't just any home, it was the one place in the world you felt safe and comforted, the best place in the whole fucking world. Every time I slid into her it was as though she'd been waiting for me to come back, like her body had missed mine and my body was grateful to have her back.

In fact, I'd been home twice last night. And if she didn't have to leave for work soon, I'd go home again.

When she slid out of my grasp again a few minutes later, I let her go. I watched as she stood from the bed, naked and gorgeous, and walked into the hallway. Her hair was messy and falling down her back, her perfect ass moving in a sexy rhythm with her steps. She disappeared from sight and I heard the water turn on, making a rushing sound, but over it I heard her humming. I smiled, letting my head fall back to the pillow, loving that she felt comfortable enough around me to walk around naked and hum to herself. Perhaps I'd get a full karaoke show when she showered.

The thought of Riley in the shower was enough to make me hard, so I decided to focus on something else.

I threw the blanket off and swung my legs over the bed. My boxer briefs were on the floor next to my suit pants, but I wasn't ready for full pants yet, so I pulled on the briefs and made my way to the kitchen. I found her coffee and started a pot, then looked in her fridge, trying to scrounge something up for breakfast. If she was anything like me in the mornings, she probably got something at a Starbucks on the way in, but I had a few minutes to spare. She had a full carton of eggs and half a loaf of bread, so breakfast was decided.

Fifteen minutes later when Riley came into the kitchen, using a towel to dry her hair, she wore a big smile.

"Did you make breakfast?"

"Yeah, but just for me. Get your own."

She dropped her towel on a chair by the table, but I kept my eyes on the eggs. The heat of her body warmed my back as she pressed against me, her hands sliding around my waist and meeting right over my naval.

"If you make me come at night and then cook me breakfast in the morning, I might keep you around forever."

I tried to keep my heart from racing at the mention of forever, but it was useless. Could two people fall in love—a real kind of soul mate love—in less than two weeks? I didn't know, but I was sure I felt things for Riley no woman had ever come close to eliciting from me.

"I made toast too," I mentioned, my voice flat, the complete opposite of the way I was feeling.

"Mmm. You're saying all the right things, Camden."

I couldn't help the smile spreading across my face. The eggs were done so I moved the pan off the burner, turned off the stove, and scooped them onto two plates already loaded with toast. I turned slowly, loving the way she kept her arms around me, and when we were chest to chest I took her face in my hands. I brought my lips to hers, but before they touched, I whispered, "There's hot coffee in the pot." Our lips were so close, they feathered against each other with each word.

Instantly, she closed the minuscule gap between us, pressing her lips against mine. She opened immediately, her tongue slipping into my mouth on a moan, her arms wrapping tighter around me. I walked her backward until she was pressed against the counter and then lifted her ass and sat her on top of it. Her legs wrapped around my waist, pulling me closer, my erection pressing right into her core. I pressed into her, making sure the ridge of my cock moved slowly over her, and I practically beat on my chest when her mouth fell away from mine on a moan and her whole body shivered.

I wasn't prepared for it when she reached between us and slid her hand between my skin and the waistband of my briefs. I gasped against her when her delicate hand wrapped around me.

"Fuck, Riley," I swore. Something about the picture we made turned me on. Her, sitting on the counter in her black trousers and purple satiny blouse, sophisticated and polished, with her hand moving up and down my shaft. Me, wearing only my underwear, thrusting into her grasp.

"We don't have time to fuck, but I'll gladly get you off." Her words only made me harder. When she'd come into the kitchen, I thought I had control over the situation, but it was clear to me that she was in charge. Her hand twisted at the head of my cock, rotating and making me gasp. I wasn't going to last long. Her thumb pressed right into the sensitive spot right below the crown of my cock and I saw stars. I moved my hand up her stomach, palming her breast, the silk of her shirt cool against my hand. I could feel the tight bud of her nipple through the soft material. I pinched it as I moved my mouth to her neck, nipping her there, making her gasp. Her breathy sounds made my balls tighten and I knew I was close.

"Faster," I managed, the words whispered against the damp skin of her neck where she smelled like soap and flowers. She complied, moving her hand up and down my shaft even faster, squeezing me even tighter. It took only a few more thrusts until I fell over the edge, warm semen coating her hand and my cock, making me groan loud enough I was sure her neighbors could hear.

My breath was panting out, but when it slowed, I moved my mouth back to hers and kissed her softly, trying to ground us, bring us back to reality.

"Scooch," she finally said, giving me a gentle push backward. I took a step back and she hopped off the counter, going to the sink to wash her hands. She came back with a warm paper towel and cleaned the mess off my dick and stomach, then gently tucked me back into my briefs. "Look," she said, new excitement in her voice. "You didn't even get any on me!" She gave me a brilliant smile and then took a step back. Sure enough, she was cum-free. "That's talent," she said with a laugh, throwing the paper towel in the trash. She opened a drawer and got out two forks, then placed one on each of the plates I'd prepared, then brought them both to the table. "Come on, let's eat."

I laughed a little, still trying to catch up after my monster orgasm, but moved to pour us each a cup of coffee. "Cream, no sugar, right?" I asked over my shoulder.

"Yeah, listen," she said before swallowing a bite of her eggs. "You've got to tone down this perfect boyfriend thing you've got going on." She said the words as she waved her fork in the air, motioning toward me. "There's only so many tricks I can pull out of my girlfriend hat to pay you back."

"You mean like jacking me off in the kitchen?" I said, sitting down next to her and placing her coffee in front of her.

"Exactly."

"If it makes you feel any better, repeat performances of girlfriend tricks are always welcome. You don't always have to come up with something new and original. If it wasn't made clear by boyfriends before me, let me reassure you—anytime a woman takes our dick in her hand and makes us come is a good time."

"Noted. Also, please be advised that morning-after breakfasts and coffee might bring forth those desired actions."

"Ms. Smith, I think we've found the secret recipe to the perfect relationship."

"Food, coffee, and orgasms. Sounds like a winning combination if you ask me."

She winked at me and I almost dragged her back to the bedroom.

"Hey, man," Justin said, walking into my office later that day. "That meeting this morning was brutal." He collapsed onto the couch in the corner of my office.

"Yes. Yes, it was," I agreed. But, to be fair, meetings in law offices were rarely anything except boring. A career in entertainment law wasn't as exciting as some might think. It was glorified contracts law.

"You going to the game on Friday?"

"I'm glad you asked." I pushed away from my desk and walked over to my door, closing it, then taking a seat beside Justin. I didn't want some of the senior members of the firm to walk by and catch us being unproductive. "Riley asked me to some fancy restaurant, something to do with picking the food for my mom's fundraiser, so we can't go. I was going to offer you both tickets."

"Both tickets? That's awesome, Cam. Thanks."

"No problem, I'll bring them to work tomorrow. Who do you think you'll take? Should be a good game."

"I don't know. I'll have to think about it. What do I owe you for them?"

"Nothin', man. But," I paused, trying to find a smooth way to transition, but gave up when I couldn't. Sometimes it was better to just be up-front. "Why don't you take Hadley?"

"Riley's friend, Hadley?"

"Yeah."

"She was hot."

I nodded, unwilling to offer my opinion on the matter. "I know she's single." I waited a beat before my next question. "Want me to ask Riley for her number?" Before he could answer, I reached into my pocket and dug out my phone. A smile spread across my face when I saw I had a text message from Riley. I opened it and immediately began laughing.

"What's so funny?" Justin asked. I turned my phone so he could see the photo Riley sent, still laughing. "Why is your girl sending you a picture of her sucking on a straw?"

"She has a thing for sending me photos of her with phallic-shaped things in her mouth."

"Marry her," he said immediately, with no humor in his voice.

"Trust me, the thought has crossed my mind."

"Are you serious?"

I shrugged. "I don't know, man. It's different with her. I've never felt this way about anyone."

"You've known her for, like, a week."

"I can't explain it. She feels like she's already mine. And vice versa. The idea of being with anyone else after her is depressing. It's never been this good and I'm afraid it will never be this good with anyone else."

"The sex?"

"The everything. The sex is, well, it's off the charts hot, but it's more than that. She's fun to be around, smart as hell, independent, likes basketball, drinks beer, and she's just *good*. I don't think I've ever met someone as decent as she is."

"But it's mainly the sex, right?" He kept a straight face for a moment, but then cracked a smile. Right as I moved to punch his arm, my desk phone buzzed.

I stood and walked over, hitting the button that would allow me to speak to the receptionist for the entire floor.

"Yes, Angela?"

"Mr. Rogers, there is a Sophia Greenway here to see you. She doesn't have an appointment but was pretty insistent I call you."

I took my finger off the call button so only Justin could hear me.

"Shit, it's Sophia."

"I thought you broke up with her."

"Technically, she broke up with me."

"Why do you think she's here?"

172

"To be difficult?"

"Well, I'll get out of your hair." He stood and walked to the door. Before he left he gave me a sympathetic smile and said, "Good luck."

"Send her back, Angela," I said through the phone. A few moments later I heard the telltale sound of heels clacking on the tile floors of the hallway and I knew it was the ridiculously high heels Sophia wore. She entered the doorway, smiling from ear to ear.

"Hello, Camden. It's so good to see you." She walked toward my desk, but I made no move toward her.

"Sophia, I'm surprised to see you here." She didn't stop at my desk like I hoped, but came right to me, leaning in and pressing a kiss against my cheek. I pulled away, clearing my throat and adjusting my tie. I circled my desk until it was between us. "What can I do for you?"

"I wanted to stop by and speak with you." She took slow and deliberate steps toward me, her finger tracing along the top of my desk. "The way we left things before was brutal, and I know we make a good couple. I think we can make each other happy if you'd give me another chance."

Her eyes locked on mine and she batted her thick eyelashes at me, trying to appear coy.

"You think we can make each other happy?" I asked, the shock evident in my voice. "Sophia, we want completely different things out of a relationship."

She shrugged. "I'm willing to make some concessions."

"I'm not," I stated flatly. "And I'm not interested in someone who feels they'll be settling for me, either. I'm not sure what you're after, but I don't think it's me."

"What's that supposed to mean?" She had the audacity to look surprised by my observation.

"It means I think you're only interested in me for my name, or the money you think I have—or will have. We were not a good match and you broke it off with me because I wasn't giving you the kind of attention you need or want."

She pasted another smile on her face and advanced toward me again. "I broke up with you because I was having a bad day and let myself get too emotional. I'm sorry for that, it was a mistake, but I don't think it's worth throwing away everything we had together."

"Everything we had? We'd been on three dates, Sophia. We were hardly even dating." I took a few steps back from her, trying not to seem like I was running from her, but not giving her the opportunity to get her hands on me either.

"Well, I think we should give it another shot."

"I'm with someone else now. Sorry." *Not sorry.*

Her face pulled back and lip curled. "With someone else? It's been a few days."

"It's been two and a half weeks and yes, I'm with someone else."

"Surely you can't be serious." She said the words as if it were preposterous. "Camden, come on. You can't be exclusive with someone you met two weeks ago. Just have dinner with me. One night. I'll make it worth your while." She sang the last part of her proposition, and I had to stop my eyes from rolling back in my head. I could think of absolutely nothing that would make spending an evening with Sophia worth it.

"We are exclusive and even at two weeks, I can tell I don't want to fuck things up with her, so dinner with you is out of the question. In fact, I think it would be a good idea for you to leave now."

Sophia stared at me for what seemed like a full minute, her eyes locked on mine, daring me to look away first, to give her a reason to think I wasn't serious. To give her any excuse to pursue her mission further. When I didn't look away, she finally relented.

"You're making a big mistake," she said as she walked toward the door. "The two of us together could make a real name for ourselves here. With both our fathers' political positions, your status and career, coupled with my beauty and sophistication, we could take this town by storm."

"Honestly, Sophia, that doesn't sound appealing to me at all. You're going to have to find someone else to fulfill that crazy and depressing fantasy with. I'm not interested."

She looked at me for one moment longer, then swiftly left, slamming the door behind her. I stood still, listening to her heels echo down the hall again until the sound drifted away. When I was sure she was gone, I let out a large breath and collapsed onto the couch again, this time letting my elbows rest on my knees and my hands cradle my head.

Never would I have imagined that Sophia would come to me and practically beg me to be with her, not after the way our relationship ended. It felt odd to even call it a relationship. When I'd agreed to call her and ask her out, it was only to get Andrew off my back about it. He'd been talking her up for six months and I was sick of hearing it. So I took her out. And then I took her out again because, honestly, I didn't have anything better to do. And I wouldn't lie about it, Sophia was beautiful. But everything about her I tolerated before, only seemed to grate on me. The way she was obviously fake, putting on a show for everyone around her, for the sake of her image, was unattractive to say the least. I shook my head at myself and couldn't believe I'd ever entertained the idea of dating her.

She was the antithesis of Riley.

Where Sophia was fake, Riley was unapologetically real and brave.

Where Sophia was manipulative and calculating, Riley was hardworking and honest.

And where Sophia was beautiful by society's standards, Riley had a beauty within her that couldn't be matched or contained. She radiated beauty.

And she was fucking hot, too.

Suddenly I wanted nothing more than to hear her voice. I pulled out my phone and listened to it ring, hoping she was still on her lunch break.

"Hello, stranger. I was wondering how long it would take you to respond to the lewd photo I sent you."

"Hey," I said with a small laugh. "I wanted to call and tell you that even though we've only known each other for a little while, I'd choose you over anyone." The words came out on a breath and I wasn't even entirely sure I'd spoken them aloud because she was silent on the other end. I waited, hoping she'd respond, but all I could hear were the breaths she was taking. "You there, Riley?"

After another silent moment, she finally responded. "Um, yeah, I'm just not sure how to respond." She paused for a beat, then asked, "Is this because I keep sending you pictures of me with things in my mouth?"

"Yeah," I laughed. "That, and because you're smart and funny. And I like the way I feel when I'm with you. I think that's the biggest and best part. You make me feel happy. I guess I didn't realize no one else had ever done that for me until you showed me what it felt like." I took in a deep breath and let it out again, hoping I wasn't making a complete fool of myself. "It's not a big deal, I just needed to tell you." Suddenly I felt embarrassed for calling her and laying it all out there, but there wasn't anything I could do about it now.

"Well, thank you. I don't think anyone's ever said such nice words to me before." I inwardly groaned, afraid she was giving me the brush-off. "Is it all right if I come over tonight and show you how much I like those words?" Her voice was soft and seductive, and I liked that much better than the shy and apprehensive voice she'd used only moments before.

"Are you going to bring the same mouth featured in all those photos you send me?"

"One and the same."

"I'll be waiting."

Chapter Thirteen

Riley

The week had been absolutely crazy. Each day was a roller coaster. At work I was stressed but productive, stretched thin but still managing to check off all my to-do boxes. After work I was transported to a daydream. Camden was more than I'd ever hoped to find in a partner. In fact, I'd never even dreamed of someone like him because I had no idea a guy like him existed. He was kind, compassionate, sexy as fuck, and went out of his way to make sure I was happy and taken care of. We'd spent every night together and when I started to worry we were spending too much time together too quickly, he put my mind at ease with orgasms. Plenty of them.

I was already running late to dinner, but I gave myself a mental pat on the back for bringing my dress with me to work so I didn't have to go all the way home to change. I was only five minutes late, but I hated to keep Camden waiting. I was technically working, and I didn't want to look bad in front of the owner of the restaurant who'd extended such a generous offer.

I found the restaurant and told the hostess who I was and was immediately escorted to the back where there was a secret room. I had to tamp down a gawk when I saw the entry to this secret room was a hidden door disguised as a bookcase.

The room was big enough to seat thirty people, but Camden was the only one inside. He stood when he saw me and my eyes ran up and down his body, loving the suit he wore. I also loved that I could picture, with extreme detail, what his body looked like under the suit. I could picture his large frame, lean and defined muscle, and that stupidly sexy and delicious V that cut across his abdomen and pointed to his most beautiful piece of equipment.

Camden stepped in front of the hostess to pull out my chair for me, kissing my cheek after he'd pushed my chair in. The thrill of his lips against my cheek was almost embarrassing. I asked the waitress for water and we were left alone.

"Did you see the cool door?" I asked as I unrolled my linen napkin and spread it across my lap.

"I did. This is some secret spy stuff right here," he said with a smile. "What kind of people use this room?"

I looked around. "I don't know. Probably people like your stepfather. That's probably why we're in here. They thought your mom was coming."

"I love my mother, but I'm really glad she's not here." He took my hand in his as he said the words, bringing the back of it to his mouth and pressing a kiss there. My face turned warm and I knew I was probably blushing. "You look beautiful," he said, his mouth still against my hand. When he finally pulled my hand from his lips, it took me a moment to respond.

"Thank you. I wasn't sure how fancy to go, but I'm glad I leaned toward the dressier side." He didn't say anything in response, but kept his gaze on me, eyes dark and unyielding. Suddenly I was unable to sit still; something inside me was restless.

The bookcase door opened and someone new came into the room wearing all white with a friendly smile.

"Good evening. My name is Antonia Rossi, the chef here. Thank you for giving me this opportunity."

"Hello, Ms. Rossi. My name is Riley Smith, we spoke on the phone a few days ago. This is Camden Rogers, Meg Rogers's son. Mrs. Rogers was unable to be here tonight, but she is very excited for our report tomorrow."

"Nice to meet you both," she said, shaking both our hands. "I have an eight-course menu planned for you tonight that should give you a vast idea of what we can offer your fantastic event. You will get a sampling of fine hors d'oeuvres, main courses, and desserts. If you have any questions or concerns, I will be back to check in at the end of the meal. I sincerely hope you enjoy what I've put together for you tonight."

"Thank you," Camden and I both said in unison. Antonia turned around with a smile and exited out the very cool bookcase door I couldn't get over.

I turned back to him. "One day I want a bookcase door," I said with a nod, like a royal decree.

"What else do you want someday?" he asked, threading his fingers through mine. "Kids? A house? Pets? Vacations? Where's one place you'd love to go more than anywhere else?"

"That's a good question. I think if I could go anywhere in the US it would have to be Hawaii. Internationally, probably Greece."

"Have you ever been to either place?" His thumb stroked over my skin and the gentleness of its movement was almost jarring. I was captivated by the way he was barely touching me, but touching me so deeply at the same time.

"Um," I stammered. "I've never been out of the US, unless you count that one time in high school I took a school trip to Canada. And I've never been to Hawaii. My family could never afford vacations growing up."

"What about everything else? Your life, what do you see?"

I shrugged, feeling a little on the spot. "I think I see what a lot of people see. Marriage, kids, a home, maybe a minivan."

He laughed, his soft chuckle spearing me. "A minivan?"

"Settled people drive cars that can hold a lot of stuff, or people."

"You want to be settled?"

It was hard to admit out loud that I craved stability, that I yearned for that life where I knew what was waiting for me when I came home. Who was waiting for me. "I know I seem like a wild and crazy gal, but deep down I'm just like any other twentysomething girl. I want someone to love me and to love someone in return. To build something with that person that no other person on the planet can tear down or wedge their way into." I paused, a little surprised I'd said so much to him, but then the defense mechanism came out. "No pressure," I said too loudly, then laughed, also too loudly. At that point I wished I had ordered wine or a cocktail.

"You believe in soul mates?" he asked without fanfare, as if he were asking if I liked ice cream.

I swallowed, my throat suddenly dry. "I didn't used to," I said quietly before my brain could filter the words out and replace them with ones that wouldn't leave me emotionally bare to a man who held a lot of power, even if he wasn't fully aware of it.

181

And then the universe saved me in the form of a waitress and our first course. Camden smiled at me and released my hand, but his eyes remained on me.

The server set our plates down and explained the dish, and then disappeared. The first course was a gazpacho with an Italian flair. And it was delicious. I'd never had gazpacho before, and if you had told me I was going to like a cold soup, I would have laughed right off my chair. But I loved it. And I loved all the courses that followed.

Antonia Rossi knew what was up. And it was food. And cheese. So much cheese.

By the eighth course I was full, even though each course was very small. Throughout the whole experience, Camden and I kept our conversation minimal, discussing the food and whether it would work for his mother's party. We talked a little about his work, but we never veered back into the heavy conversation we'd abandoned when the food arrived. I was secretly glad we weren't in a good place to overanalyze our new and unusually serious relationship.

Ms. Rossi did come back into our secret room at the end of the meal and we told her how much we enjoyed the meal and the experience, and she thanked us for coming in.

"Please stay as long as you'd like, we kept the room free for you all night, so there is no hurry." She spoke to both of us, but then turned to me. "Please let Mrs. Rogers know I am looking forward to hearing from her."

"I will. And thank you again for all this. It was exquisite."

Antonia Rossi gave me a gracious nod of her head and then disappeared through the bookcase door.

For the first time since we'd started our meal, the room was suddenly tense. We'd stepped on some relationship land mines before dinner, and now we were left with the wreckage.

"You're awfully quiet," he said after a few moments of silence.

"Am I?" It was the only response I could come up with. What did he want from me, exactly? To say, *again*, that I was starting to fall for him? That I wanted him to be the one I knew was waiting for me at home every night? That I wanted him to be the person who gave me the stability I craved? Well, he had another think coming. I'd already put myself on the line and I wasn't eager to do it again.

The bookcase door opened again before either of us could say anything more and I couldn't have been more grateful to our faithful server, who returned with a dutiful smile.

"Can I get you anything else? More water? Coffee?"

"Actually," Camden said, his voice strong and smooth. "Can we get some champagne? Go ahead and put it on this card." He slid a card across the table to the server in a way that seemed way too smooth. The server smiled, took his card, and then left again.

"Why in the world are you ordering champagne?" The confusion in my voice was clear. And I scrunched up my eyebrows for good measure.

"We're going to celebrate." He said the words as if they were explanation enough.

"What are we celebrating?"

"We're celebrating the fact that you've broken through one of your barriers by behaving in a sexual nature in public."

Had I been drinking, I would have had a spit take.

"What in the world are you talking about?" I looked down at myself. *Yup. Still clothed.*

"I want you to stand up and go to the restroom. While you're in there, I want you to remove your panties and bring them back to me."

First, my eyes widened in surprise. Then they narrowed in understanding. Finally, my breath hitched with repressed anticipation. I leaned forward so I could whisper to him, "You want me to go in the bathroom and take off my underwear, and bring them out here to you?"

"That's what I said."

Smug, sexy bastard.

"Why?"

"Because it's dirty and illicit. Because you've never done anything like this before and I like watching you get all worked up even though you don't think you're supposed to." His expression was calm and challenging, as if he didn't think I'd do it. Or he did, and he was really getting off on the idea. "You think it's wrong, but you're excited and aroused. I know it's confusing, but it's also sexy as hell." He paused for a beat, but then continued. "So, are you going to do it?"

I held his gaze, my eyes still narrowed. "What's in it for you?"

"Babe, you're not a guy so you probably won't understand this, but walking out of a busy restaurant on a Friday night with your girl's panties in your pocket? It's the sexiest fucking thing I can think of and I'm hard already just imagining it."

"Wait, really?" I whispered, leaning closer to him, surprised by his reaction. I was definitely damp downtown, but I honestly couldn't pinpoint why.

He reached over and gently took my hand, then brought it to his crotch where there was definitely a straining erection beneath his suit pants. Then, because he's a sexy asshole, he moved my hand to his thigh—the one part of his body he knew I was stupid over—and pressed my open palm against the thick muscle there.

"I want you to go in the bathroom, take off your panties, and then we're going to leave. I'm going to take you back to my condo, eat you until you come, then I'm going to watch you ride my thigh until you come again. Then, I'm going to slide into you and fuck you until I come."

I watched his face, hard like stone, and it was only in his eyes I saw lust. The need. He said he was doing this for me, to give me an experience I'd never had, to broaden my sexual horizon—my very own, personal, sexual Mr. Miyagi—but I could tell he wanted it too. That realization brought a little confidence back to me, made me feel a little bolder.

I leaned toward him, whispering close to his ear, "Wanna know what I think, Camden? I think you're gonna do all that anyway. But I'll play your game." I stood up, letting my hand drift against his cock, and placed my napkin on the table. Then I walked out of the room, knowing his eyes were on me, zeroed in on my ass, which I happened to know looked phenomenal in the dress I'd chosen. All right, it might have been the very reason I chose it.

I left the secret room and saw our waitress coming toward me with our champagne.

"Could you point me toward the restroom?" I asked her, trying not to look like I was a sexual deviant. She pointed me down a hallway to my right, and when I made it to the bathroom, I was disappointed to see it was not a single-stall room. Luckily, though, it was empty. I took a look at myself in the mirror, noticing the blush of my cheeks. I rolled my eyes at my reflection—she was such a hussy—and walked into a stall. I carefully peeled my black lace panties down my legs, hid the evidence, and then heard the door opening. Another woman took the stall next to me and I got the overwhelming urge to flee. I flushed the toilet for the sake of appearances and washed my hands too, then scurried out of the bathroom before the other person could see me. The last thing I needed was a witness to my debauchery.

As I walked through the restaurant, I tried my hardest to not give myself away. I walked at a normal pace, I used my normal gait, and I kept my head high. It was all for naught though, because I was pretty sure everyone in the room could tell I didn't have anything on under my dress. At least, that's how it felt. When I found Camden again, he looked cool as a fucking cucumber. Well, until I walked in, anyway.

As soon as he noticed me, his gaze shot straight to my sex and the hunger in his eyes was potent.

"Come here," he growled. I walked slowly toward him, making sure my hips were swaying, that every part of my body from the waist down that could move was keeping his attention. I came to stand right next to his chair, my belly a hairbreadth from his shoulder, and his arm wrapped around my waist, pulling me flush to him. His hand started at the small of my back but slowly smoothed its way down over the curve of my ass. It stalled there and he gave me a squeeze. "I believe you have something for me." His voice was still all growly, but the corner of his mouth was turned up into the tiniest of grins. That tiny smile was like a breath of fresh air to me. This was a different Camden, a man I hadn't met before, but that grin—I knew that man. This was just another side of the man I knew I was falling hard for, and I wanted to know all of him.

I reached my thumb and forefinger into my cleavage and pulled the black lace from my bra, and then I watched his eyes bug out of his head. His hand on my ass gripped me tighter and he pulled me even closer.

"We're going home. Now." His voice was more urgent than before, but that only made me hotter. He reached down to the table and grabbed a flute of champagne, handed it to me, and said, "Bottoms up."

"Hopefully," I replied with a wink. Not a wise move, I realized a moment later when both his hands were roaming down my ass, flirting with the hem of my dress. "No, no, no, Camden," I sang, shaking a finger at him. "You said I had to take off my panties and give them to you, and then you promised me a ride. I'd like to collect." I stepped backward out of his grasp, trying desperately to look as though I wasn't as affected by the whole scene when, in reality, I was thoroughly turned on. Ready to go. Green lights as far as the eye could see.

"Oh, I'll give you a ride." He laughed, giving me more proof that the Camden I'd gotten to know since that first basketball game was still very much with me. I downed my champagne and then took his hand in mine and led him from the room.

He'd taken a cab to the restaurant, so we both headed to my car. I suddenly realized I was disappointed we wouldn't be taking the Batmobile, because I loved watching Camden drive that car. When we reached my car, he held out his hand for the keys and I didn't argue giving them over. He wanted to be in charge and I wanted that too. I had relinquished control the moment I pulled my panties off and stuffed them into my bra.

Camden drove safely but quickly to his condo. The doors to the elevator were hardly closed all the way before he pushed me up against the wall, his mouth completely devouring mine. It was the kiss I'd been anticipating since we left the restaurant, the kiss that would lead to all the other fantastically sexy things he'd promised. It was an unusually clear night in Portland for the late fall, and it would have been beautiful to look out the elevator and see the mountain glowing in the moonlight, all the recently fallen snow like an iridescent blanket covering the peak. But instead of a breathtaking view, I'd gotten a breathtaking kiss. An all-consuming kiss.

His mouth slanted over mine and our lips fused, meeting perfectly and melding together with precision. Like we were fucking made to kiss each other that way. One of his hands came to my neck, moving back into my hair that was swiftly coming free of its loose knot and tangling up in his fingers. His other hand was finding its clever way between my thighs, inching upward. I spread my legs a little farther apart, giving him the access he wanted, and he groaned as his fingers made contact with my bare skin.

"You're wet," he rasped against my mouth.

"Duh," I responded.

He let out a short laugh, but it was snuffed out by the way his lips sealed over mine again, this time his tongue darting into my mouth at the same time he plunged two fingers inside of me. I was so keyed up, the anticipation driving me wild, I was almost surprised I didn't come on the spot. It was close, though. The combination of his mouth and his fingers, playing me like his favorite instrument, it would have been too much to handle for too much longer, but the door opened and we stumbled into his condo.

Our lips didn't part as he led me to the living room. No lights were on, but the moon was bright enough to light the way. Camden's hands were busy ridding me of my jacket and purse, tossing them somewhere along the way to the couch. I felt the edge of the couch at my calves and let out a yelp when I was pushed down, forced to sit. Just as quickly as I landed there, Camden was kneeling on the floor in front of me, his hands behind my knees, yanking me forward so my ass was on the very edge.

His eyes locked on mine and he slid his hands around from the back of my knees up to the top of my thighs, his fingertips slipping underneath the hem of my dress. He continued, his eyes still locked on mine, until my black skirt was pushed all the way up, exposing me to him from the waist down.

"How did it feel, walking through the restaurant knowing you were bare under your dress?" His hands ran lightly over my legs, teasing me.

"I felt naked." I squirmed on the couch, my body still on the precipice, wanting him to finish what he'd started.

"And?" He moved his hands down to my knees, gently squeezing me there.

"And dirty, like everyone knew what was going on."

"Mmm," he growled, leaning forward and pressing his mouth the inside of my thigh where the flesh was soft. "I'm the only one who knew." He said the words and then bit me just hard enough to make me yelp, but then he kissed the spot to soothe the ache. "I knew you were naked under your dress and that it was all for me—that you'd do that for me—it was a gift."

189

"You're supposed to say thank you when someone gives you a gift." I not-so-subtly lifted my hips, offering him the most tender part of me, hoping he'd make good on his word. He gave me a lopsided grin—the one I loved—and then slowly kissed his way to my core, pressing kisses everywhere except right where I wanted him most. When he finally used his tongue to spread me open, I almost cried out in relief, but instead I cried out in pleasure.

He made happy, hungry noises as he kissed and licked me, using every part of his mouth to get me off. His tongue was swirling, his lips were sucking, and his bearded chin was the last piece of the perfect trifecta of orgasms. I came hard, clenching around his tongue, my thighs tightening around his head, my fingers pulling on his hair, and he was there between my legs growling in approval.

Before I was even all the way over my orgasm, he left me. I made a strangled noise in protest, unable to form words yet, but I promptly stopped complaining when I saw he'd stood up to take off his clothes.

Yes, please.

Take it all off.

I watched as he hastily unbuttoned his shirt, dropping it to the floor, then pulled his undershirt off over the back of his head in that sexy way only guys can do. And is there anything sexier than watching a man unbuckle his belt while his eyes are trained on you? Nope. There isn't.

When he was completely naked, massive erection and all, he pulled me up from the couch and yanked my dress over my head. Then, without any words, he sat on the couch and pulled me down to straddle him. Then his hands were everywhere again. Grabbing, pulling, caressing, and my hands were doing the same. His hands cupped my breasts as my hand wrapped around his cock. I stroked him, marveling at how hard he was, but how soft his skin felt. My mind went blank as his mouth captured my breast, sucking me in deep. I moaned loudly and my hips moved reflexively, rocking back and forth, searching for friction, the ache between my legs growing with every tug his mouth made on my nipple. He growled around my breast and his hands moved to grip my hips. Then, one knee fell away and suddenly I was straddling just one of his legs.

Two things happened next. The thought of my bare sex against his thigh sent immediate and electrifying shock waves through me, starting at my core and ending there again, making my inner walls clench, wetness seeping from me. Also, I was overwhelmed with a sense of embarrassment and shame. The idea that I would rub myself on his thigh to get off seemed strange, I knew it was, but it was so fucking hot, I chased myself around in circles. I wanted so badly to use his body to bring mine pleasure, but there was a mental wall I couldn't climb over.

His hands came back to my breasts as his mouth fell away, and he peppered my skin with kisses up my chest and over my neck.

"Don't overthink this, Riley. My body is yours, any part of it, all of it. Use it."

I groaned while slowly grinding against him, taking in gasping breaths as more shockwaves rolled through me. It felt incredible. His hard thigh rubbed my clit in just the right way; it was all I could do to keep a slow pace. A part of me wanted to lose control, to shamelessly use him, to abandon myself and my notions of propriety, and simply fuck his leg. I don't know if he saw that in me or not, but he spoke regardless.

"Jesus, babe, you're so wet. I can feel it on my leg. I can feel you moving over me and it's so fucking hot. Don't stop." His hands moved back down to my hips and he gripped me hard enough to make me gasp. But the pain was slight and only heightened everything I was already feeling. He pulled me down on him, and my eyes rolled back with the added friction. My hands jumped out, seeking something to find purchase on, something to ground me, something to hold on to, to keep me from floating away. I held on to his bicep and shoulder while his hands moved my hips back and forth, pushing me toward a spectacular orgasm.

When it finally hit, my body was already in crisis mode. I drifted from coiled tension to limply sated, every muscle from the waist down pulsing in convulsions. Even my toes were twitching. It would go down in the history of Riley as one of the best orgasms ever. But Camden wasn't finished with me.

He picked up my limp body and carried me to the bedroom, laying me down gently on the bed. I watched through hooded lids as he reached into his nightstand and took out a condom. I forced my eyes open at that point because watching Camden put a condom on was one of my most favorite pastimes. Even though I'd just had the biggest orgasm I could remember, my body was instantly alert at the sight of him touching his cock, sheathing himself, and then looking for me, at me, ready to take me.

He crawled over me on the bed, stopping for nothing, and plunged into me on one long thrust. My back immediately arched and my lungs emptied on a groan. He pumped into me a few times, roughly, but fantastically, then his hands scooped me up under my back and brought my face up to his, my legs instinctively wrapping around his waist.

"Tell me it's never been like this with anyone else." His hand tangled in my hair and one arm wrapped around my waist. He drove into me as he said the words, but his eyes remained trained on mine.

"Never," I managed, the word falling out on a sigh. "Only you."

His hands moved over my skin, stopping at all his favorite places, pulling, pinching, and tugging. His mouth latched on to my neck, kissing, biting, and sucking. He did all of this while fucking me within an inch of my life. Eventually, one hand moved to the back of my neck and pressed my head to his shoulder, pulling me into an embrace while he pushed into me over and over until he came. He normally wasn't vocal when he came, but that time he let out a few surprised-sounding moans, as if his own pleasure caught him off guard.

"Fuck," he whispered against my hair as he lay me back on the bed, letting his body rest on top of mine. "Goddamn, Riley," he said, right before his mouth found mine. "If you're not careful, I'm going to fall in love with you."

My heart stopped at his words, terrified of them being both true and something just said after sex, words thrown away and meant as a transition. The entire evening had been building toward something, and I thought it was the crazy orgasms we'd both had, but obviously, I was wrong. Apparently, the night had been building toward a moment of pure panic.

"Don't freak out," he said, pushing my hair from my face, his body still covering mine, the warmth of it stupidly comforting. He kissed me again and then pulled back, catching my gaze once more.

"Have you ever been in love?" I blurted out, shocked by my own words. My eyes darted back and forth between his, trying to find the answer there, but all I saw were the corners of them wrinkle as he smiled.

"I used to think I'd been in love, but now I'm not so sure."

"No?" Never had a word been whispered quieter.

His face dipped down and every single part of me melted as he ran his nose gently along the length of mine. He kissed me slowly, then pulled back far enough to say, "I'm beginning to think whatever I've felt before was only a fraction of my capacity to love someone."

"Oh."

He laughed and then rolled off me. I tried not to watch as he removed the condom and disposed of it in the trash can under his nightstand, but everything about him captivated me. When he finished, he came back to me, pulling me to his side. I went willingly, and I knew I always would. If his arms were open, I was supposed to be in them. Nothing in the world had ever been clearer to me than that.

After a few minutes of silence and his hand running up and down my spine in a way that had my eyes drifting closed, he finally spoke.

"Are you all right with everything that happened tonight?" He sounded wary and nervous.

I shifted so I was propped up on an elbow and could see his face.

"Yeah. Why?"

He curled a lock of hair behind my ear, his eyes now showing the worry that had been in his voice. "I don't want to push you into doing something you aren't comfortable with."

194

"Oh, you mean the underwear thing?"

"Yeah. Was that too much?"

"Surprisingly, no. If you had asked me a month ago if I'd ever do that with a guy, I would have said no."

"Then why didn't you tell me no?"

I shrugged. "Because I wanted to say yes. I liked the way your eyes were alive when you asked me, and I wanted to know what it would feel like to let you take control like that, to trust you in that way."

He was silent and his face was unreadable, until that sexy grin appeared. "It was fucking sexy as hell, Riley."

"Yes, well, don't think just because I took my panties off for you in public means I'll be doing much more. I do have boundaries. They're in there somewhere. I think when you smile at me they melt away, along with my inhibitions."

"I like you uninhibited."

"Clearly," I said with a laugh. I thought back to all the things I'd done with Cam that I normally wouldn't have done, and I suddenly found myself blushing. One would think walking through a restaurant without panties would have been the height of boundary pushing, but no, I managed to outdo myself on that too. Images of myself, and what I'd done with him, flashed through my mind and I couldn't hold his gaze any longer.

"Hey," he said, his finger pulling my chin back up to look at him. "What happened? What shut you down just now?"

Unable to say the words while looking at him, I buried my face in his chest.

"I came on your leg." My words were muffled against his warm, damp skin.

"What?" he said while laughing, making his chest bounce, my face also bouncing as a result. "Come on, talk to me."

Like ripping off a Band-Aid, I lifted my face a little and clamped my eyes closed, saying, "I came on your leg."

"Damn straight you did. It was hot as fuck, too."

"It was ridiculous," I said, my voice sullen.

"Why? You've used my hand to get off before. And my dick. What's the difference?"

"I don't know," I muttered, rolling away and finding a reason to inspect my fingernail. "Fingers and dicks are *typically* used in sex. Quadriceps? Not so much."

"So the fuck what? If it makes you feel good, and I can provide it, I want you to ride every part of me, baby. You can bet I'm going to stick my dick between your boobs at some point."

I couldn't help but laugh.

"This is a ridiculous conversation."

"It might feel ridiculous, but I want to be able to talk to you about your needs and wants. I want to give you everything. Sure, today you might have gotten off on my leg, but tomorrow it might be something more important, and I want us to be able to talk about it. About anything."

"Okay," I whispered, still a little embarrassed.

"Good," he said, rolling me over and pulling my back into his chest. He snuggled into me and it was so easy to relax against him, to let his big body envelop mine and keep me warm and safe. After a few quiet moments, he asked, "Do you need anything before I fall asleep?"

"No," I said sleepily.

"You sure? Water? Extra pillow? My other leg?"

He was laughing and rolling away before I could smack him. But I caught him. Eventually.

Chapter Fourteen

Camden

As I pulled up to my mother's house, I remembered the last time I was there and introducing Riley to my parents for the first time. I thought about how nervous she'd been and I caught myself gripping the steering wheel too hard. She was always so hard on herself. She'd gone into that brunch thinking she wasn't good enough for me, or that my parents would think that about her.

We'd come a long way since then, especially since my mother has been working with Riley for a month now to plan her gala. My mother was closer with Riley than any other woman I've ever been with, and that was great, but I couldn't wait for them to have more than just a professional relationship. For that reason, I was looking forward to dinner with my mom. She'd called and invited us over, not wanting to spend the entire evening alone as my stepfather was out of town at a conference. The fact that Andrew wouldn't be there was another reason to accept the invitation.

My mother's driveway was empty and I felt the disappointment immediately. The closer the gala got, the busier Riley was, and I wanted every minute with her I could steal.

I parked the Batmobile and walked into the house, not bothering to knock.

"Hey, Mom, I'm here."

"In the kitchen," she called.

I slipped my jacket off and hung it on the hall tree, rolled up my sleeves, and sought out my mother.

"Hello, there, my handsome son," she said with a smile as I entered the kitchen. She was standing at the island mixing something in a bowl. I moved to her, kissing her on the cheek, then swiped a crouton from the salad she was tossing.

"Stop sticking your dirty fingers in the food, Camden." She said the words like she was angry, but I could see her smile so I knew she wasn't actually mad at me. "Where's Riley?"

"She said she'd meet me here. She had a late conference call at work."

"She's working too hard." My mother's voice was full of concern. I reached for another crouton, but she slapped my hand before I could get hold of one. She scowled at me and I laughed.

"Well, here's the thing. I think this is Riley. She has a strong work ethic. I know she's trying hard to make a good impression on you and her boss, but I kind of think she would be working this hard regardless of who the client was. She's worked hard her whole life."

My mother was quiet so I looked over at her.

"You really like her, don't you?"

In the past, this was where I would have scoffed and told my mom I was too young to be serious about a woman. I would have laughed and said it was just casual. But I couldn't fathom putting Riley and the word casual in the same sentence. Nothing about my relationship with her was casual. It was all-encompassing, new, scary, deep, fulfilling, rewarding, and the sex was off the charts, but my mom didn't need to know that part.

"I do. A lot. And I think the feeling's mutual."

Mom smiled and then her eyes welled with tears. She wiped them away quickly, trying to hide them from me, but I laughed and put an arm around her. "She likes you too, Mom. And not only as someone she's working for. She thinks you're great."

"I like her too," she said, her voice squeaky and soft.

"Don't cry, Mom. This is a good thing. Maybe I'm really a grown-up now."

"Well," she said, her voice a little stronger, "let's not go *too* crazy."

We laughed together, I stole another crouton, and my phone rang. I saw Riley's name on the screen and I knew it was bad news.

"Hey, babe, my mom and I were just talking about you."

"Uh, that sounds horrifying."

"All good things. What's up?"

"I'm so angry right now. My conference call was postponed for an hour and then Rose said she wants to status afterward. I don't think I'm going to make it for dinner and I feel really shitty about it."

"Well, that is shitty, but it's not your fault. Don't worry, I've had dinner alone with my mom a ton of times, I can probably make it through another."

"I know, I just don't want your mom to think I'm flaking out on her."

"Mom doesn't think you're flaking out on her." I turned to my mother and asked, "Do you?"

"Of course not, dear," Mom said without batting an eye.

"Can I talk to her?" Riley asked. My eyebrows shot up in surprise. I don't think any of my previous girlfriends ever asked me to hand the phone to my mother before.

"Uh, sure." I held the phone out to my mom. "She wants to talk to you," I said, my voice slightly laced with confusion. Mom took the phone from me and put it up to her ear with a smile.

"Hello, Riley," she said sweetly. "Oh, I'm so sorry to hear that. Of course I understand." She walked to the fridge and pulled out a pitcher of ice water. "Don't worry about it, dear. There will be plenty more opportunities for me to feed you." She laughed and I could almost swear I heard Riley's laughter through the phone. "Don't work too hard though, I worry about you." I watched as my mother went about preparing dinner while talking to my girlfriend on the phone. "Okay, well, I'll send a plate with Cam so you will have a home-cooked meal to come home to." Then she laughed. "Yes, I'm aware he doesn't cook." My face pulled back in shock at her words. *I cooked.* "All right, I'll see you on Thursday for the menu finalization and place setting approval. I'm excited to see what you've come up with. Okay. You too. Bye, sweetheart." Mom pulled the phone from her ear and tapped the screen.

"Did you hang up?" I asked, a little upset I didn't get to say good-bye.

"She hung up first. She had to go." She handed the phone back to me and I couldn't help the way my eyebrows scrunched and my mouth pulled to the side. "Stop pouting, Camden, and help me set the table."

"Fine," I muttered, feeling like a big baby. It never would have bothered me before to not get the chance to say good-bye, but I wanted that with Riley, wanted those moments where I could tell her I missed her, or tell her I wished she were here, and that I'd see her later.

I was putting the plates down when my phone buzzed in my pocket.

**Sorry I had to go so quickly, Rose needed me. Plus, I didn't want to say dirty things to you when I knew your mom was just feet away. But rest assured, I will make missing this dinner up to you. And by that, I mean you're in for the best blowie of your life. I miss you. See you later.* *

**I miss you too.* *

"You're wearing a lovesick smile, Camden." Mom's voice was all-knowing, and I tried to keep myself from smiling, but it was impossible.

"What can I say? I can't help it."

We brought the rest of the dishes to the table, this time sitting in the nook in the kitchen since it was only the two of us, and then sat down to eat. We ate in silence for a few minutes, talking about nonconsequential things every now and then. Honestly, I was too interested in my mother's meatloaf to pay much attention to anything in particular. Mom was right about a home-cooked meal.

"Andrew is looking forward to spending some time with Riley soon." I looked up at my mother after she'd spoken those words, a little confused. My confusion turned to suspicion when I noticed my mother was avoiding my gaze.

"Something tells me you're speaking for him, Mom. Besides, the last time Riley and Andrew were in the same room, he was an asshole to her. I'm not sure she would even feel comfortable having dinner with him anytime soon." And the fact of the matter was, I was on her side about it. If she was uncomfortable, I'd keep her away to protect her, to make sure he didn't say any other asinine things to her.

"You have to give him a break, Camden. He wasn't trying to offend her, or you. I know for a fact, deep down in his heart, Andrew wants the best for you and even though his methods might need a little guidance, he's always looking out for your best interests."

"That's where we disagree, Mom. His first priority is himself and his career. I already became a lawyer because he wanted me to. I refuse to let him control who I fall in love with. I have to draw the line somewhere." I didn't like speaking to my mother that way, but something about Riley brought out the protective bear in me. I set my fork down with a clang and rubbed my hands over my face. "Look, Mom. I'm sorry. I know you mean well, but where Riley's concerned, you've got to keep Andrew away until she's comfortable. Please. It's important to me. *She's* important to me." I looked up and saw my mother gazing at me, resignation on her face but sadness in her eyes.

"I wish I could have done a better job bringing you two together." She shook her head and then looked at the ceiling, and I knew she was close to tears. "He's always cared about you, Camden, but he's not good at showing it. When he interferes, that's his way of loving you." I scoffed and picked up my napkin, wiping my face harshly, trying to keep myself in control. No matter how I felt about Andrew, my mother was an innocent in all of it. "He truly wants what's best for you, and anytime you've ever felt railroaded, it was him thinking he knew what that was. He loves you, Cam. He thinks the world of you. He thinks you're smart and funny, and he's so proud of the man you've grown up to

203

be, we both are, sweetie. He just shows how much he cares in a strange way."

"By insulting my girlfriend when I bring her home to meet you? No, I don't buy it, Mom. That was a shit move and I can't just forget about it because you think he means well. I'm sorry. I can't put Riley in that position. Andrew is going to have to prove that he won't hurt her and he'll have to do that on Riley's timetable. Not mine, not yours, and not his."

I held my mother's gaze for a moment, both of us trying to implore the other to see our side.

"Okay," she finally said, her voice a whisper. I watched as she reached up and wiped away a stray tear. I hated that she was crying. I never wanted to cause my mother pain, but this wasn't an area of my life I was willing to compromise. When her cheeks were dry, she gave me a weak smile and said, "Riley is lucky to have you." Then she started crying all over again, that time in earnest. I pushed my chair back and went to her, pulling her up into a hug.

"Mom, don't cry. This isn't the end of the world. Everything will be fine."

"Oh, sweetie, I know it will. I'm just having a hard time. I want you and Andrew to get along, and I want Riley to feel comfortable here, and I also can't believe how good of a man you are."

I pulled back and put my hands on my mother's shoulders. "You taught me how to treat a woman. I'd never let anything happen to her. Or you." I hugged her again because I could tell she was still upset, but after a moment she pulled away, taking in a deep breath and seeming to calm herself.

"Let's sit down and finish our dinner."

"Okay, Mom."

We managed to finish our meal without any more arguing, and it ended up being a pleasant evening. I couldn't remember the last time I hung out with just my mom. True to her word, when I left she sent me home with a plate piled high with food. I wasn't sure if Riley liked mashed potatoes and meatloaf, but it didn't matter because I would totally eat it if she didn't want it. I think my mom knew this because she sent an extra plate home for me too.

I'd been home for a few hours, showered, and was lounging in a pair of gym shorts when I heard the elevator open and Riley's heels click through my condo.

"Cam?" she called, her voice tired.

"Back here, babe."

She walked in as though the weight of the world was on her shoulders; slumped down, arms hanging at her sides, eyes half-closed. She walked straight to the bed and collapsed facedown, making the mattress bounce.

"You okay?" All I got was a groan in response, muffled by the mattress. "I'll take that as a no." Rolling off the side of my bed, I wandered over to her, took each of her feet in my hands, and slipped her heels off one at a time. Grabbing her by the hips, I flipped her over and laughed when she flopped onto her back, resembling an obstinate toddler.

"I feel like I've been awake and on my feet for an entire week." She folded her arm over her eyes as she spoke, still rather tantrum-y.

"That's because you basically have been. You need a break."

"I need this event to be perfect."

I took her foot in my hand and pressed my thumb into the arch.

"Oh, God...." Her hands dropped to the blanket below her and her back arched up as she moaned.

"Feels good?"

"Fuck, yes."

I shifted on my feet as my dick reacted to the words she was saying and the tone she was using. I kept it under control though, focusing on her and her needs, wanting to make her feel a little bit better. After a few minutes, I switched feet and the whole show started all over again. She writhed and gasped, and I hardened watching. She was lost in sensation, but if she had looked up she would have seen my erection tenting the front of my gym shorts.

I rubbed her feet as long as I could, until I ached for release, but I didn't want to push her, knowing she was exhausted. I moved my hand up her calf, under the fabric of her pants, rubbing the muscle there, listening to her moan some more.

"Baby, let's get you something to sleep in." I pulled my hand out and had reached to unbutton her pants when her eyes met mine.

"I promised you the best blow job of your life."

"You did," I said with a laugh. "But I can take a rain check."

"You don't want a blow job?" Her bottom lip stuck out in a pout.

"That's not what I'm saying, babe." Her pants slid down her slim hips as I pulled on the legs. Of course she was fucking wearing some lacy underwear. Not once had I caught her in regular cotton panties. I was beginning to think she didn't own them. And that was fine. I mean, I loved seeing her in lace and satin, but right then, I needed her in some granny panties. "You're tired. Exhausted. I want you to get some rest. You're going to make yourself sick."

"So what you're saying is," she paused while she pulled her blouse over her head, showing me the bra that matched her panties, "you're willing to forgo a blow job so that I can get some rest?" She slid up to her knees and made her way toward me at the edge of the bed, her fingers sliding up the bare skin of my chest.

"Uh, yeah," I said, not completely sure I'd made the right choice. She looked me in the eye for a few tense moments, the fingers on one hand twirling in the hair at my nape.

"You better be careful, Camden."

"Why?"

"You're going to make me fall in love with you."

Her expression was guarded, as though she was afraid of what my reaction would be to her words. I leaned down and kissed her softly.

"Maybe that's my plan."

She held my gaze for a moment more, then rested her cheek against my chest.

"I really am tired," she whispered.

"Come on," I said, moving to my side of the bed and opening the covers for her. I tried not to groan in agony when she slipped her bra off and then curled into me. Instead I pulled the covers up over us and then reached over to turn off the lamp on my nightstand, shrouding us in darkness. I held her, running my hand through the ends of her hair the way I knew relaxed her, and listened until her breaths were deep and even. Only when I was sure she was asleep did I kiss the crown of her head and whisper, "I think it might be too late to stop me from falling in love with you."

Chapter Fifteen

Riley

"Just when you think you might have everything nailed down, something else pops up at you." Jasper said the words as he read an e-mail on his phone, shaking his head.

"Is it anything I want to know about, or are you going to handle it so I can remain blissfully unaware?" I asked the question without turning my head from my computer screen.

"Oh, honey, I've got this covered. It's funny how some people see me and think I won't throw a bitch down."

"I have no doubt, *honey.*" I did look at him then, smiling, even if it was a tired smile. We'd been working for weeks on this party and it was now only days away. *Days.* And what Jasper was talking about was true. For any event, you could get to a certain point where you felt as though you had everything under control, but there's always those little tiny loose ends that popped up and made you want to find a clown and kick it in the junk.

Clowns were scary, okay?

"Riley, you've got a delivery at the front desk?" Our newest intern, Robyn, said, barely poking her head in my office before she ran away. Rose was working her over and I think she feared that if she stood still too long, she'd be fired.

"I bet you one of the vendors got something mixed up and is delivering here instead of downtown."

"Want me to handle it?" Jasper asked, ready and willing to do my dirty work for me.

"No, thanks, I've got it. I need to walk anyway, I've been sitting in this chair for over an hour." When I got to the front desk, I saw a man standing right outside the elevators with a large floral arrangement. It was beautiful, but it was all wrong. We'd ordered small, tasteful, white and blue arrangements for the auction tables. This was almost embarrassingly large and very, very red.

"Are you Riley Smith?" The man was peering at me from behind the flowers.

"Yes, but I think there's been some sort of mistake. All flowers are supposed to be downtown on Saturday, and we didn't order anything red."

He gave me a puzzled look, but then displayed an expression I recognized from Jasper. He'd decided I was crazy and he only wanted to do his job.

"Listen, lady, I'm not sure what you're talking about. I've got a delivery here for Riley Smith, so if that's you, then please take this so I can get to my next delivery. Every minute you argue with me about receiving flowers, my tip goes down from the next lady who's actually glad her man sent her roses."

"These aren't for the Rogers gala downtown?"

He looked at me like I was stupid. "Are you deaf? These are for Riley Smith. Is that you?"

"Yes."

"Then for the love of everything holy, just sign for them." He held out a little palm device and I took it,

210

signing my name with the little stylus, then handed it back to him. "Here you go, tell your man I said good luck."

I was so taken off guard, I didn't realize he'd insulted me until he was already in the elevator, but I caught his eye before the doors closed and I flipped him off. I almost dropped the heavy vase in the process, but he didn't know that. I made it back to my office with the huge arrangement and set it down on my desk.

"Those are all wrong," Jasper said, standing and walking around my desk, eyeing the flowers with worry.

"That was my first thought too, but I don't think they're for the gala." I finally spied a card hiding in the mass of roses and plucked it out.

Riley,

Tonight you're mine. Give me 30 minutes' notice and I will have a car waiting for you when you're ready to come to me.

-Camden

"Someone's getting laid tonight," Jasper sang after reading the card over my shoulder. Ignoring him, I looked over the flowers again in a new light.

"They're so beautiful."

"Boyfriend didn't spare any expense, either. These must have cost a fortune."

I chose not to respond to that either. Jasper was right, though. The flowers were beautiful and probably expensive. I took a moment to realize it might have been the first time his money didn't bother me. Six weeks ago, had I gotten these flowers, it would have made me feel inadequate and unworthy. It would have sent my head into the sand, questioning whether or not Camden and I were good for each other. But now that I knew him and his heart, I knew right down to the center of me that Camden didn't send me flowers with a price tag, he sent me flowers with his soul. He wanted the flowers to evoke a feeling in me, not make me realize how much money he might have spent on them.

If there was one thing Camden was good at, it was being ignorant of his wealth. He had money and he used it when he needed it, but it wasn't an asset to him, it was simply there. And while that would have caused me concern before, now it was almost endearing. When we first started dating, I was so afraid of his money and was irritated that he couldn't see why, but now I knew it was simply because he didn't see money. He just saw me.

"Have you seen my boyfriend? He doesn't have to send me expensive flowers to get laid."

"That's my girl," he replied with a laugh. "Did he fuck up? Are those apology flowers?"

"I don't really know what they're for. The card says a car will pick me up tonight."

"Mysterious *and* hot. You're living the dream, Riley."

Here's hoping I don't wake up.

I gave Cam the thirty-minute notice and couldn't help but smile when I walked outside my building to find him leaning against a sleek black stretch limo.

"What is all this for?" Walking toward him, the butterflies came to life, flittering through my belly, as if they were trying to soar right out of me, straight to him.

"Do you trust me?" His voice was calm, and his grin was tipped up at the corner, but I could tell he was a little nervous.

"Trust you?"

"Yeah." He leaned forward and kissed me slowly, not touching me anywhere else but on my lips. I moved in, trying to get closer, wanting more of his mouth, but he pulled back. "Do you trust me?" That time he whispered the words.

"Yes. Of course."

"Good, then turn around."

I wanted to ask why, to figure out what was going on, but I knew he wanted me to let go and let him lead. So I did. I turned, taking in a deep breath, unsure of what would happen next. Suddenly a dark cloth covered my eyes and my fingers came up to feel satin wrapped around my head. My pulse thundered away, chest pounding, at the idea of Camden blindfolding me. I felt the satin tighten around me, felt the tugs on the fabric as he secured it, and then my hair swept over my shoulder and his mouth was on my neck.

"You just made me extremely happy, Riley. Come with me." He took my hand and led me toward the limo. I took a few faltering steps, obviously unaccustomed to walking blindly, but he was very good at making me feel safe. He directed me into the limo, got me situated, and then told the driver I had yet to see that we could depart.

"Where are we going?" I whispered.

"Don't worry, it's a surprise."

I jumped when his hand landed on my knee. My hand came to my throat and I tried to let my heart return to its normal beat.

"You don't have to worry, baby. I've got you." As he said the words, his hand crept up my thigh and his fingers slid under the hem of my skirt, and my breath caught. His hand moved farther up but then stilled and grasped my thigh tightly. "Are you wearing a fucking garter belt, Riley?"

Before I could even answer, he pushed my skirt all the way up to my waist, exposing me to, well, I didn't know what because I couldn't see anything.

"Cam, are we alone?" All I could think of were all the movies I'd seen with people in limos and there was always a screen that could go up or down. I swallowed thickly and prayed it was up.

He didn't answer me, but instead replaced his hands with his mouth and began kissing my legs, his lips moving over the lace tops of my thigh-highs and even farther up.

"Always in fucking lace," he said before pressing a kiss right against my panty-covered opening. I gasped at the sensation. The way his lips felt against my sex, the way the limo bounced along the road, the sound of the tires moving over the pavement, and the way his hair felt between my fingers as I threaded them through, it was all sensory overload.

The limo continued to drive us to our destination as he continued to drive me wild. He seemed to be on a mission to tease me. He touched me everywhere, except where I wanted him most. His mouth and fingers danced around my core, but never actually touched me there, always grazing me. I rolled my hips and arched my back, trying everything I could to convince him to touch me, to give me some sort of release, but he wouldn't be swayed. I couldn't see him, but I would have bet money I could feel him smiling against my mound as he teased me.

I felt the limo stop and the ignition cut, and Camden was pulling my skirt back down my body.

"I have plans for you, but they don't involve sex in the back of a limo."

"Really? Could have fooled me," I grumbled, adjusting my skirt. I heard the door open and felt the rush of cold air float into the limo, then Camden was taking my hand and leading me out.

"Where are we?" I asked, listening for any clue I could find.

"You'll see," he said, right before pressing a kiss to my temple. I heard a door open and then the press of his hand on the small of my back, urging me through. The wall of warm air soothed me, but my heart was pumping, thinking about the unknown. We could have been anywhere. It was a rather short ride, and in Portland you could get almost anywhere in twenty minutes.

Whatever building he'd brought me into, it was quiet. The only thing I could hear was the buzz of electricity. His hand still held mine and he led me along, telling me when I would feel the floor change from tile to carpet and when I had to turn. Finally, we stopped, and I listened again, trying to figure anything out. When I heard the unmistakable sound of coins my ears perked up. Camden then took my hand and made me hold it out, open, and palm up. A bag was placed in it, and I heard the coins again. The bag wasn't terribly heavy, but its weight caught me off guard so I quickly brought my other hand up to help support it. The coins were in a plastic bag and they moved between my fingers in a familiar way.

"Why is there a bag of coins in my hands?"

"Think about it, baby. There's only one place you could be where you'd need a bunch of coins."

I put an overly excited smile on my face and said, "Are we at a laundromat?"

"Ha ha, smart-ass. Try again."

"I don't know, Camden, I'm standing here blindfolded, still stupidly turned on from your fun in the limo, and I have no idea where I am. Put me out of my misery. I've played your game long enough."

"Funny you should mention games," he said as he reached up and pulled the blindfold off my eyes. It took a moment for my eyes to adjust to the light, but mainly because there were different colors of light everywhere. Bright, flashing lights.

"You brought me to an arcade?"

"Happy anniversary," he said sweetly.

"Anniversary?" I couldn't keep the confusion from my voice. I dropped my hands and brought the bag of nickels to my side.

"Mmm hmm." He stepped up closer to me, his hands winding around my waist and clasping behind my back. "Two months ago tonight I sat next to a sexy stranger at a basketball game and the Jumbotron made me kiss her." He leaned down and pressed his mouth to mine, angled perfectly over my lips, his tongue barely tasting me. He pulled back and that gave me a moment to take in my surroundings with all the new information. My eyes landed right over his shoulder and I smiled.

He must have noticed my smile and stepped away, revealing the row of Skee-Ball machines. Suddenly I realized there weren't any other people in the arcade.

"Is this place closed? Did you break in to a nickel arcade?"

"No. I rented the entire place for the night. We have the whole place to ourselves."

I looked around as if I needed further confirmation. "You rented a nickel arcade for our two-month kissing anniversary so we could play Skee-Ball alone?"

"Well, yes. But," he said, raising a finger, "I also had the place stocked. There's Chinese takeout and Hef waiting for you when you get hungry."

"Are you for real?" I blurted.

"What?"

"I mean, is this for real? Are you serious?"

"Well, yeah," he said slowly, sounding confused and looking worried. "Do you not like it? I thought it would be something fun and different—"

He didn't get to finish his sentence because I jumped him. I launched myself at him and kissed him stupid.

"This is the sweetest thing anyone has ever done for me," I whispered against his lips after showing him how much I appreciated it with my mouth.

"Well, before you get all mushy, I should share that I have some ulterior motives."

"Oh, really?" I carefully unfolded my legs from around his waist, but left my arms draped over his shoulders, not wanting him to get too far away.

"I'd like to make our evening interesting." His fingers slipped right below the waistband of my skirt over my ass, dipping in a little. The feeling of his fingers against my skin only ignited a fire that had been stoking ever since he put that damn blindfold on me.

"A wager?" I giggled. I couldn't help it. I couldn't remember a time when I'd been that happy. "I don't want to take away from your endgame here, but I'm kind of a sure thing." His hands pulled at my ass, dragging me as close to him as I could get while still clothed.

"We'll each take a shot, and whoever gets the lower score on each ball has to lose a piece of clothing."

"You want to play strip Skee-Ball?"

"I'm up for it if you are."

I looked around, part of me wanting to make sure there wasn't anyone around. Was some pimple-faced high schooler hanging out in the breakroom? Surely they wouldn't just hand the business over to Cam and leave him alone here. "How sure are you that we're alone?"

"I am 100 percent sure we are the only people in this building."

My eyes roamed, as I tried to concentrate but was distracted by his hands again.

"What about surveillance video? There have to be cameras in here somewhere."

"Part of the rental contract explicitly stated the cameras were to be offline during my time here. I watched the owner shut the cameras down. We're all alone. No one can see us."

The funny thing was, part of me wanted there to be cameras. I didn't necessarily want someone watching us, and I didn't want some sophomore in the backroom jerking off while I had sex with my boyfriend, but the idea that there might be a camera on us, that we might be filmed, surprisingly turned me on.

"I play better when I'm drunk, so I'll need those beers."

He smiled broadly then smacked a playful kiss on my lips.

"Follow me."

The next hour was spent laughing more than I had in a long time. We ate and drank, but then made our way around the arcade, playing all kinds of games. Camden was competitive, which didn't surprise me, but it did surprise me that when I was better at a game than him, he didn't sulk and complain; he wanted to play it again until he got better. As long as he was progressing and getting better, he had a blast. One game he couldn't outscore me on was pinball. He made up some excuse about women being better multitaskers, therefore making it easier for me to manage all the different levers and multiple balls.

I barked out a laugh when he managed to say "multiple balls" with a straight face.

"So," he said, leaning up against the Whack-a-Mole game I was currently annihilating. "Ready for a round of Skee-Ball?"

I narrowed my eyes at him. "Do I get any sort of handicap? You pretty much wiped the floor with me last time." Without breaking eye contact, he slipped his shiny shoes off and pulled his tie free from around his neck.

"There. That's two. Think that'll be enough?"

I laughed. "Probably not. You'll most likely still beat me."

"One can only hope."

I walked past him, taking the tie from his hand and slipping it over my head. "Let's do this, Rogers."

"Okay, rules are, we both get one ball to make the best score. Whoever gets the highest score of that round, gets to pick the piece of clothing the other person loses." Camden tossed a wooden ball up and caught it without looking. "We play until one person loses all their clothes."

"*All?*"

"All."

"All right." *I can't believe I'm going to do this.* On the way to the Skee-Ball games, I grabbed my coat and scarf from our table.

"Ladies first," he said, making a sweeping motion toward the game where our balls had already been racked.

"How gentlemanly." I grabbed a wooden ball, rolling it around in my hand, lined up my shot and took it, a little surprised he hadn't tried to distract me. I scored a decent fifty points, but I knew what this game was about, and it wasn't sinking the balls in the holes with the highest points. I knew he'd beat me, and he knew it too. This was about him pushing my boundaries and giving me another experience. At some point I had accepted it, and knew what was coming. Sure enough, Camden sunk his perfect ball right into the hundred-point hole.

"Coat." His single word was a demand, and fuck me if his steely tone and bedroom eyes didn't make everything below my waist warm up.

The next five balls played exactly the same way. I tried for the hundred-point hole but never could make it. He made it every time.

"Scarf."

"Shirt."

"Heels."

"Blouse."

"Skirt."

I stood in the middle of a nickel arcade wearing only a bra, panties, thigh-highs, a garter belt, and his tie. This seemed like every brace-toothed nerd's dream.

"Was this, like, one of your teenage fantasies? Did you have wet dreams about beating pretty girls at Skee-Ball and making them take all their clothes off for you?"

"I've had plenty of fantasies throughout the years, Riley. But none of them compare to you."

"I want to change the game," I said suddenly, taken off guard by his words.

"Oh, really?"

"Yes, this is too easy for you."

"What are the new rules?"

"New rules, we play until one of us is naked, but the difference is, if you *don't* make a ball in the hundred-point hole you have to take something off. Sink the ball, and I'll take something off."

"So all the pressure is on me?"

"Yep," I said, popping the *p*.

"Deal." He reached for his next ball and I perched myself at the end of my Skee-Ball lane. I crossed my legs slowly and then leaned back until my elbows hit the wood. He paused, hand inside the alley where the balls dispense, eyes glued to me and my body. I watched as he weighed his options. At that point, he knew what my intention was. To distract him. I figured he was weighing which he wanted more: to beat me or fuck me.

He picked up a ball and took his stance. I brought my finger to my mouth, letting my tongue dart out and lick it, then slowly ran the wet tip down my chin and neck, over my breast, and down my torso.

He watched me the entire time, but right before my finger made it to the edge of my panties, he took three steps forward and launched his ball.

"Fifty points," I said, trying not to smile too hard. "Lose the shirt." Luckily for me, since he'd been so sure he would win, he hadn't bothered to layer up like I had, and had left his suit jacket at our table. He took his time unbuttoning his shirt, watching me with rapt attention as he did. "Take your next shot, Camden," I said once his shirt was on the ground next to most of my clothes.

He grabbed a ball and prepared to fire. I uncrossed my legs and spread my knees, running my hand down my center. I did it for his benefit, to throw him off, but I couldn't deny I was aroused, wet even. "I'm waiting," I teased.

"*Fuck*," he swore, his hand coming up to run through his hair. I watched him steel himself, line up his shot, and launch the ball. I smiled when he got a gutter ball.

"I'll take the pants, Rogers."

His gaze was pinned on me as he pulled open his belt, and I found my fingers pressing harder against my sex, adding more friction. I gasped, surprised at how turned on I was. This wasn't my wheelhouse. I didn't like adventure outside the bedroom, but apparently, I was wrong. He pulled off his pants and stood there, still a good eight feet away, panting and nailing me with his gaze. His boxer briefs were stretched with his erection and the sight only made me hotter. I slipped my fingers underneath the lace of my underwear, gasping as my two middle fingers slid between my lips.

"Oh, God," I moaned, unable to play the game anymore. At first I was trying to bait him, to make him lose the game he so clearly thought he was going to win, but now I was too turned on to continue. I felt his hands on my thighs before I realized he was in front of me, but even though I knew he was there, I continued to work my hand through my sex.

"What do you want?" he rasped, his eyes darting all over me. From my hand and its work between my legs to my breasts, to my face, he was feasting on all of me.

223

"I want you to touch me."

He pulled his undershirt over his head, knelt, and placed his hands under my knees, pulling me to the edge of the lane. He slid his hands up my stocking-covered legs, only stopping when his fingers reached the elastic of my underwear. He tugged at the same time I lifted my hips, and in an instant, my sex was bare for him. I reached for my garter belt, but his hand landed on mine.

"Leave it on." Before I could agree, his mouth descended on me. His tongue claimed me, licking me up and down, hungry for every part of me. His hands were wrapped around my thighs, holding me open, giving him unfettered access. He kissed me, sucked me, and licked me, constantly moving, always teasing. When his lips latched on to my clit, sucking with surprising pressure, my body's instinct was to pull away—it was too much. But he held me down and didn't let up. I cried out, then opened my eyes and looked down at him, nearly coming at the sight of his mouth—the mouth I knew so well—latched on to the most intimate part of me. He caught my gaze and let up a little, running his chin back and forth through my folds, making me cry out even louder.

"I can't...," I whimpered, afraid I would combust.

"You will." His hand left my body. One hand pulled on the cup of my bra and he roughly palmed my breast. The other hand moved south and two fingers sank into me. That was all it took to send me flying, spiraling through the most intense orgasm I'd ever had. He didn't let up though; he pumped his fingers in and out of me, sucked my clit, and squeezed my breast until I had come down from my high. Even then he didn't let up.

He pulled away, wiping his face on the back of his hand, then grabbed me by my armpits, hauling me up to stand. My legs were weak, my head still spinning in a different orbit, but I watched as he pulled down his boxer briefs, his impressive length springing out of the waistband like it had been held captive. I reached for him, wanting to feel his hard shaft in my hand, but he grabbed my hand before I could make contact.

No words were spoken between us as he walked backward toward the lane. He sat down, then lay back, pulling me over him. I didn't ask questions; there was no need. I knew what he wanted, and I wanted it too. I climbed over him and, wasting no time, situated him beneath me and then sank down, feeling him enter me, slowly and fully.

"Jesus... fuck...," he spat, his hands roaming everywhere he could reach. I'd never felt that full before. Something about the wooden lane we were on, the fact that there was no give, it made him push against me harder, made everything feel better. Even the slightest rock of my hips was like an electric shock to my clit, which was already overly sensitive, thanks to his mouth. "You've got to move, Riley," he said, sounding almost as if he were in pain.

I did as he asked, pushing up and letting his cock slide out of me, then sinking back down, loving the way he stretched and filled me again, gasping at how sublime it felt. It became obvious I wasn't moving fast enough for him when he grabbed my hips and quickened my pace for me, using his ridiculously strong arms to manipulate my body for his pleasure. I wanted that. I wanted him to find his fucking nirvana in my body, use it to reach that high, over and over again. I wanted him so addicted to me that he never wanted anyone else, never thought of anyone but me.

I took his hands off my hips and brought them to my breasts. He took the cue, using his fingers to pull and pinch, to knead and grab. I placed my open palms on his chest, using him for leverage, and then I forced my hips down, putting every ounce of pressure I could on my pussy, and rocked against him.

"Holy fucking shit," he growled. I wanted to see the look on his face as he spoke, to see the way his face contorted when he was close, but my concentration was on the way my hips were grinding into his, the shocks of pleasure that rocketed through my body as my clit rubbed against his pubic bone. My eyes cinched closed and my lungs worked overtime.

The warmth between my legs built, sparking and igniting, and without much warning, I was coming. My back arched as I came, letting out a loud moan, and it was followed closely by Camden's own shout of release. I stilled, my head lolling back, my hands still gripping his pecs, a bead of sweat rolling down my temple and onto my neck.

After a few silent moments, Camden finally spoke. His words were pushed out between panting breaths. "This is not good."

The words themselves might have made me worry, but I could see the smile on his face so I knew he didn't regret what we'd done.

"Now I'll never be able to look at another Skee-Ball game the same. I'll always get an erection at arcades. That's really not cool."

I laughed, collapsing onto him, loving the way I could still feel him deep inside me. His hands trailed up my back, which was slick with sweat.

"This was your idea, remember?"

"Best fucking idea I've ever had. You," he said, one of his hands cupping my cheek and bringing my face up to meet with his. "You're a fucking goddess, Riley. I've never seen you like that before. It was so fucking sexy." He kissed me then, the kind of kiss where teeth meet because you're both smiling.

"I'm not sure what came over me. I think I got carried away." My cheeks warmed at my words and I knew I was blushing.

"Well, promise me you'll get carried away again soon."

"I'll try."

We lay there for a few more minutes catching our breath. But soon the moment passed and our heartbeats leveled out, and the dampness of our skin turned cold.

"Let me take you home," he said softly against my ear.

I didn't know if he meant my home or his, but it didn't matter because I already knew I'd be at home if I was with him.

When we walked out to the waiting limo, it was the ultimate walk of shame. I probably looked as though I'd been thoroughly fucked, but I couldn't find it in me to care. And to his credit, the limo driver didn't seem fazed by it. Since I could actually see the inside of the limo, I took a moment to look around, noticing it was top of the line. This was no limo used for bachelor parties or proms, it was an expensive vehicle.

Camden slid onto the seat next to me, wrapping his arm around my shoulders and pulling me close, and I couldn't help the smile that took over my face.

"Hey, so," Camden said a few minutes later. Uncertainty laced his voice, and that wasn't a word I'd use to describe him, so I turned to him with concern.

"Yeah?"

His free hand came to rest on my knee and it went a little ways to soothe me, but his voice still had me worried.

"We didn't use a condom back there." He looked right into my eyes as he said the words, and then his gaze searched mine.

"Oh." He was right, we hadn't. And I hadn't realized it at the time, but right after, the realization had hit me. "Um, I'm on the pill."

"I'm really sorry, Riley. I'm sorry it happened that way. I don't want you to think I did it on purpose. I didn't. I have a condom. I have one on me at all times since we started dating, but I got caught up in the moment. That's a terrible excuse, but I want you to know that I'm sorry."

"It's okay," I said, my voice small and confusion now completely taking over. Being with him, with nothing between us, had felt natural and wonderful. And, yeah, we probably should have discussed it, but I didn't think he'd done it on purpose. "Mistakes happen." It was all I could think of as a response. I hated the icky feeling that was now coursing through me.

"I'm clean," he said suddenly, his tone urgent. "Shit," he said, pushing his mussed hair off his forehead. "I didn't mean for this to go down this way."

"I'm clean too, Cam. It's fine. We can move on. Pretend it didn't happen."

"That's not what I want. I've wanted to talk to you about this for a while, but you've been busy and I didn't want to add to your stress. Listen." He turned on the seat, facing me, reaching up to push my hair behind my ear. "I care about you and I want to stop using condoms. But only if that's something you want."

"Have you been with a lot of women without one?"

"Never."

"Never?"

"Nope. I've never been with anyone who I even thought about it with."

"So, what's different now?"

"You are." His answer was short and to the point, but it was enough to stop my heart. "When I think about you, I'm not thinking about our next date or what we'll be doing next month, I'm thinking about our life together. I'm thinking about all the ways I can show you how much I care about you, and all the things you do that make me happy." He reached down and laced his fingers through mine, looking down at our intertwined hands, but I left my eyes on him. "Making love to someone without a condom is a big deal to me, Riley. It's always been something I thought I would share with someone special, someone I saw a future with, someone I could fall in love with. Taking away that barrier, for me, means trusting someone with myself, my body, and my heart. Maybe it's dumb, maybe I'm being a big idiot, but I've been saving this for someone in particular, and that's you."

His thumb trailed gently over the back of my hand, and I tried to put some words together to explain how I was feeling.

"Giving all of myself to you is something I've struggled with in the past, but there are no barriers between us now, Camden. What you see for us, in the future? I want all that. With you. And being with you tonight, really connected, it means the world to me." I reached up and pressed my hand against his cheek. "I trust you with my body and my heart."

He placed his hand over mine and pulled it down, placing a kiss right in the middle of my palm.

"I don't know what I did to deserve you, but I'm going to do everything I can to keep you forever."

"Forever sounds good."

Chapter Sixteen

Camden

I woke up reaching for her. It had become a habit. Every morning if she wasn't pressed up against me, I reached out, found her, and pulled her over, wrapping myself around her. But this time, when I reached for her, all I felt was cold sheets and empty space. I cracked an eye open, noticing it was still dark outside, sunrise still a few hours away. Sure enough, the other half of my bed was empty. I closed my eyes again, and finally made out the sound of the water running in the bathroom.

Riley was up and showering at five in the morning. It took me a moment to figure out why in my still-sleepy morning haze, but then I remembered it was the day of the party. My mother's party. And Riley was probably in there freaking out.

I moved the covers off me and swung my feet to the floor. I padded to the bathroom and walked to the shower. Ever since Riley started spending nights at my house, I'd thanked the construction gods for all-glass walls in showers. There was never, in all of history, a better sight to wake up to than Riley showering.

"Hey, babe," I called out. I opened the glass door and poked my head in. She turned and gave me a pretty pathetic smile. I knew she was nervous and I'd anticipated a less-than-bubbly Riley this morning.

"Did I wake you up?" she asked, leaning her head back into the water falling from the rainwater showerhead. I watched as she smoothed her hands over her hair and the way her perfect breasts moved as she did.

"I only woke up because you weren't there."

"I swear, starting tomorrow, I'm going to sleep for a whole week."

"Sounds good," I appeased her, but we both knew she'd be up by ten on Sunday morning, bored, and ready to start a new project. "You want breakfast?"

"You don't have to make me breakfast. I feel bad enough you are awake right now."

"Well, I am awake, so you can either let me make you breakfast, or I can come in there and distract you with various parts of my body. Which will it be?"

She narrowed her eyes at me. "You know I don't have time for that right now."

"What I know is that an orgasm or two will seriously calm you down. But I also know that you feed off this nervous energy, so sex might actually mess up your epic event planning game. So, I'm going to go make you breakfast. Okay?" Her expression had softened as I spoke and by the time I finished my diatribe she was smiling.

"All right, but no coffee."

"I'm sorry, have we met? I thought you were my girlfriend, Riley Smith, but my girlfriend drinks coffee like she's being paid to do so. I think there's been some sort of mix-up."

"Ha. Ha. I'm serious. I have enough nervous energy running through me to power a small village right now, and coffee will only upset my stomach."

"Got it. No coffee. Any other requests?"

"Just a good-morning kiss."

"Now that's a request I can accommodate." I opened the door wider and stepped into the shower slightly, watching as she came the rest of the way to me. She pushed up onto her toes and pressed a sweet and wet kiss to my lips, and both our mouths moved into a smile simultaneously.

"You're the best," she said, grinning at me.

"Says the naked woman. I think that makes you the best."

She laughed, but shook her head and walked away. I could have stayed there all day and watched, but I knew that wouldn't be productive, so I left and walked into the kitchen instead.

Thirty minutes later when Riley emerged, she looked like a classy business professional. Not a hair out of place, sophisticated makeup, and a killer pantsuit.

"You look great, babe," I said as she came directly toward me and reached up for a quick kiss.

"Thanks. This is my lucky suit."

"I thought you had a dress for the party tonight."

She groaned. "Your mom insisted I buy a new dress. Usually, for a client's event, I'm background noise. I am not supposed to be seen. If you see me, it's bad, it means there's a problem. I'm a behind-the-scene kind of gal. But your mom is adamant about the fact that she wants me to enjoy the party like a guest—which will be impossible, by the way."

"My mom wants you to have a good time." Riley shrugged and then sat down at the bar of the island in the kitchen. "Here," I finished putting the last of her food on her plate and set it down in front of her. "You're going to need a lot of energy today, so eat up."

She looked down at the plate, then her gaze bounced back up to me. "I can't believe you went to all this trouble."

I scoffed and said, "It's just pancakes, eggs, and bacon."

"It's amazing. Thank you." Her eyes were soft and her head was tilted to the side slightly.

"Anytime." I winked at her and loved the way her cheeks turned pink. "So, you're going to come back here to change before the party?"

"Um, no," she said with a mouth full of bacon. Was it just me, or did all guys get turned on when their girls try to talk with a full mouth? Never mind. "Hadley is meeting me there and bringing my dress. And my shoes. And an entire arsenal to turn me into Cinderella."

"So, I won't see you until the party?" I brought my coffee cup up to my mouth to take a sip, waiting for her answer.

"No," she said as she put her fork down on her plate. "I'm sorry. I don't have time to come all the way back here and get ready."

"It's fine. I just wanted to know. And since I do, I can give this to you now." I pulled open the drawer everyone had in their kitchen that held a wide array of contents. It had takeout menus, batteries, a flashlight, and a few paper clips. It also had a skinny, long, black box. I picked it up and held it out to her.

She looked at the box and then looked up at me. "What is that?"

"It's a present."

"A present?"

"Yeah. You know, a gift."

"For what?"

I shrugged. "Nothing. Everything. I wanted to give you something to show you how proud I am of you. You've been working tirelessly for six weeks on this, and I know you've sacrificed a lot."

She stared at me for a moment, gaze never wavering from mine, but then her eyes started to well. "Why did you have to go and be all sweet? Now I'm going to cry and ruin my makeup." She dabbed at the corner of her eyes and ran her finger under them.

"Babe, open the box."

She finally reached out and took it from me and then slowly opened it. I watched her eyes as they landed on the bracelet, widened, then welled some more. Placing my cup on the counter, I walked around the island to her and took the box from her hand.

"I wanted to get you something you could wear with your dress tonight, something that you would see and remember that I'm behind you, supporting you, all the time. Even if you can't see me. I also wanted to give you something that would make you think of me. That might be selfish of me, but I don't care." Gently pulling the bracelet from the box, I turned her wrist over and clasped the bracelet securely on her. "The saleswoman who helped me was pushing this tennis bracelet," I said, running my finger

235

over the sensitive skin where her pulse was beating. "But I looked at all of them and thought they were plain and boring. This one, however, looked more like you. The way the central diamond is surrounded by smaller diamonds, and how they all flow out in kind of a wave? That made me think of you. There's nothing ordinary about you, Riley. You're my twirling diamond." I pressed a kiss right over her wrist and then leaned in to kiss her lips, our contact tainted by the salty taste of the few tears she'd shed.

"How am I supposed to get any work done with those words running through my mind and the reminder of you on my body?"

"I don't know, but I'm glad it's you and not me." I kissed the tip of her nose and walked back to my coffee.

"You should really stop while you're ahead," she said with a laugh.

"Oh, I plan on it."

Chapter Seventeen

Riley

"Guests are starting to arrive, Riley." Rachel's voice rang through my earpiece, and I tried to settle the nerves pinging around in my belly. Deep breath in, hold it, breathe it out slowly.

"Okay, team," I said into my mouthpiece as I pushed the button down that was clipped to the neckline of my dress. "It's showtime, people. We've been planning this for weeks and know exactly what we're doing. If for some reason you need assistance, get ahold of Rachel, Jasper, or myself. There will be no panicking or alerting the clients that there is a problem. *Find me.* And have fun, everyone."

One by one, my team chirped in and gave encouragements, but I knew we were all going to have to work our asses off.

"Riley, darling, there you are." I looked up to see Meg walking toward me, arms outstretched. I walked into her embrace, accustomed to the idea that she was a hugger. "You look ravishing," she said as she held my shoulders at arm's length. "Has Camden seen you in this dress yet? He won't be able to keep his eyes off you."

I blushed at her words, but also loved the wave of warmth that washed over me. It meant a lot to me that Meg liked me, and that she seemed happy Cam was with me. In fact, it meant more to me than I ever expected it to.

"Thank you. You look beautiful too." Meg had chosen a classic little black dress. She'd paired it with all things sparkly and it looked amazing. I had barely finished my sentence when Andrew came to Meg's side, offering me a warm smile, and I tried to put on a brave face.

"Good evening, Mr. Rogers. It's good to see you again." My words weren't cold, but they weren't warm either. They were professional. That was the best I could give him.

"Please, call me Andrew." He continued smiling and took a moment to move his gaze around the room. "This is incredible, Riley. Meg has been doing nothing but singing your praises for weeks now, and I can see why. You've put together something really spectacular here."

"You haven't even seen the best part yet," Meg said excitedly. "There's another ballroom downstairs set up for the silent auction. We'll have dessert and cocktails down there after dinner, and then come back up here for the main event."

"I still can't believe you managed to get Indigo Ale here," Andrew said.

"Well, someone on my team had a favor to call in and luckily they were available. They're immensely philanthropic and this event fits right into their wheelhouse. They were happy to do it."

"Still, it's impressive." He winked at me and I wanted very much to believe in this Andrew, to think that he was on my side, but I was still wary. I did offer him a more sincere smile, but I couldn't put my guard down 100 percent.

"Have a good time tonight, both of you." I pressed my finger to my ear as though I was listening to someone, and then gave Meg an apologetic look. "I'm sorry, duty calls."

"Of course, dear. Don't work too hard."

I did a lap through all the guests areas and then through the vendor areas as well. Everything seemed to be running smoothly, only tiny fires popping up that I could have fixed with my eyes closed and hands tied behind my back. When I walked back into the main ballroom, which was set for dinner, my eyes fell on Hadley standing in the corner. Meg had insisted I invite her, wanting me to feel as though I had a friend here I could relax with if I got the chance. It was a nice gesture, and I appreciated it, but at that moment I was holding back laughter.

Hadley was in the corner and Justin looked as though he would eat her up given the chance. Her back was to a wall and his arm rested next to her face, his own face a hairbreadth from hers. Justin and Hadley were in relationship purgatory, as I liked to call it. They both wanted each other—Justin a little more forthright with his feelings than Hadley—but they couldn't seem to get on the same page. From what Cam had told me, Justin wasn't usually an all or nothing kind of guy. He liked to play the field and enjoyed being single, and she was the same way. But when it came to Hadley, he was desperate to claim her, to snatch her up and make sure no one else got even a whiff of her. He'd pee a circle around her if he thought it would work.

She needed time and he needed to prove that she wasn't just a challenge, that he wanted her for more than only her body, and that she wasn't a trophy to him.

"I've been looking all over for you." I heard his voice and, like always, something inside me shifted back into place. It was incredibly inconvenient for my independent heart, but when Cam was around, I became whole again. I turned toward the sound of his voice and when I saw him, I tried really hard not to drool.

He was clean-shaven with a brand-new haircut, and he was wearing the sexiest tuxedo I'd ever seen.

I was an event planner. If I'd seen one man in a tux, I'd seen a million. But Camden Rogers in a tuxedo was a wet dream. Put his image in the middle of a magazine and I would gladly wallpaper my room with it. The lines of the tux made his shoulders look even broader than normal and I wouldn't have thought that was possible. He'd skipped the traditional bow tie and opted for a long tie, and it just so happened to be the exact same forest green as my dress.

"Well, you've found me." My words came out like a breathy whisper and I knew I was already blushing, but there was no hiding my immediate and complete attraction and arousal. I wanted to take his tie off him and let him use it on me.

His eyes darted down to my wrist where he saw the extravagant bracelet he'd given to me earlier. Two months ago, had he given me the same bracelet, it would have made me run. I would have convinced myself it was a sign of our differences and I would have bailed. But that morning when I saw his expression, the emotions behind his words, as he explained why he'd bought it, well, I never wanted to take it off.

And it was sparkly as fuck.

He took two more steps toward me, his hand coming to my hip and his mouth landing on the shell of my ear. "You. Look. Edible." I felt his grip tighten on my hip. Electricity coursed through me and I wavered on my feet. I leaned my cheek into him, and the smoothness of his face lit me up inside. I was used to scruffy Camden. And while I liked the feeling of his beard, I couldn't ignore the need to feel his smooth skin between my thighs.

"How'd you get a tie that matched my dress exactly?"

"Hadley."

240

"Ahh. Well, you look pretty delectable yourself, Mr. Rogers."

He smiled and then looked around the ballroom. "Riley, this is spectacular. You should be really proud of yourself."

I took a moment to take in the view as a party guest. It *was* pretty impressive. I gave a one-shoulder shrug. "It'll do." He laughed and kissed my temple at the same time, sending swarms of butterflies soaring in my belly. I slid my hand around his waist, coveting the softness of the expensive fabric of his tux. Everything about him felt good and right. Raising my chin, I met his gaze, and I wanted to tell him I loved him, that I'd been falling for weeks, but I couldn't push the words out. I didn't want to tell him that in a room full of strangers.

"Looks like those two are getting rather cozy with each other." Following Camden's gaze, my eyes landed back on Hadley and Justin.

"Think he's wearing her down at all?"

"I don't know. She seems like she's only resisting him on principle, and he is picking up on that. He's waiting for her to crack, to give him something—anything—but he won't wait around forever."

"Well, regardless of what happens between them, can we agree not to let it affect our relationship at all?" Pressing in closer to him, I looked up, wondering how he felt about it all.

He looked down and pressed a kiss against my forehead. "Never," he whispered, his lips still warm against my skin.

"I should probably get back to work."

"If you must." His hand slid down my arm and captured my wrist where my bracelet was. His thumb ran over the diamonds and then his gaze met mine. "I think you're seated next to me at dinner."

My eyes rolled in exasperation. "Your mom is so funny. I know she wants me to feel like a part of the party, but if my boss ever heard that I'd *sat down to eat* at an event, it would be my last one."

"Well, I'll fight off anyone who tries to sit there regardless."

"Fine," I said with a laugh. I reached up for a kiss, loving that he didn't hesitate, that he wasn't the least bit concerned about kissing someone wearing an earpiece who was obviously working the event.

"Promise me you'll at least give me one dance, though."

I pretended to think about his request, but then a smile broke out over my face because I absolutely could not wait to dance with him. Even if I was technically on the clock.

The dinner progressed without any large issues. People enjoyed the food and I could see conversations happening throughout the room, against the backdrop of quiet classical and jazz music. I managed to sneak a few minutes to sit down at the Rogers's table, only to have Meg rave about me to everyone there. She told everyone I was the event coordinator, but then she continued on to tell them all I was also Camden's girlfriend. He rested his arm over the back of my chair, leaning in close to me, and I tried not to blush. Andrew sat next to Meg, smiling broadly the entire time she was boasting about me. Something about the situation sat funnily with me. It could have been Meg's verbose bragging about me, or it could have been Andrew's sudden lack of hatred toward me, but put together and combined, it was unsettling.

I managed to get a few minutes at the table and then sneak away. As I walked away, Camden tugged on my arm and brought me back for a small kiss, making everyone at the table swoon and let out simultaneous *awwwws*.

When the dinner portion of the event was coming to a close, the lights dimmed and a video began playing on the main stage about Angel House. The dim lights were perfect to disguise the wait staff clearing tables while the guests were being informed on where and what their donations would go toward. I'd seen the package before, and it was compelling. The foundation did a lot of good work for families that were victim to domestic abuse. Even though it may have been a meager amount, I was planning on donating toward the cause as well. One would have to be heartless to work on the project and not feel compelled to help. And that's exactly what we were hoping the package would do for the guests—make them feel good about giving.

The video ended and I saw a few women dabbing at tears in their eyes. The guilt of making them cry was far outweighed by the hope that those tears would transform into dollar signs. Six weeks of working on this project had given me a renewed sense of responsibility. This was good work. Sure, from the outside in, it looked like decorating and picking the right floral arrangements, the right food, but good work on my end equaled more help for those in need. That was a responsibility I took very seriously, and I hoped at the end of the night I could see great results for everyone involved.

The lights went up and the announcement was made that dessert, coffee, and cocktails would be available downstairs, along with the silent auction. Guests stood and I watched as my team got to work.

"Riley, Riley, come in, Riley." I smiled at Jasper's excited walkie lingo.

"I'm here, Jasper. You only have to say my name once."

"Well, this is important. Indigo Ale is here and they are ready to set up."

Jasper's excitement was now running through me. "Excellent timing. The top ballroom is ready for them."

The next hour was a blur of commotion, excitement, and surprising panic. The silent auction was going well, fueled by full bellies and liquor, and the mood in the lower ballroom was jovial. Everyone seemed to be having a good time. I heard titters of people loving the silent auction packages, but also anticipation for the live auction coming later in the evening. I was glad people were excited for the live bidding, but I was also worried people would hold back from bidding on the silent auction.

"How's it going?" I asked Jenny, an intern who'd been assigned to help with the event. "Have we gotten a lot of bids?"

"I think so. I'm only in charge of these four tables," she said, gesturing around her, "but there has been a steady line of people dropping bids. I think it's going really well so far." She smiled brightly at me and I patted her shoulder.

"Great job. Thanks for your help tonight."

"No problem. This is exciting."

I smiled back at her, seeing a little bit of my younger self in her, and made a note to work with her in the future. I could always use an eager and bright woman on my team. Right as I was about to turn to check in on the other tables, a familiar hand came to my waist and slid around to my belly, pulling me back against an equally familiar chest.

"Watching you work is really fucking sexy. You're in charge and it does naughty things to me." He whispered right against my ear and the air brushing over my neck was doing naughty things to me.

"You're going to have to control yourself for a few more hours, Cam." There was a slightly apologetic tone to my words because, honestly, I was a little sorry. I wanted the event to go well, but I also wanted to sink into bed with him, and let him sink into me.

"If you wanted me to behave myself, you should have worn a different dress." His words did a good job of sending shivers down my spine and making goose bumps pop up all over my arms. "There has to be a utility closet somewhere in this building I can drag you into." He said the last words against my neck, and my nipples tingled as they hardened. I was not wearing appropriate clothing to combat hard nipples, so I turned in his arm and pressed my chest up against his, not that it would make my nipples calm down, but at least it would hide them for a moment.

Get it together, nipples.

"We can't, Cam. Not here."

"I know, but a guy can dream."

"When this is all over, you can take me home and do whatever you want to me."

"Oh, is that right?" He smirked as he said the words, his hand smoothing over the curve of my ass, taking a handful and giving it a squeeze.

245

"Camden?" I watched as his eyes moved up away from mine and landed on something he wasn't pleased to see. Or someone. I turned, finding the voice familiar, but couldn't have prepared for what I would see when I turned around.

"Sophia." Camden's voice was angry and irritated, and his arm tightened around me, even though I was fully turned toward her. "What are you doing here?"

"Your father invited my whole family." She said the words with forced innocence, batting her eyelashes. Her eyes fell to me, then to Cam's hand around my waist.

"My stepfather," he corrected, anger thick in his voice.

"Riley, we've got a situation in the kitchen." Rachel's voice in my earpiece made me jump, but before I could stop myself, I reached for the button and responded, "I'll be there ASAP." I realized my mistake almost immediately, and even if I hadn't, Sophia made it clear she'd noticed what was going on. She looked at my earpiece and everything clicked.

"You're fucking the help?" She smiled as she said the words, her mouth pulling wickedly into an evil sneer. "Is that why you wouldn't go out with me when I came to your office a few weeks ago? Because you're slumming it?" She laughed then, a loud, obnoxious, irritating sound that matched every opinion I had of her.

"I need to go," I said to no one but myself.

"No, wait," Camden said, grabbing my wrist, keeping me from walking away. "Don't listen to her, Riley. She's just trying to start trouble."

"It doesn't matter," I said with forced coolness, which never sounds cool. It sounds like you're pissed and trying to hide it. "I have to go."

"Let her go, Camden, sweetie. She has work she has to do."

I dared to shoot Sophia a withering look, but then continued through the ballroom, heading for the kitchen. My heart was pounding, threatening to beat right out of my chest, and my lungs were working overtime. Breaths dragged in and then shuddered back out. By the time I made it to the kitchen and out of sight of guests, I was barely holding back tears. I headed straight for the walk-in freezer, needing a moment to compose myself. The cold air wafted over me and for a moment it felt good against the hotness of my face, the red flush a product of warring emotions.

Sophia represented everything I was insecure about in my relationship with Camden, and even though I hated her simply for being a bitch, I couldn't ignore the fact that what she'd said in the ballroom validated every fear I'd already had. People, the kind of people Camden and his family surrounded themselves with, would never see me as anything other than the help. I would always just be the girl trying to claw her way out of lower class.

The worst part of the whole situation was that I was pretty confident in myself before I met Camden. Insecurity wasn't something I was terribly familiar with. I knew my place in my world and I blossomed within its confines. I reached for dreams within my grasp. I never wished for Camden, but once he was in front of me, I was tempted by him, tempted to open myself up to this kind of hurt just to be with him. And, fuck, it hurt.

I could handle Sophia being at the event, but I couldn't handle hearing they'd seen each other knowing Camden hadn't mentioned anything to me about it. I'd

247

never felt unstable before, and Camden had pulled the floor out from under me.

I let the tears fall, wiping them away quickly, and when I had my emotions under control, I walked back into the kitchen to find Rachel. I sucked it up and got back to work.

When I found Rachel, she was too engrossed in whatever issue she was dealing with to notice I was a mess.

"Oh my goodness, I'm so glad you're here. We have a problem."

"Lay it on me," I said with a sigh. As soon as she started talking, Jasper came to stand next to her, our little triad ready to take on whatever obstacle stood in our way.

"The Renegades player who was supposed to be in the live auction just called and said he had a family emergency and can't make it."

"Damn," I whispered. The Renegades had generously offered to auction off a tour of the locker rooms at the arena, accompanied by one of their top players, and then tickets to a playoff game in one of their suites. It was an incredible package and I thought it would bring in one of the highest bids of the evening. "That's a big loss."

"Well, his agent said the Renegades were still willing to offer the experience, they just can't get a player here tonight. They're still up for everything, there's just no one here to offer the experience."

"It's not as great of an experience without a player here to offer it."

"What about your boy toy?" Jasper asked.

"Who?"

"Your boyfriend. The mayor's handsome son would be a suitable escort for the Renegades experience. He's hot and he knows a lot about basketball. He'd be great."

The emotional roller coaster was real. One minute I was feeling insignificant and unworthy of Cam, and the next I was ready to claw the eyes out of any woman who would *dare* try to go on a date with him. *He was mine.* Well, I wanted him to be mine, but after what Sophia had said a few minutes before, I wasn't sure he and I were on the same page anymore. But, the success of this fundraiser was hanging in the balance. That particular experience was our biggest ticket item, and it would definitely sell better with a hot man attached to it.

"You guys want me to auction off a date with my boyfriend?"

"Oh, Riley, he'd be perfect!" Rachel's eyes were wide with hope.

"This sucks," I whispered, my gaze falling to the floor.

"Is everything all right?" Jasper's voice was softer than usual, and I felt his hand on my shoulder.

"No," I said quietly as I shook my head. "But there's nothing I can do about it right now." I sucked in a deep breath and let it out in a whoosh. "I'll ask him."

"I can do it if you want me to," Rachel added sweetly.

"No, it's fine. He'll probably say no to anyone but me anyway. Hell, he might even say no to me."

"If you need anything...." Jasper trailed off, but I knew he was trying to be supportive, and I appreciated it.

"Thanks. Any other issues we should sort out while we're here? There's only about an hour until the live auction starts."

"Everything is good on my end," Jasper stated.

"That was my only issue. Everything is running smoothly, I think. It's a great event, Riley." Rachel's voice was kind and I could see the sincerity in her eyes, but also the concern. She knew something was up and I couldn't have that.

"Thanks. It was a team effort though. We just have to get through the next few hours and everything will be all right. Keep me posted," I said as I tapped my earpiece.

"You got it," Jasper said with a smile.

"Hang in there," Rachel said.

I gave them a weak smile and then turned, took in a deep breath, and walked back into the ballroom with my head held high.

Chapter Eighteen

Camden

"What the fuck is your problem, Sophia? You think being rude to my girlfriend is going to make me change my mind about you?"

She had the nerve to laugh and it made my blood begin to boil. "You can't seriously be upset about *her*. She's nothing, Camden. I understand the need to sow your wild oats, to pretend you're interested in the girl to fulfill some need to feel better about yourself, but there's no need to ruin the good things between us for some *nobody*."

"First of all, there is no us. There never was, and there never will be. And secondly, I'm not slumming it with Riley. She's the best person I've ever met. It doesn't matter what's in her bank account, or mine for that matter. I'm with her because she's good and beautiful and smart. Why would I give all that up for you? You're none of those things."

I thought I saw a tiny flash of hurt cross her face, and I almost felt bad about it, but then her porcelain façade fell back into place and she was fake as fuck again. "We both know she's just a phase, Camden. And even though I don't appreciate the way you've spoken to me, I know you'll come crawling back when you realize what a mistake you're making."

I had no response to her insanity, so I chose to walk away and try to find Riley. I pushed past Sophia and bolted in the direction Riley had gone, but couldn't find her anywhere. I weaved through the kitchen, back up to the main ballroom, I even looked in the coat check room, but I couldn't find her. The only place I hadn't looked was the bathrooms, and I didn't think it was a good idea to cross that boundary. If she was hiding from me, it was probably better to let her cool off before we spoke. But we would speak.

I grabbed a glass of champagne off the tray passing by and drank it down in one long gulp. The memory of Riley's face when Sophia mentioned coming to my office flashed through my mind, and I wished for a stronger drink. I'd wrestled with telling Riley about Sophia's random visit, but it meant nothing and would have caused her more stress. I was realizing now that perhaps I should have told her at the time, that we could have avoided all of this.

I thought I'd been doing a good job over the past few months of convincing Riley that whatever abyss she imagined between us, the big black hole she attributed to my family's abundance of money and her lack of it, was a nonissue. Nothing would have stopped me from pursuing her after that kiss at the basketball game and listening to her smart, sassy mouth. She was the complete opposite of every woman I'd ever dated, and I fucking loved it. I loved her. Obviously, some part of her had never let it go, never believed me when I told her that I wanted her for her, and for no other reason. I walked to the bar and ordered a whiskey. I'd just dropped a bill in the tip jar when I felt a hand on my shoulder.

"Your girl's doing a fantastic job, Camden." My stepfather's words were full of praise and sincerity, but I couldn't appreciate them in that moment.

"Did you invite Sophia and her family here tonight?"

A look of confusion passed over his face and his eyebrows drew together. "Not personally, no. They're on the list of contacts who automatically get invited to all our functions. Her father is a friend of mine."

"Did you invite them on purpose to try and put Sophia between Riley and me?" My tone was angry, and I wanted more than anything in the world for him to be honest with me. "Just tell me the truth."

His hand came back to my shoulder and he gave it a squeeze. "I would never do that to you, Camden. And I'm sorry that you think I would. Sure, I wanted you to date Sophia, but your mother and I have never seen you as happy as you've been with Riley. I would never try to sabotage you in that way."

Fuck me, he looked sincere. I was glad he felt that way about Riley, but it almost was worse because it meant that Sophia was a crazy bitch and she'd been purposely trying to cause trouble. I ran a hand down my face then took a deep swig of my drink.

"She said something to Riley and now, shit, I don't know how to fix it."

"Sophia said something to Riley?" His expression moved from concerned to curious, and I was about to jump into the story, but Riley appeared beside me.

"I don't want to talk about anything right now, but I need a favor." She looked miserable, as though talking to me was painful and the last thing she wanted to do.

"Anything," I said without hesitation. It was the truth, I would have done anything for her.

"The player from the Renegades can't make it for the auction, but the organization would still like to offer the experience. We just need an escort. Do you think you could do it?"

"Do what?"

"Get up on stage and be the person whose company we auction off for the experience. You'd have to take whoever bid the highest to the arena and then go to the game with them." The entire time she was talking she never looked me directly in the eye. She was either looking over my shoulder or down at her shoes. I wanted so badly to grab her and make her talk to me, but I knew it wasn't the right time or place. "You'd get to sit in the suites, and I'm sure you'd get a free jersey or something." It hurt that she thought the box seats and swag would be the reason I would help her. I wanted to help her because I fucking loved her.

"I'll do it on one condition," I said, using my finger to tip her face up to meet mine.

"What's that?" she asked, her voice practically trembling, as if she were close to tears.

"You have to let me take you home tonight and we have to talk this out."

She held my gaze, never wavering, and eventually asked, "That's the only way you'll help?"

"Yeah," I said, purposefully running my thumb over her bottom lip, using the way her shoulders shivered as proof that she was still affected by me even in anger and hurt. That gave me hope.

"Fine." She turned and walked away before I could respond, and my heart sank a little as I watched her go.

"She looks like she's in a lot of pain, Cam. She looks like she loves you." Andrew's words pulled me back to reality and I turned to look at him.

"Here's hoping." Raising my glass, I clinked it against his.

The next hour passed without incident. I stood around with Andrew and my mother, trying not to look as though my dog had been run over by a car. But in truth, I was miserable. I needed the party to be over so I could take Riley home and talk to her, explain to her what happened with Sophia, get everything out in the open, tell her that I loved her and wanted nothing more in the world except for her to be with me and to love me back.

I wasn't sure what she was going to say to all that, but I knew I would never be happy unless I laid it all out there for her. She needed all the information and then I'd let her make the decision. But I'd be damned if I was going to let Sophia be the last person she listened to when it came to our relationship. Fuck that noise.

The party continued and eventually one of the girls I recognized from Riley's office came to me and said, "We need you upstairs for the auction."

"Sure thing," I mumbled, swallowing the rest of my whiskey—my second whiskey anyway. I followed her up the stairs, leaving my empty glass on the tray of a waitress as I passed her by.

"We really appreciate you stepping in like this, Camden. I hope it's all right if I call you that. I'm sorry, I'm not usually this babbly."

"Camden is fine. You're Rachel, right?"

"Yes, hi. Like I said, we're grateful. I know Riley didn't want to ask you to do it, but it was kind of an emergency situation."

"Well," I said on a sigh, "Riley knows I'd do pretty much anything for her. I'm happy to help." Rachel led me backstage and explained the process. My personal auction would be last—kind of like the big finish.

"So, you basically hang out back here until you're announced by Jasper, and then walk out on stage, smile, and try to look like you're excited to hang out with whoever buys your time."

"Got it," I said, giving her a half-assed smile. I just wanted to get this part over with and take Riley home, make her talk to me, make her see what she meant to me.

"Listen, she'd probably kill me if she knew I said anything, but I just want you to know that Riley is really upset. Whatever happened between you two tonight, it upset her. She cares a lot about you and I hope you two can work it out. I've never seen her as happy as she's been the last few weeks." Rachel looked genuinely concerned for Riley, and that made me soften a little toward her.

I forced a small smile and tried to reassure her. "I'll work it out with Riley, don't worry. And I won't tell her you said anything."

"Thanks," she said, half laughing and half sighing. "Like I said, wait until you hear your name and then go out there and smile. You'll knock 'em dead."

"Got it. Thanks."

She smiled again but then left me standing backstage with a few other people. After a few minutes, I could hear more people starting to trickle in, the noise level of the room rising, the murmurings of conversations floating backstage. I was suddenly tired. Exhausted, even. I rubbed at my temples, aggravated by the dull throb emerging there.

"Are you feeling all right?" I heard Riley's voice, and my head snapped up. Just seeing her face made me feel better, but then I noticed she looked even more tired than I felt.

"No, I'm not." She looked around and then motioned for me to follow her and she led me to the corner of the backstage area where only the light from the stage was present, making it dark and quiet. "I don't like whatever is happening between us." She listened, but her head dropped down and I wanted so badly to reach out to her, to draw her close, but I didn't want to anger her or push her farther away. I waited for her response, for her to give any indication that she felt the same way, and I got my answer when she reached her hand out and looped her pinky finger around mine. I accepted that little inch she gave me, but then I took a mile, threading my fingers through hers and pulling her into me, my other hand cupping her cheek.

"Why didn't you tell me she'd come to your office?" she whispered, eyes searching mine, full of hurt I knew I was responsible for.

"Because it didn't matter. And because I didn't want to stress you out."

"It can't be both, Cam. It either wasn't a big deal, or it was and you knew it would bother me."

"It didn't matter *to me*, but I knew it would matter to you. I knew you would be upset about it and it would cause friction. But it wasn't worth it to me to cause that kind of trouble with us. I've hardly gotten to see you these past few weeks, and when I do see you, I want it to be about us, not about her. She's nothing." I bent my knees to bring my face level with hers. "*She's nothing.*"

Riley met my gaze and kept it, locking her eyes with mine for a long moment. Finally she let out a large breath. "I've never felt this way about anyone, Camden. I've fallen in love with you and it's scary. I'm scared you're going to realize I'm not the right person for you, that we're too different, and that you're going to end it, and where will that leave me? Completely and desperately in love with someone who doesn't feel the same way. So, it scared me when I heard she'd been to see you and you didn't tell me. Her, of all people." She let out a sad laugh, using a finger to wipe the tears from her eyes. I moved my hand to the back of her neck, wanting to pull her close. "I'm not used to feeling insecure, but she does that to me."

"You love me?" I asked quietly, watching as she pulled her face back to see me a little better.

"After that whole speech, that's your first question?"

"Do you love me?" I asked again, bringing her hand up to my mouth and kissing the back of it, waiting for her answer.

"Yeah, I do." Her eyes were darting back and forth between mine, and I could tell she was frozen, waiting for me to say something that would either make her happy or break her heart. I knew I would never be able to break her heart, but now I had to make her see that as well.

"I knew the instant we spoke I was going to fall in love with you so hard, Riley. I might have been in love with you the minute you refused to give me your phone number. I love that you're spunky and hilarious and witty. I love that you're soft and kind and *good*. You're the best person I've ever met, let alone been with, and I love you so fucking much, I'm just glad you've finally caught up with me."

She laughed again, a real laugh, and a few tears slipped down her face. I wiped them away, hoping they were the last ones of the evening, and then I pulled her close.

"Can I kiss you?"

"You better."

She tipped up on her toes to meet me halfway, and our mouths touched. I kissed her, loving the way she tasted salty and sweet, the way she arched into me, and the way I could feel her love in the kiss. I wrapped one arm around her waist and picked her up off the floor, turning us so my back was to the stage and she was pressed against the wall, both of us hidden in the shadows of the ballroom.

I pressed into her, using the force of my body to hold her up, freeing my hands to roam over her body and the smooth fabric of her dress.

"Cam," she said on a breath, "I have to go back out there. The auction is about to start."

As she spoke, I moved my mouth to her neck, nipping her there, loving the way her heartbeat pulsed beneath my tongue.

"I can't wait to take you home," I rasped against her neck.

"Me either."

I moved my mouth back to her hers, kissing her deeply but letting her feet fall back to the floor. When I pulled away, I rested my forehead against hers. "I love you."

"I love you too." Before I'd met Riley, I never would have thought those three words would affect me the way hearing her say them did. My heart soared, my pulse thundered, and my mouth smiled. It was the best feeling, hearing her say those words. I wanted to listen to her saying them forever. I kissed her again, but only a small, fast one, then stepped back.

She looked like the happy Riley I'd spent the last eight weeks with. She looked like the woman I fell in love with.

"You have to leave because otherwise, I won't be able to control myself any longer." I kissed her forehead, trying to appease my need to feel all of her but respect the fact that she needed to work.

"Okay." She smiled. A brilliant, dazzling, sexy as fuck smile, and I couldn't believe how lucky I was to have her, to be the one she chose to love and let in. I was a lucky bastard. "I'll be right off the stage to your right during the auction. Jasper is the auctioneer. After it's over the band is up, and then I am a free woman."

"You still owe me a dance."

"I know." She smiled again, then turned and started to walk away, but I grabbed her wrist and pulled her back. My hands framed her face and I searched her eyes.

"I'm sorry. I'm sorry about everything. I'll never keep anything like that from you again."

"Thank you," she whispered. "I love you, and I forgive you. I'm sorry I pulled away. I'll work on running to you instead of away."

"That would be amazing," I said, pressing a kiss against her lips one last time before I let her go again.

Chapter Nineteen

Riley

Holy fuck.

He loved me.

I walked through the dark backstage area, my fingers pressed against my lips, smiling, and floating on a fucking cloud.

He *loved* me.

And I loved him too.

We were in love.

Holy fuck.

I saw Jasper and walked to him, trying to wipe the stupid grin off my face. I failed, obviously, because he lit up when he saw me.

"Well, you look a lot happier than you did an hour ago. Did you let your boyfriend tap you in the bathroom?"

"What? No!" I laughed, partly because Jasper was funny, but also because I was so happy, laughter was simply falling out of me. I had no control over my happiness.

"Well, whatever he did to you, tell him to do it all the time. Every day. You look good happy."

"Thank you," I said, blushing. "So, are you all ready to go?"

"I am. Is it weird that doing this is fulfilling some sort of weird western, cattle ranch auction fantasy I've always had? I want a good old-fashioned bidding war to break out. I want paddles flying and people yelling."

"First of all, we don't have paddles. Secondly, you're insane. This isn't a cattle auction. This is a sophisticated event, and I'm sure everyone will act accordingly."

"Party pooper."

"Okay, I think you're up, Jasper. Knock 'em dead. Make sure you wring all the money you can out them. Be your charming self and hit them in the wallets, right where it hurts."

"You got it, boss lady."

Jasper took to the stage and commanded everyone's attention. I knew he was an attention whore and that's why I knew this part of the job would be perfect for him. He thrived when he knew everyone was watching him.

"Good evening, ladies and gentlemen. I am sure you've all had enough time to loosen your inhibitions and your money clips." He paused for the laughter that he knew was coming, and I had to admit, the audience ate him up. He had them in the palm of his hand. "Tonight we have some excellent packages for you all to bid on, and remember, all these packages are donated to the Angel House, so 100 percent of your money goes directly to the cause. There are no middlemen, no red tape, no hoops to jump through. Your money will immediately go to help women and families who have been affected by domestic abuse, so let's open those wallets and have a good time."

Polite applause filled the room and I smiled at Jasper, so grateful for his help.

"The first package is dinner for four at Portland City Grill. Your package includes a five-course meal, dessert, and all you can drink service. A limo will pick you up and take you home, ensuring everyone has a safe and pleasant evening. The bidding for this package will start at seven hundred and fifty dollars."

Hands flew up immediately and Jasper did a great job keeping the momentum going and goading people into bidding again when they were on the fence. In truth, that was a great price for the package to begin with, but when the bidding got up to two thousand dollars, I was practically jumping up and down with excitement. The bidding slowed, but Jasper pressed on, squeezing another five hundred out of the top bidder.

"Sold for twenty-five hundred dollars!"

Everyone around us clapped, but you could tell people were waiting for the next item to bid on. I held my clipboard, making sure I kept track of what was going on, trying to keep a tally on the final bids, wanting to have a clear figure of the funds raised by the live auction.

The next five items all sold for thousands of dollars and I had to contain my excitement. Meg was going to lose her mind when she saw our final total. That very moment the girls were downstairs tabulating the silent auctions and we would announce the winners after the live auction and be able to deliver a final donation total.

"This whole event couldn't be going any better, Riley. You should be really proud."

I was startled by the voice so close, and even more surprise came when I saw Andrew Rogers standing next to me. He was smiling at me, but my smile had faded away.

"Thank you," I said curtly, turning back to the stage.

"I wanted to talk to you, if you don't mind. I think I owe you an apology."

His words surprised me, but I didn't have any spare time to give him. "I'm not sure what this is about, but I'm a little busy."

"I know, and I'm not trying to bother you, but it's important you hear what I have to say."

I huffed out a breath. "I don't think I owe you anything, Mr. Rogers, but I can't go anywhere either, so if you feel the need to speak, I can't stop you." I purposefully trained my eyes on the stage, trying to give him the impression that I wasn't paying attention, when in fact I was. Acutely.

"I had set Sophia and Camden up originally because I thought they would make a good match."

I didn't even attempt to hold in the groan that came from me as I spun to look at him. "Mr. Rogers, please don't. If you can't support my relationship with Camden, then you're going to have to take it up with him. I'm done trying to please you, or impress you, or prove anything to you. I love Cam, and he loves me, and if you keep pushing Sophia at him, you're going to lose him. I don't want that. But I can't talk to you anymore if you're going to constantly be trying to push me out of his life. I'm not going anywhere."

There was a pause where neither he nor I moved, just held each other's gazes. But finally, Mr. Rogers smiled.

"You are the perfect woman for him." He said the words through laughter, smiling and reaching his hand out to place it on my arm. I looked at it in confusion, wondering what in the ever-loving world was happening. "I have never heard anyone, and I mean *anyone*, defend someone with such passion. And I was a lawyer, for Christ's sake!" He laughed even harder, but I still kept the puzzled look on my face.

In the distance, I heard Jasper say Camden's name and then suddenly the entire ballroom was filled with women hollering at *my* man.

"Camden Rogers will be your guide on this amazing adventure. The winning bidder will be accompanied by Mr. Rogers on an all-expenses paid trip to tour the Renegades' locker room, the Loda Center Arena, and also receive a catered meal in the owner's box suite. This is the perfect package for not only a basketball fan, but any fan of spending a day with a handsome man."

The women in the audience went crazy again. I was torn between rolling my eyes or joining in with the screaming.

"Riley." I heard Camden's stepfather call my name again, so I turned to look at him, wondering what in the world more he could have to say to me. "What I was going to tell you was that I was sorry. I want to apologize to you for the way I treated you the day we met, and for not trying hard enough to make you feel comfortable with me. I did set Camden up with Sophia, and I was disappointed it didn't work out, but after getting to know you, there's no one else I would rather see him with. You're his perfect match. I also wanted to tell you that I didn't invite her here tonight to sabotage your relationship. Her father is my friend and their family has always been on the list of automatic invites. It was never my intention to undermine your relationship with Camden. He's happier with you than he's ever been with anyone."

It was stupid how sincere he sounded and how hard I found it to stay mad at him. The Rogers men were fucking fabulous at apologies. Damn them.

"I appreciate that," I managed. I was distracted, however, by the bidding war that had started over my boyfriend. Jasper had started the bid off at one thousand dollars, but it quickly shot up to eight thousand, then ten. There were a few women who were vicious, outbidding each other within milliseconds. Poor Camden looked like a deer with headlights bearing down on him. He looked around, finding me at the edge of the stage where I said I would be, and I gave him an encouraging smile. He was raising a lot of money for us.

"He looks miserable," Andrew said from beside me.

"He does."

"Fifteen thousand dollars." I heard the words and immediately the rage consumed me. Sophia had her hand raised and a sickly sweet smile on her face as she bid a fucking *wad* on my boyfriend.

The fucking nerve.

"I have fifteen in the back," Jasper said, motioning toward her. Camden's gaze fell on Sophia and I almost laughed as he visibly rolled his eyes. A few whispers floated through the ballroom but then a blonde woman raised her hand.

"Sixteen," she said confidently.

"Seventeen," Sophia countered.

"Eighteen," the blonde huffed.

"Twenty."

Holy shit.

"Twenty to the lady with the resting bitch face," Jasper said so quickly, I almost didn't hear him. More murmurings filled the room, everyone wondering if anyone else was going to bid against Sophia. Camden was a catch, for sure, but twenty thousand dollars? That bitch was out of her mind.

"Bid," I heard Andrew say behind me.

"Twenty going once," Jasper announced.

"What?" I turned back to Andrew with confusion.

"Bid on Camden. It's on me. Please. It will make me feel so much better about the whole situation."

"I can't bid using your money," I said, shaking my head.

"You can, Riley. Please, it would be my honor. I was going to write a check to the foundation tonight anyway, we might as well make it worth our while, right? Go on, bid twenty-five."

"Twenty thousand going twice."

"Are you sure?" I asked. He seemed insistent, and if I was being completely honest, the idea of bidding against Sophia was thrilling.

"Do it, Riley. Quickly, before it's too late."

"Twenty-five thousand dollars!" I held my hand up and yelled out my bid, smiling widely. First at Camden, but then I turned to look at Sophia. If I'd had twenty-five thousand dollars to my name, I would have spent every penny to see the look on her face. Her mouth gaped open, then her eyes narrowed at me.

"Twenty-five to the gorgeous brunette in the front!" Jasper said with a laugh. Camden was looking at me with confusion and I winked at him.

"Twenty-six," Sophia yelled angrily.

"Go on," Andrew said with kindness.

"Twenty-seven," I said with a laugh.

"Twenty-eight," she practically screamed.

"Bid fifty, Riley. I was going to write the check anyway."

"No," I gasped, turning back to him. "I can't bid fifty thousand dollars," I whispered to him.

"Riley, please. This is the most fun I've had in ages, and I swear I was going to donate that amount anyway."

"Twenty-eight going once," Jasper said insistently, shooting daggers at me with his eyes.

"It would make me so happy to see you win this, Riley."

"Twenty-eight going twice," Jasper groaned, obviously biased as an auctioneer.

I spun around, threw my hand in the air and yelled, "Fifty thousand dollars!"

The entire ballroom gasped and Sophia shrieked, "What?!"

"Sold to the most beautiful woman in the room for fifty thousand dollars!" Jasper yelled above all the commotion in the ballroom, not even waiting to see if

Sophia was going to outbid me. If he'd had a gavel, I was sure he would have banged it loudly.

The excitement of the moment overcame me and I ran up the steps to the stage and right into Camden's arms. He welcomed me, kissing me fiercely as soon as I was close enough. There were more gasps and even a few expletives throughout the ballroom, but it didn't matter in that moment because I was in Camden's arms.

"Where'd you get fifty thousand dollars?" he asked as he ran the backs of his fingers over my cheek.

"Andrew. He apologized and then she-bitch started bidding, so he told me to outbid her."

"Really?"

"Truly."

"Sounds like he approves."

"It would appear that way."

He gave me another kiss, this one not as deep and not as sexy, but still perfect, and then pulled me from the stage.

"That was the most excitement I've seen in a while, right, everyone?" Jasper asked the guests as we made our way off the stage. "We'd like to thank everyone for their donations, and as a special treat, I am pleased to introduce Indigo Ale!"

Everyone clapped as the band took the stage. Camden led me to Andrew, who'd been joined by Meg, and both were smiling at us.

"Looks like you got the girl," Andrew said, reaching out to shake Camden's hand.

"That's a lot of money, Andrew. I feel a little responsible. Let me cover half."

"You absolutely will not," Meg said insistently. "If you feel badly enough you'll make your own donation. But Andrew did the right thing." Meg turned to me and took my hand in hers. "We hope this can be the beginning of a stress-free relationship between all of us. We love you, Riley, and we want you to feel comfortable with us."

"I do, and I can't tell you how much this all means to me. But, truthfully, it was water under the bridge before the bidding war started."

Meg pulled me in for a hug and whispered in my ear, "It was so worth it to watch her mouth fall open. She completely deflated when she realized how much money you'd bid. It was incredible."

"Best moment of my evening," I said, laughing as I pulled away.

"You still owe me a dance," Cam said sweetly, pulling me to his side, his hand landing at the curve of my waist and making my heart flutter at his touch.

I reached for the button on my mic, pressed it, and said to my team, "This is Riley. I'm off radio for fifteen minutes. Find Rachel or Jasper if you need anything." I didn't wait for a response and pulled the earpiece out. He led me to the dance floor and then pulled me against him, one hand on my back, the other holding my hand against his chest. I rested my hand on his shoulder and looked up at him.

"It's been quite an eventful night," I said with a laugh.

"But it's still been an incredible event, baby. I'm so proud of you."

I let out a large sigh, trying to process the idea that it was almost over. "Thanks." I'd never worked this hard on a project, and it was great to feel like I'd pulled it off. Well, if you ignored the whole bidding war incident. "I hope Rose doesn't get wind of the fact that I made the highest bid of the night. She'll think she's overpaying me."

He laughed and pressed a kiss against my forehead.

"You know," he said a few minutes later. "I didn't want to tell you I loved you for the first time after a fight. I don't want you to think I used my feelings for you as a playing card."

"I don't think that," I said, moving my hand from his shoulder to thread it through the hair on the back of his neck.

"I want you to know I love you unconditionally. Whether we're getting along or fighting, making love or sitting on the couch. I love you. Through anything. With anything. Without anything. In any way. I love you in all the ways."

"Shut up."

He smiled and then kissed me. It was the good kind of kiss. The best kind. The kind felt all over my body. The kind that took my breath away and made parts of me ache with need. The aching was the best part. The desire, the want, the anticipation—it was all wrapped up in that kiss. When he finally pulled away, I had to force myself not to pout.

"You're a good dancer," he said, whispering the words against my ear.

"Really? I'm just standing here, following your lead."

"Hmm, maybe I like the way you're pressed up against me."

"Mmm, I like that too."

"I think we need to take a vacation. Maybe in the new year we can get away for a week."

"Mmm, I like that too."

"You're very agreeable."

"You're only saying things I agree with."

"Move in with me."

"What?" I stopped dancing, stopped breathing, stopped thinking about anything except the words he'd said.

"Move in with me. Live with me. Be with me. I hate bouncing from my place to yours, we spend every night together anyway, and I love you. *Move in with me.*"

Okay, heart. This is it. Try not to explode. Or melt. Keep it together!

"I've never lived with anyone before. What if I'm bad at it?"

He shrugged. "Then I'll kick you out."

I blinked at him and pulled my face back. "Are you serious?"

Laughing, he pulled me close again. "Of course not. You can't be bad at living with someone if you love them. Besides, I've put up with you so far. I want to spend every moment I can with you. I promise it won't suck."

"Well, there's a ringing endorsement," I said, laughing along with him. "Okay, I'll live with you, but there's one condition."

"What's that?"

"I don't want to live in your condo."

His eyes gazed into mine and I watched as he considered my words. "Babe, I love you, but your place is tiny. And there's no place to park the Batmobile."

"I don't want to live in my apartment either. I want us to find a new place. Somewhere new that's only ours. And I want us to be equals. I'm not going to live off you. I want it to be fifty-fifty. That means you're probably going to have to lower your living expectations a little. I can't afford high-rise condos."

"Okay, I hear you," he said, his brow furrowing as his hand slid down my waist and feathered over my ass. "But would you consider a twenty-eighty split?"

"You're negotiating?"

"It's in my blood."

"Forty-sixty."

"Twenty-five-seventy-five," he countered, kissing the tip of my nose.

"Give me thirty-seventy, and you've got a deal."

"Deal," he said, right before he spun me out in an elaborate twirl. When he pulled me back in he leaned me back over his arm, dipping me, and placed kisses all up and down my neck. When I was upright again he pulled me even closer, every part of my body tucked impossibly tight to his. "Arguing with you totally turns me on," he said, his lips so close they moved over mine with his words.

"You just negotiated for a live-in lover. Sounds like she's going to get a pretty good workout living with you."

"You better believe it," he said, kissing me again.

"I love you," I said between kisses as the song came to an end.

"All of me?"

"Every part."

"I want to show you all my parts."

My head fell back as I let out a loud laugh. His chest shook with his laughter as well. "Give me a few hours and then I'll be happy to see every single part of you."

"You're going to love them."

"I know."

Epilogue

Riley

You'd think, for fifty thousand dollars, I could at least get some lights on in here.

I stood in the middle of the basketball court at the Loda Center after following an elaborate trail of notes and directions, left for me by my overpaid escort.

"Hello? Cam?" I heard nothing in response except the creepy silence you hear when you're alone in a giant room, the silence that makes you freak out. It was too quiet. "This isn't funny, Camden Joshua Rogers." I tried to use his middle name to intimidate him, but I knew it wouldn't work. I also knew he was probably not far away, watching me freak the fuck out. He'd wait until I was thoroughly wigging out, then swoop in and save the day.

Damn him.

It would work.

"Hey, baby," I heard him say from behind me. I turned and gave him a nasty look, but all my attempts at irritation faded when I saw him.

He walked toward me, wearing another fantastic three-piece suit, with a six-pack of Hef in one hand and a single peony in the other. His jaw was scruffy with the beard I'd made him grow back, and his smile was sexy enough to melt even the most flame-retardant panties right off my body.

"What are you doing?" I asked, dropping my hands to my sides. I'd thought I knew what I was in for this evening, but Camden always seemed to find a way to surprise me, and those surprises usually involved me falling even more in love with him.

"I'm bringing you some of your favorite things." He walked right up to me and dropped a kiss on my waiting lips. "Beer and perennials. I know the way to my girl's heart."

"Yes, so well in fact that once you got there, you never left." I reached up and kissed him again. I took the peony and snapped off most of the stem and then tucked it into my ponytail, then, pulling a beer from the cardboard box, I found the bottle opener on my keychain and made quick work of the cap. I took a healthy swig. "Where's my tour? I want every tiny bit of experience Andrew's fifty thousand dollars paid for."

"Oh, you'll get your tour. Joshua Baxter will be here in twenty minutes to show us around before he has to warm up for the game."

"Joshua Baxter? *The* Joshua Baxter? Are you serious?"

"As a golden retriever."

"What?" I said, choking on both laughter and beer. "That's not how the saying goes. Golden retrievers aren't serious."

"Tell that to one when it's trying to retrieve something." His face was stone cold and he meant every word he said. It only made me laugh harder.

"Okay, seriously, what's going on?"

"I don't know, I thought it would be kind of fun to come back to the place it all began. Come with me."

He held his hand out to me and I took it—of course—and followed as he led me up into the stands. He looked as though he knew exactly where he was going, so I followed without question. Finally, he brought me in front of a seat and told me to sit down. I did, carefully so as not to spill my beer. Once I was settled, I smiled up at him, watching as he took the seat next to me.

"This is it." Turning to look at me, his face lit up with a sweet smile, I couldn't help but lean over to kiss him.

"This is what?" I asked, my mouth still pressed against his.

"This is where we were sitting that night. I was here, you were there, and you couldn't stop looking at my thighs, you were eavesdropping on my date breaking up with me, and then you fell madly in love with me."

"Oh, that's how you think it went down?" I said dreamily, leaning my head against his shoulder and taking a pull from my Hef.

"That's the best version of the story. The part where you run away from me makes everyone sad. It was a bad move on your part."

"Clearly."

"Hey, look," he said, pointing up to the roof of the arena. "We're on the Kiss Cam."

I looked up and, sure enough, the Jumbotron was lit up and flashing the words KISS CAM, below which was a live video feed of us.

"Did you set this all up?" It totally sounded like something he would do. He had all these strings he could pull, and if he didn't know someone personally who could

277

help him, he'd seek someone out and charm the fucking pants off them to get what he wanted. I was exhibit A of that argument.

"I did. Does that earn me a kiss?"

I scoffed at him. "No. I believe I paid *you* a vast amount of money, and therefore, I shouldn't be the one putting out tonight. I expect to do very little work tonight and reap a ton of reward."

He smiled at me, and I knew it was because I was arguing with him and he got off on it. I smiled back because I got off on it too.

When his lips met mine, it was exactly like the first time. He was tentative at first, barely brushing his mouth over mine, but then he dove in and took everything he wanted from me. My hands slid into his hair and his arm wrapped around my waist. When he sucked my lower lip into his mouth, I groaned. That must have flipped some sort of switch for him, because suddenly his arm around my waist tightened and I was being lifted into his lap. He brought my legs to either side of him, leaving me to straddle him. It wasn't the worst thing in the world, but in the commotion, I dropped my beer on the floor of the arena. His hands came to my face, holding my mouth right where he wanted it, and I moaned again, feeling his thighs beneath me.

He had me in one of my favorite positions, but usually I preferred to be naked when I straddled him. The fact that I was wearing clothes totally didn't stop me from rocking back and forth against him. I pictured what we must look like up on the Jumbotron and I almost stopped, embarrassed of what someone would think, but then I realized that it was really fucking sexy and I wanted so badly to turn around and look, but I didn't want to stop kissing him.

"Fuck, I love you, Riley," he said as he moved his mouth to my neck, licking, biting, and kissing his way down and across my collarbone. His hands moved down over my ass, pulling me even closer to him, forcing my core to rub against the bulge in his pants. "Jesus Christ, baby," he hissed, keeping one hand on my ass and moving the other to my breast, cupping it over my blouse.

"Maybe," I said, but had to stop to bite my lip to keep in a loud moan as I rocked against him. "Maybe we should skip the tour and the game and go home. I'd like to be naked right now."

"No," he said against my chest where he was panting. "We can't go home. This was fifty thousand dollars. And Joshua Baxter is expecting us."

"Weirdly, you saying another man's name while I'm trying to orgasm makes the need totally go away." I looked at him, and he laughed, pressing his forehead against my chest again.

"Come on, let's go wait by the locker room." He tapped my backside, so I gave him one last kiss and then eased my way off his lap.

"I dropped my beer," I said, my tone forlorn.

"It's okay, baby. I have five more."

"There's the way into my heart."

He laughed and took my hand, leading me back down to the floor. We walked silently through the arena, his fingers entwined with mine, and I had a moment of overwhelming love for Camden. It happened often, actually. We'd be somewhere together, or even when we were apart, and it would crash over me, like a tidal wave, how much I loved him. I leaned into him and without missing a beat he took my weight, and we continued that way through the darkened hallways.

"Can you believe it's been three months since that party? I've been looking forward to this night for so long." I looked up at him, smiling, and watched as he leaned back against the wall next to the doors that said Locker Room above them. He set the beer on the floor and then pulled me to stand between his legs.

"Why? To meet a player?"

I shrugged, leaning farther into him. "I like being here with you. It's nice."

He pushed a loose strand of hair behind my ear, giving me the sweetest smile he had, and I rested my cheek against his palm.

The door to the locker rooms opened and I tried to pry my mouth off the floor when Joshua Baxter walked out, beaming at us. He introduced himself and I mumbled my way through my name, giggling like a little girl. He didn't seem fazed by it though. He was probably used to fans being all stupid around him.

He led us on an amazing tour and we each got jerseys from the store and I nearly fainted when Joshua signed mine. He walked us to our suite, thanking us for our amazing donation to Angel House, and then left us with a huge gift basket of swag and our own personal bartender. He had to warm up for the game, and I was sad to see him go—not before I took a ton of selfies with him, of course— but once we were alone, I had the epic freak out I'd been holding in for the past hour.

"That was amazing," I squealed, jumping up and down. "I can't believe Joshua Baxter laughed at one of my jokes!" I hopped up and down, finally able to release all the pent-up excitement. "And he was so nice! I didn't even feel like he was just fulfilling an obligation, he was genuinely glad to show us around! I love him even more now," I said, putting my hand on my heart.

"So it's the perfect night?"

"Perfect," I replied, dreamily.

"Worth 50K?"

"Definitely."

"Good."

He was so stupidly handsome when he smiled, especially when the smile was only there because I was smiling. He was so genuinely happy when I was happy, it made me happier, and it continued in some sick, twisted, insanely sweet, happy cyclical pattern.

"I love you," I said, wrapping my arms around his neck. "Thank you for having a crazy ex who broke up with you at a Renegades game and then followed you around like a sick puppy and tried to break us up, forcing me to spend fifty thousand of your stepfather's dollars in a figurative pissing match against her."

"Aw, you're welcome, baby. No one pisses better than you."

"Truer words were never spoken."

"Kiss me," he said with a smile.

"Anytime."

The suites were rather posh. The one we were in might have been nicer since it was the owner's, but

281

regardless of how amazing the others were, I was convinced watching basketball games in the suites was the best way to go from here on out. You could either sit in a spacious, comfortable room, in plush chairs, watching the game on large television screens, or you could sit at the bar and watch, or you could even go out onto the veranda. Camden and I took our drinks and our snacks and made our way out onto the veranda. I preferred to watch the game with the other fans. Sure, we were a good ten feet from them, but I still wanted to feel like I was a part of the game, and it was hard to do that from a recliner in the back of the suite.

Halftime rolled around and, of course, the Renegades were winning, so I took a few minutes to load a picture of me with my new bestie Joshua to Instagram. Some hopeful was out on the floor trying to make a half-court shot for ten thousand dollars. He missed, but they gave him a T-shirt, so he seemed pleased with that. The overhead lights dimmed a little, and a spotlight started zooming around the arena.

Everyone started clapping and hollering as the Kiss Cam came on the Jumbotron.

A year before, if you'd asked me how I felt about the Kiss Cam, I'd have told you it was the worst part of the whole basketball game experience. But now, as I sat next to Camden and watched people who loved each other kiss—whether they be friends, lovers, family, or even strangers—it made me think about kissing the man I loved and how all it took was that one kiss.

So when the Jumbotron flashed a live photo of us on the screen again, I laughed, thinking the odds of that happening more than once were slim to none, but I kissed him nonetheless. He held me against him, making the kiss slow but sweet, and when he finally pulled away, it was only far enough to press his forehead against mine.

"Riley," he whispered, his voice strange and shaky.

"Yeah?" Something was wrong with him. He seemed nervous, and he never got nervous.

"I have something I want to ask you."

Suddenly the entire arena went berserk. Everyone was yelling and screaming, clapping and stomping. I had no idea what was going on, only that Camden was slowly making his way to the ground.

"What's wrong?" I yelled over the enormous volume of the crowd.

"That's just it, Riley. Everything is right." Suddenly, it occurred to me what was happening. Camden was on one knee and behind him, I could see the Jumbotron where the words Kiss Cam had been replaced with Engagement Cam. I looked back down at him and he'd produced a ring from somewhere and was holding it up to me, a wide and nervous smile still on his stupidly handsome face. "I love you, Riley. I love you more than I ever imagined I could ever love someone else. And I know it's only been six months since we started dating, but every day we spend together only cements for me that I only want to do this with you. I will never find another crazy person I want to spend all my time with, share all my beer with, and beat every time at Skee-Ball. Will you, please, say you'll marry me and make me the happiest fucking man on this planet?"

The crowd was chanting "SAY YES SAY YES SAY YES" and my heart was beating out of my chest, but the only thing running through my brain was "Of course. Yes."

In an instant he was standing and I was in his arms, being kissed stupid. The arena erupted into thunderous applause, practically shaking the whole building. He gently put me down and slipped a beautiful and perfect ring on my finger, then leaned in for another kiss.

"I love you," he whispered against my ear. I pulled back so I could hold his face and look into his eyes.

"I love you too. So much."

"More than Hef?" he asked, smiling.

"Definitely more than Hef."

More Books by Anie Michaels

The Never Series

Never Close Enough

Never Far Away

Never Giving Up

Never Standing Still

Never Tied Down

The Love and Loss Series

The Absence of Olivia

The Presence of Grace

Stand Alone Novels

The Space Between Us

Instead of You

The Private Serials

With A Kiss Series

Kiss Cam

How to reach Anie

To get updates about new releases, sales, and events, sign up for my monthly newsletter here.

Please feel free to follow me on all media platforms!

Facebook

Twitter

Instagram

Join my Facebook group for readers here.

Acknowledgements

I would first like to thank AJ Harmon and Heather Carver for inviting me to be a part of the Passion in Portland anthology that inspired me to create Riley and Camden in the first place.

Big thanks to all my beta readers – Andrea, Rachel, Michelle, Danielle, Joanne, Ali, and Becca. Also, thanks to Andrea, Stefanie, and Kelly for your assistance during the final stages and helping me find the errors that no one else's eyes could find.

To all the readers in my group, Reading With Anie, I am so grateful to have a place to share my ideas and just talk books. Reading is my therapy and I'm so happy you're all there to be my therapists.

To Anie's Awesome Teamsters – I would not be half as sane as I am without you all (and I'm not terribly sane to begin with). I know I post some crazy stuff and ask a lot of you, but it really is the biggest help and deepest well of advice I have available to me. Thank you for all your opinions and for sharing them with me.

Thanks to Cassy Roop at Pink Ink Designs for creating the cover for Kiss Cam – it's everything I wanted the cover to be.

Thanks to Lindy Zart for always being available to answer questions and give advice when I am unsure and need someone to push me over the edge.

And Becca, again, for not only your friendship, but also all the help you offer me. From advice on cover decisions, to beta reading, to teasers, I couldn't do this without you.